DOUGLAS COWIE

NOON IN PARIS, EIGHT IN CHICAGO

First published in 2016 by

Myriad Editions
59 Lansdowne Place
Brighton BN3 1FL

www.myriadeditions.com

First printing
1 3 5 7 9 10 8 6 4 2

A CIP catalogue record for this book
is available from the British Library

ISBN (pbk): 978-0-956559-97-5
ISBN (ebk): 978-0-956792-67-9

Designed and typeset in Sabon LT
by WatchWord Editorial Services, London

Printed by CPI Group (UK) Ltd, Croydon CR0 4YY

For Bob Eaglestone

Prologue

1981

THE ARTICLE APPEARED a few pages into the culture section. Nelson Algren, American writer, had died. Newly elected to the American Academy of Arts and Letters. On the bedside table stood a photo of the two of them standing in tall dune grass with a background of trees, she in one of the Guatemalan or Mexican dresses, he standing behind, both of them holding the oars to the little dinghy he liked to row around the lagoon in Miller. Next to the photo, a stack of his letters, the most recent of which had arrived in 1965, sixteen years ago. Almost as long as the time she'd known him. She read the article a couple of times and folded the newspaper closed. For twenty minutes or more she sat silently, clasping the newspaper on her lap. The younger Castor – 'Simone,' she heard him say in his nasal Midwest voice – would have cried now. Would have cried until Sartre – also now dead – gave her a large glass of whisky. She stared into the middle distance, not at anything, and looked at the photo. She'd felt old then, until she'd met him. She permitted herself a wry smile.

Later in the afternoon her sister phoned and said she was sorry. Don't be sorry, she replied. Are you not sorry? Hélène asked. She was not. He'd written so many terrible things about her after her memoir, even though it was now years

3

ago. No, she couldn't feel sorry or apologise. I can live my life without apologies. There's no use apologising or feeling sorry for the dead, anyway. She could feel sad, though, she admitted to herself. She touched the silver ring, turning it once around on her finger, and looked again at the photograph and stack of letters on the bedside table.

Part One

February 1947–January 1949

Chapter One

HE PROBABLY should've thrown out the beef stew a couple of days ago, but it hadn't grown any spores, so he lit the gas underneath it for the seventh dinner running. He shook the match and tossed it in the pail, and rinsed a bowl and spoon, wiping them dry with the flap of his shirt. Snowflakes danced on the gusts that rattled the fogging window. Maybe after he ate he'd go down to the Tug or, if nobody was there, the lockup. Something to do, anyway. He looked at the empty typewriter, the pile of letters behind it. Yeah, the Tug. Why not? No more work getting done tonight.

The stew wasn't hot enough yet, but its farty aroma had begun to fill the room. He placed the needle on the record and Roy Acuff started playing 'The House of the Rising Sun'. The phone rang.

He got it on the third bell. Acuff was asking for glasses to be filled to the brim. Whatever the voice was saying on the other end, it wasn't English she – he? – was gasping down the line. Not even Polish, he knew that much. He told the caller and operator they'd connected the wrong number and set the phone back in the cradle.

The stew started to bubble. Should've bought some bread on the way home from the Y. The phone rang again. Dammit.

He dropped the ladle back into the boiling stew and caught the second ring, Acuff now singing the only thing a rounder needs. More incomprehensible rasping: wrong number again. Back to the pot, a hint of something burning seeping into its scent. But before he could touch the ladle, the phone again. He ran the few paces, picked it up before it could holler again, Acuff telling his brothers to shun the house in New Orleans, and this time he didn't even listen or say anything, but dropped it back into the cradle and listened to the last chords of the song.

Half an hour later it rang again. He was halfway through a second bowl of stew.

An American voice said this is the operator and don't hang up. There's a party on the other end of the line who would like to speak to you. Please hold the line.

He shovelled another chunk of beef into his mouth and waited.

'Hello? Hello. I have obtained your telephone number from our friend.' Same voice as before, but now the woman was speaking more comprehensibly, or at least more slowly.

'Our friend?' he repeated, still chewing.

'It is Mary who has given to me your telephone number.' Mary G., that was it. He'd forgotten. 'I am visiting Chicago. She has said to me that Monsieur Algren knows Chicago.'

He looked at the fogged window, and the snow. 'I suppose Mary doesn't lie.'

'*Pardon?* I am sorry?'

'Never mind.'

He listened to the crackle of the line and wondered if the operator was having fun listening in.

'Perhaps you would like to come and meet me?'

'What – now?'

8

'Yes, when you have some free time. Or tomorrow?'

'No time like the present.'

'I am sorry?'

'I could meet you in half an hour or so.'

'*Bon*. Yes, good. I am in Palmer House; I can meet you there, in the Little Café.'

He finished the stew and put the bowl and spoon in the sink. Palmer House. Fancy lady. Damned if he knew what the Little Café – Leetle Café, she'd pronounced it – was, though. Mary's letter was in the pile next to the typewriter and he found it and reread it. Yes, she'd mentioned this Frenchwoman. Simone. A writer of some kind. Was Mary G. pimping? Him or her? Didn't matter. He'd go find this Leetle Café and meet the frog. Something different from the Tug or watching the parade of addicts and thieves at the clink. Why not? He took his overcoat from the hook on the door.

There wasn't much activity in the opulent and overlit Palmer House lobby, but at one end, past the concierge desk, the clusters of chairs standing on ornate carpets, past the lobby bar, was the entrance to Le Petit Café. He was still laughing as he pushed through the revolving door. There was not speaking French and there was not speaking French, but even at the lowest estimate there were chances with translation she could've probably taken. A few tables were occupied but only one of them by a woman on her own.

So this must be him, the blondish hair, grey wool overcoat – this must be Monsieur Algren. She lifted her hand and forearm in a tentative wave, and he caught it, nodded, his smile showing a couple of teeth, and strode to her table. She reached out her hand to shake as he dropped into the chair opposite. He wasn't like the New York people, she could already see that; Mary G. hadn't been wrong. They shook hands and now he was taking off his coat, and already talking, but her English couldn't stretch to his rapid speech and Chicago accent. She nodded and tried to smile and pick out at least some of the words. His shirt was plaid and his wool trousers were held up with leather braces – pants, suspenders; she mentally Americanised her English. It made him look a little ridiculous, or anyway, different from the other men in the bar of the Palmer House. She interrupted him to excuse herself to go to the ladies' room. She didn't really need to, but couldn't think of another way to make him quiet.

Maybe I should shut up for a while, he thought as he watched her bustle out. Not even sure what I've been rattling at her, anyway. She was short, wearing a navy blue dress, her hair piled in an elaborate twist of a bun on the top of her head. Her fingernails were painted purple; he'd noticed that as they shook hands. A bow-tied waiter came over and he ordered two bourbons and a glass of ice. She hadn't come back when the waiter returned with the drinks. Be an expensive evening, in hourly rate terms, if she stays away, he thought.

But she returned. They each put a single ice cube in their drink, and she said *à votre santé* and he said *skål* and then he said something about Marseille and the war and she nodded but once again struggled to understand another word of what followed. She tried, but his pace was a sprint, and Marseille and war made her think of Paris during those years, and how they'd lived. But no – she watched his mouth as he talked, watched his blue eyes behind his round glasses, watched his arm wave the tumbler with its single ice cube bouncing against the side – no, Mary had made a good judgement: he wasn't like the New York people.

She told him, when he finally closed his mouth, or at least paused long enough to take a drink, that she'd been in New York City since the end of January. She was giving lectures, and discovering American culture. She didn't notice him roll his eyes at that. But her hosts out in New York, they wouldn't take her to see what she wanted to see. There were places they told her weren't safe, and there were places they called slumming it, where, they told her, it was unfashionable or uncomfortable for them to go. So she had to go to those places on her own; she'd walked the Manhattan grid alone and eaten in drugstores and drunk whisky in dark and filthy bars. She'd told Mary she'd die of boredom in Chicago if it were to be more of the same: fancy dinners in fashionable restaurants, but only uncovering the real city on her own. She put down her empty glass and signalled the waiter for another round.

'I want to see the real city of Chicago,' she told him. 'Not just hotels with thick tablecloths.'

He knocked on the tabletop. 'The Leetle Café of the Palmer House seems real enough.'

She didn't get the joke. The waiter arrived with their drinks. *Santé*; *skål*.

'Why do you say *skål*?' she asked.

'My people are Swedish, on my father's side.'

She nodded. 'Mary said you know the neighbourhoods where the real people live.'

'Okay.' He drank his bourbon in one. 'Go get your coat and I'll take you someplace real.' She smiled.

She hadn't noticed the sneer in the way he said 'real'. He wasn't trying to condescend, he thought as he watched her cross the bar to the revolving door, but still. Whoever this lady was, she didn't know what she meant when she said real. Mary'd sent him a doozy all right. It'd be the Tug and the lockup after all tonight.

11

A few minutes later she returned, wearing a dark blue coat. 'Where will you take me?'

He smiled and she noticed for the first time his crooked teeth. They were somehow nice. 'I'll take you to a bar that doesn't have tablecloths,' he said. 'Now tell the waiter your room number and we'll go.'

They walked through the revolving door, across the lobby to another revolving door and out on to the cold sidewalk of Monroe. The doorman hailed a cab and they began driving north.

Barusz held up a hand in greeting when they walked in the Tug. A boxing match flickered from the television mounted above the far end of the bar. Almost directly underneath it somebody or other was clutching a beer and squinting at it. The jukebox stood silent at the other end. Barusz poured two beers and two whiskies and winked at Nelson as he set them down. The single booth in the front corner was open, so they crossed the small room and sat there.

So here was someplace real for her. They sat saying nothing for a few minutes. It wasn't spite, but he felt like making her sit there and look at the place. When she'd drunk half her beer, the whisky still untouched on the table, he started talking, some of it true, some of it less than real, but so what.

She listened as again he began talking, too quickly, but she understood a little better as she got used to his pace and accent. The man with one leg at the bar had lost the other underneath a streetcar. The young man at the pool table trying to play a shot from the corner that was too close to the wall, his elbow high in the air, his hat pulled low over his eyes, had come back from the war addicted to morphine. His opponent never drank anything stronger than coffee and made his living doing armed robberies. The old man in the other corner with the enormous hands had been a wrestling champion.

He'd never seen the pool players before, but for her they might as well be what he made up. It'd give her something to put in a lecture. A fattish man and a skinny kid, both with grey rings beneath their eyes, came in from a door behind the bar and nodded towards the booth as they passed on their way out. No, they weren't his friends, exactly; Barusz ran a poker game in the back room, he told her. Those two were lousy players, too lousy even to cheat. He signalled Barusz for another two beers and pulled the whisky glass closer.

'What about women?' she asked. 'There are no women in this bar.'

'The only women who come in here are whores.'

She felt a small shock of – accusation? He felt it, too. Not what he'd meant but now it had been said. Too late. Barusz set the beers in front of them and returned to the bar, wiping his hands on his apron. But for the single click of colliding pool balls, the Tug suddenly felt silent as a library to both of them.

'I mean they're actually prostitutes,' he said. 'Most of them. They tend to come in later.'

Whether it made her feel less like he'd called her a whore he wasn't sure. Nor was she, although she hadn't felt quite as though he'd called her one, but more the possibility of it. Perhaps it was language. And that she was tired, or simply feeling foreign. She watched the pool players, sipped some whisky, and watched as the one-legged man crutched to the restroom. The man at the bar groaned as one of the boxers on the television dropped to the canvas, and Barusz said something sympathetic. She looked over at Nelson, frowning into his beer, the whisky glass now empty.

'There are so many prostitutes in Chicago?' she asked.

13

His eyes twitched to her. 'Around here, anyway,' he said, shrugging. 'Seems to be the going business.' She nodded, and he smiled with one side of his mouth. 'What about we drink up and go look at some other real corner of Chicago?' he said.

'Corner?'

'Not a street corner.' He laughed. 'Come on, we'll go see someplace with a little more life.'

It had stopped snowing, but the wind was gusting down the north–south street. They pulled up their coat collars simultaneously. He walked fast and she had to move at a speed close to a trot to keep up with his long strides. Was he trying to lose her? No, because now he was stopping at a corner and turning to say something again, fast, and hard to hear over the wind and the streetcar rumbling past. He pointed up at a building and she saw a woman in a pale lighted window of the second floor, her shoulders bare, and even from the street Simone could see her breath condensing on the glass. In the doorway beneath, a man leaned his shoulder against the frame, one leg folded over the other, a fedora pulled low over his forehead. They crossed and walked past him, and he flicked a coin in the air and caught it.

They passed a drugstore and she thought of all the lunches she'd eaten on her own in Manhattan in those places, 'french' fries and bacon, lettuce, tomato and glass bottles of ketchup and mustard on vinyl-topped tables. She thought of asking him if he ate his lunch in drugstores, but as the question formed it seemed foolish so she didn't. Two or three of the taverns they passed had neon signs that flashed BEER but there were several others with painted signs or no sign at all. Most of the other shops or businesses were closed, and had bars across their windows and doors. They turned at a corner and walked one more block before turning another, and again at the next corner they turned. It was like Manhattan, another grid of streets, but even so she felt as though she was walking in a maze of bricks and fire escapes, neon signs and billboards, jailbarred shopfronts and alleyways she couldn't see down. She buried her cold hands in her coat pockets. He hadn't said anything since he'd pointed out the prostitute in the window, and they'd walked several blocks, the wind at her back, the wind cutting across and stinging her face, now again at her back.

He stopped in front of a stairway that led to a basement doorway. A painted sign at street level, surrounded by light bulbs, had a word or name she didn't understand, and Nelson was talking to a boy – he must have been a teenager from the look of him – wearing a ridiculous straw boater. A jazz club, she thought as he beckoned her to follow him down the stairs, and her thought was confirmed as the door swung open and she heard the kick of a drum, a cymbal crash, the semi-dissonant harmonies of trumpets and saxophones. He handed some money through a window and received change and two paper tickets, one of which he handed to her. It was printed only with a number. She followed past the window and through a curtain.

It wasn't a jazz club. They sat at a small table near a stage bathed in red and blue light. The band played in the far corner. The woman on the stage wore a tiara plumed with peacock feathers and her eyes were thick with kohl. She danced with large painted fans, her wrists oscillating, the fans flickering with a precision that kept her body hidden even as they exposed it. Drinks were set in front of them – she hadn't noticed he'd ordered. They touched their glasses and she noticed again his crooked teeth as he smiled. No, the Manhattan people wouldn't have brought her to a place like this. The music reached a crescendo of horn blasts and tacky drum fills and there was applause for the dancer, or her bare breasts, or both, and as she departed the stage the next performer took it and the band found a new rhythm and the show continued. The room was dark enough that it was hard to see Nelson, but she could tell that just over half the tables were occupied, mostly with men, but a few women as well. The whisky and cigarette aroma competed for supremacy with the sour tang of the performers' make-up and sweat. They watched the show for an hour or more – she had no idea of the time – as it continued, one dancer after the other, then several together, the band hardly stopping, the drinks arriving seemingly without the need to order. He paid for each round without allowing her – or without her finding – the opportunity to offer. As the band built another cheap crescendo and she stared glassily at the admittedly impressive rotation of tasselled nipples, he was abruptly on his feet, picking up his coat and heading towards the door. Had he said something? Possibly, probably. She lifted her own coat from the back of the chair and quickly followed through the curtain, through the door into the cold and up the stairs where the boy was still hustling in his boater, calling and gesturing at each person remotely within shouting range, though, she noticed as she looked around, there weren't many people out.

'Are you hungry?' he asked when they'd reached the corner, and she realised she was. They turned back the way they'd come, Nelson nodding at the burlesque barker as they passed. Another block this way, turn on this corner that way – she really had no idea where she was any longer, not even in relation to the first tavern, let alone her hotel – and they were entering an overlit diner, the air hot and thick with grease and coffee.

They sat at a table next to the window. On the other side of the diner a young and thin man read a folded newspaper while chewing on a toothpick, but he was the only other customer. Without looking over at the man, Nelson told her he did shakedowns for the mob, which she didn't understand, so he explained. The waitress filled their coffee cups and took their order. Simone asked him if every person in Chicago was a criminal.

'Even the mayor,' he said.

The waitress set a half-sandwich and bowl of soup in front of Simone and boiled chicken legs and vegetables in front of Nelson. She ate the too-hot and over-salty soup slowly, but he shovelled the vegetables down, and was already eating the second chicken leg before she was even half-finished. He began to eat the bones, biting through and sucking out the marrow before chewing the rest. She watched astonished, forgetting her soup until he'd left his plate empty.

'Is it not dangerous, eating the bones?'

He grinned and shrugged, and wiped his mouth with the paper napkin.

Outside the diner he hailed a cab and they were now heading she didn't know where. He said something about more criminals, and she wondered what this city was, and who this man was Mary had sent her to. Again she was watching the city with no real idea of what she was seeing or where she was. For a while the cab drove directly under the elevated train tracks, then it turned away from them again, and soon enough it stopped, and Nelson paid, and they seemed to be visiting a police station.

'Cook County Jail,' he said as they walked up the few steps. At a desk inside he took a piece of paper from his wallet and showed it to the uniformed policeman. 'You have to have a ticket,' Nelson explained to her as she followed him down one corridor, then another. They stopped outside a door.

'Ticket?' she repeated finally.

'To see the line-up.'

'How do you get a ticket?'

'You have to be the victim of a crime.'

She felt a shock. 'You are a victim of a crime?'

'A couple years ago. I got rolled. I hang on to the ticket so I can come watch the line-up.'

'Rolled?' She didn't really understand any of what he'd said.

'Mugged.'

She shook her head and raised a hand, palm upwards.

'Robbed. By a man with a gun.' He made a gun with his finger and thumb, and poked her ribs with it.

He knocked and the door opened: another uniformed policeman inside. Two rows of benches lined the back of the small dark room, and at the front a policeman sat at a desk, facing a large window that looked on to a brightly lit, white-walled room. Only three people occupied the benches. Nelson gestured to Simone to sit on the front bench, next to the wall. The officer at the desk called, Next! and after a few seconds a young black man walked into the white room, squinting against the light, shading his eyes against it.

Drop your hand, the officer said. I can't see nothing, man! the young man responded. Drop your hand. He let his hand drop, and his eyes squinted harder. What did you do? asked the officer. I didn't do nothing, man. What were you arrested for? Standing on a corner. Says here you were standing on a corner outside a diner at midnight, holding a gun while the diner was being robbed. The young man shrugged and said nothing. Get a lawyer, son. You're not leaving my jail tonight. Next!

The young man walked to the other side, a police officer just visible in the white room as he reached out his hand. An old, bearded man shuffled into the centre of the window, also squinting, and craning his neck forward and back.

Vagrant, said the officer. Put him in the drunk tank. Next!

A thin boy, not too different from the one in the diner, and then again, not too different from the pool players in the Tug, sloped into the room, his eyes on the floor. Nelson whispered that it was a one-way mirror, that the perps had to stare at their reflections while they were berated by this cop. This one was accused of shooting his girlfriend. Simone shifted in her seat as the officer described details from the report. When he'd finished making the suspect listen to his crimes, the officer again shouted Next! and another appeared, this one accused of pickpocketing. He was dispatched quickly and a rapist replaced him. Then another armed robber, followed by a murderer, an arsonist, a petty thief, someone who'd been in a fight, another who'd stabbed his wife. Nelson sat erect like an eager schoolboy listening to a lesson, oblivious, it seemed to her as she continued to shift in her seat, to anything beyond the faces and voices of these criminals and their interrogator, oblivious to her discomfort, which, as brutal details of violent crimes piled up, was growing into a feeling of illness. Her thick wool dress felt too hot, too heavy in this close room. Everyone laughed as a teenager explained that he hadn't meant to steal the money but the cash register was open and he thought he should hold the cash to keep it safe, and that when he'd pistol-whipped the store owner it was because the man had overreacted, and he was defending himself, and the money; but Simone didn't laugh. She wiped her forehead with her sleeve, and she leaned against the wall. She felt sick – it was sick; this room was sick. She reached towards Nelson and tugged his sleeve. 'I do not feel well,' she said, and he could see even in the darkened room that she was pale, her forehead prickled with sweat. He helped her up and put his hand on her back as they left, retracing their path down the corridor.

Before they turned the corner he stopped, and pressed his face to the glass window of another door. 'Hey, here, look at this.' He drew her close, and tapped on the glass. The room was dark, but she could make out a large wooden chair with bulky arms and a high back, straps draped over it. 'It's the electric chair,' Nelson said, and she could hear a note of excitement in his voice.

But he looked down at her and dropped his smile. He could see she really didn't feel well. 'Let's go outside,' he said, and again placed his hand on her back and led her down the corridor.

The cold air did help a little, but they both realised that the physical symptoms were really because she was overwhelmed and exhausted. He hailed a cab and they drove north. She could lie down at his apartment, he said, and he'd fix her a drink.

She didn't notice anything about the neighbourhood – she hadn't recognised the Tug as the cab passed it – nor did she notice anything about his building. She let him guide her up some stairs and then he was unlocking a door and turning on a light. It smelled of overcooked meat and vegetables. He led her through a small room – there was a desk, she noticed, and books and a stove – and into another, smaller room with a bed and nightstand.

'Just a moment,' he said, and disappeared into the first room.

There was nowhere to sit so she took off her shoes and lay down on the bed. She heard his footsteps on the wooden floor and after a minute he returned, a bundle of sheets in his arms.

'I was going to give you clean sheets,' he said.

'I don't need them,' she said.

She might want them if she knew when they'd last been changed, and who else had done what in them, but he wasn't going to argue. 'Would you like a drink?'

'No,' she said, propping herself on one arm, 'I feel I have had enough to drink. Tell me, is this what all Chicago is like?'

'Like this apartment?'

'No, these criminals, these prostitutes, these people.'

'It's not what the guidebook will tell you, but that's what I've known my whole life.'

'I see.' Thinking of the one-legged man in the bar, of the whore in the window, the parade of criminals at the jail, she began to cry.

'Hey,' he said, and again, 'hey.' He dropped the sheets and walked to the bed, sat and reached a hand to her shoulder. 'It's okay.' Which was something to say, at any rate.

She took hold of his hand and squeezed it and tried to make herself stop, tried to make herself stop, she hated it when she did this, and now in this strange apartment in this strange city, with this strange man, she was shaking and she couldn't stop. His lips brushed lightly on her cheek. She opened her mouth and inhaled sharply, then bit into her lip again. His mouth moved to hers and she let it, softly, and it made her feel better, not strange, somehow, she thought that it should, but it didn't, and so she let the thought go and her sobbing slowed and she brought her hand to his shoulder, and felt his slide to her breast, down to her hip and then her thigh, pushing her coat away, her dress up, and soon her clothes were a tangle sliding over her head and she was

21

pulling at his shirt buttons and he was on top of her and she felt only her body, and his. Some hours later she awoke and looked over at him and put her hand on his chest and before long he too awoke and they started again and this time – oh! – this time it was more, there was something else, it pounded in her temples, her pulse she meant, she gasped, couldn't get enough air, and felt herself convulse beneath him as though she wasn't there, but no not like that as though she was too much there, heat pushed across her skin, and her fingernails digging deeper into his sides and she couldn't stop shaking, harder and her eyes pressed harder shut against or with the sensation and she was lifting off the bed, stretching towards him, deeper, away, and she dropped back on to it. Exhausted. She wanted to think – no she didn't, and that was strange, no she couldn't – she touched her burning forehead with her palm. Never before.

He'd made her apple pancakes, and gone out into the street in his grey slippers, only wearing his bathrobe, to hail her a cab back to her hotel. It was mid-morning. She didn't have any appointments until the consulate in the afternoon. She watched the daylight city from the cab window, cars and trams and the El, people with hats pulled down over their ears, hands gloved or clutched in pockets, and when she was finally back in her hotel room she collapsed on the bed without removing her clothes and slept.

The limousine picked her up at noon and drove her to the consulate on Michigan Avenue, where she was introduced to several men; they were always only men, no women. The same at the consulate in New York. After forty or so minutes of knocking on office doors, shaking hands, looking at this painting or that photograph, she was ushered back into her

22

limousine with an apparently select group of cultural attachés and personal assistants and they drove to a restaurant. The carpet was thick, and the waiters all wore bow-ties and waistcoats, and they combed the crumbs from thick linen tablecloths. Her hosts discussed their plans for exhibitions and other events and she nodded at the right times, but mostly she thought of Nelson Algren, of his bewildering tour of Chicago, of him sucking marrow from chicken bones, the men in the Tug, the burlesque fan-dancer, the thieves and murderers and the electric chair. And of his body on top of hers, moving inside hers – she'd never had that, not with Sartre, not with Bost; never before had she come like that – of his apple pancakes and grey dressing gown. They had the good grace to wait until the second course before raising the topic of Sartre, and she had the manners to tell them what they wanted to hear. But she could only think of Nelson Algren, Nelson Algren, this strange crooked-toothed crocodile smile of Nelson Algren. When she'd arrived in New York, she had been determined to find some kind of affair to make her happy, though she couldn't imagine who in America would want her. She had almost found someone there, but the timing was wrong, and they didn't manage to meet again. Now there was this unexpected stranger of a man in Chicago – and she was leaving on the night train.

She excused herself from the afternoon meetings by saying she had to visit an unwell friend. They insisted on sending her in the consulate limousine when she told them where she was going. The driver didn't know Wabansia Avenue, and in truth neither did she – a taxi would've been easier. She kept her eyes on the streets in hope of finding a landmark from the night before. Would that help? She'd been lost the whole time. She started to feel a little hopeless, a little too desperate. He might not even be home, after all; she didn't know what he did during the daytime. Oh, but she needed to see him once more. And wait, wait: there was the tavern. The neon sign was turned off but it said THE TUG, and she told the driver it must be nearby, they must be close. Sure, the next street sign said Wabansia Ave, and the driver turned left – she guessed, it seemed more correct – and the limousine trawled slowly past the brick buildings, wooden porches, a billboard that said SCHLITZ – the billboard, yes, and stop here; that's the building. She was almost certain, certain enough to try.

He'd managed half a page so far, which wasn't bad. Should've just gone to the Y and boxed for a while and then come back to write, but there was always later, or tomorrow. The stew was definitely off now; he'd flushed it. Have to go out and get some chops or something later. He got up and put on the radio to fill the place with some noise. Just as he sat back down the doorbell rang and he looked out the window. Black limousine? He went down the stairs to see what the hell this was about.

'You crazy frog!' She stood on the sidewalk, her coat collar turned up against the wind, her feet wet from the uncleared snow. He'd been concentrating on work since her cab had driven away this morning, but now he knew how much he'd wanted to see her again.

'I didn't want to leave without seeing you once more,' she said without moving.

'Crazy frog,' he said again, and laughed, showing his teeth. 'Come in, come in.'

She followed him up the stairs to his apartment and when the door had closed she was slipping out of her coat and reaching her mouth towards his, both at once, and he was

24

leading her into the tiny bedroom and they were taking off their clothes and falling to the bed.

'You'll ruin my reputation in this neighbourhood.' Her head was pillowed on his shoulder, her arm across his belly. 'Showing up in a limo. Everybody will think I'm rich. There'll be a line out the door of Polacks asking for loans I can't afford and they can't repay.'

'I have caused you trouble?'

'No, no.' He laughed. 'But the neighbours already think I'm a suspicious character, since I don't go to work.'

He asked her to stay for dinner, but she had to meet the consulate men, and then she would be on the train to California. They dressed and stood close to each other in the doorway between the apartment's two rooms.

'I would like very much to read one of your books,' she said. 'I can buy them, yes?'

'I'll have them sent to your hotel. I can call my publisher.'

She reached her hand to his face. 'When shall I ever see you again?'

'You can always come back to Chicago,' he said. 'Or maybe one day I'll visit Paris.' He went over to his desk and grabbed the first thing that seemed reasonable, a nice enough red fountain pen, and handed it to her. 'Kind of a gift, I guess.'

She took the pen and kissed him on the lips. 'I will never forget you,' she said, and walked down the stairs and out on to the snowbanked sidewalk, where her limousine waited to take her back to the Palmer House, to another expensive dinner, and to Union Station where the train for California would depart.

Chapter Two

THE TRAIN MOVED slowly westward from the station, away from downtown, before arcing southward through the stockyards and the manufacturing plants and into the prairie. Simone watched the cityscape change to landscape, or, more accurately, watched the lights diminish into darkness, and there was nothing left to look at of the city she'd barely known, but which had marked her deeply. She couldn't be quite sure if it was the city and the things she'd seen of it, so unlike any place, anything she'd seen before – even the burlesque, even the bar, were unlike any burlesque or bar in Paris – or whether it was simply this man, whom she barely knew, but who had bewildered her, and overwhelmed her. She took his book from her bag – he hadn't sent any as he'd promised, but she'd found this collection of short stories in the train station book stall. She started to read the first story: it sent her back to that jailhouse, the police captain taunting and consoling and dismissing the criminals in equal measure and sometimes in the same words, and she could see, reading and reliving, that this man and this city had everything to do with one another and that she wanted to see them both again. She lay in her sleeping berth reading until she was too tired, and when she awoke in the morning she picked up the book and continued, and later that evening as she sat in the dining car she took out a piece of paper and the red fountain pen and began writing: *Dear Nelson Algren.*

Nelson Algren spent his days as he had before: going to the Y to work the heavy bag and shower, going home to continue writing this new novel, picking up pork chops on the way home, making stew or lasagne, going to the Tug for a few drinks, sometimes a game of poker, though he hadn't really been gambling much lately. He'd thought of the frog now and again, of her ridiculous accent, almost impossible to understand, of whether she'd understood a damn thing he'd said anyway, of her navy blue dress – apparently her only dress – of her naked in his bed. Of course it'd been too late to get his books sent before she'd left, and he figured she'd be sore about that. But then her letter from the train arrived – *I'll try to write in English* – and asking if maybe she might visit in April, and he thought of her arrival in the limo, and holding the letter and thinking of it he began to laugh aloud; yes, there was something about this crazy frogwoman, and if she wanted to come back, then he wanted to have her. So he wrote.

It'd only been about a week since the letter, and he'd sent his to New York, so he knew she hadn't read that yet, but the doorbell rang in the middle of the afternoon and his first thought was of Simone. He went to the window and looked out. No limo stood idling on Wabansia Avenue. That was just as well; once was enough. He didn't really expect to see her at the door when he opened it, but nor did he expect to see Mary G.

Two large suitcases stood next to her on the front porch. She was smiling, her teeth showing, her eyes slightly squinting. Nelson stood in the doorway in his bathrobe and slippers and said nothing.

I've moved from New York, she told him. Her smile remained. Can I come in?

He took her suitcases and she bounded up the stairs and into the apartment. Once inside, she asked, smile undiminished, if he wasn't going to kiss her. He set the suitcases by the door and she stepped to him and kissed him on the lips, and he returned it, though he broke away first.

She said she was hungry and they should go out and get something to eat. He tugged the hem of his bathrobe and suggested he wasn't dressed for it.

Oh, go and change into some clothes, you silly man, she told him, giggling, so he went into the bedroom and changed, tossing his bathrobe on to the still unchanged sheets. Mary G. looked as though she was moving in to stay, or at least for longer than he really wanted her. As they walked out of the apartment he glanced at his desk. A half-written page curled from the typewriter. A stack of letters stood next to it, the one on top from the California train.

The snow was congealing into slush. They walked along Wabansia to Ashland, and down to Pierce to a diner, and sat at a table in the middle. Mary was talking the whole way but he wasn't paying much attention. The place was half-full. He'd finished his grilled cheese and most of the fries, and she was still only halfway through her pork chop, when she asked him about the frog. He'd been waiting for it.

Did Simone de Beauvoir call you?

She did. He pushed a french fry through the ketchup puddle. She's some lady.

Mary wanted to know what they'd done.

He waved the fry, and ketchup spattered the table. Showed her the sights. She wanted real Chicago so that was what she got.

Mary told him that in New York nobody would take her to the Bowery, and he said that in Chicago she'd gotten overwhelmed by Bucktown. He laughed, and she chuckled too, and thanked him for taking her around; she hadn't been sure if it was such a great idea, foisting her on him.

He shrugged and ate another fry. He couldn't decide whether he pitied Mary or just didn't want to be around her, but either way he was going to have to put up with her for a while.

Over the next several days he took her to bars, he took her to cheap restaurants, they went to Maxwell Street, they went to jazz clubs, they walked around town without aim. A few times he managed to enlist Stuart or Studs to go along with them. Mary was fun and all, but he wanted to be writing, and, if he wasn't going to be writing, he'd at least rather be entertaining the frog than Mary, who seemed to think it was a marvellous adventure, who seemed to think she was welcome to stay for as long as she liked, or till death did them part – it wasn't clear on what evidence Mary was fooling herself, but it wasn't his doing. He wondered when she'd notice his indifference – though he supposed he'd have to stop fucking her for that. They went to Indiana for a few days to visit his friends there, and the awkwardness between them – between everybody – finally gave Mary the hint; when they got back to Chicago she was upset, and asked him what he wanted from her, so he told her to leave. She yelled at him, and she cried at him and she told him she'd moved all the way from New York City for him, and he pointed out he hadn't asked her to, or even hinted it might be fun, and that there was a big difference between a small affair and being Mrs Nelson Algren, if that was her idea. He could see she was trying to be dramatic as she jammed her things into the suitcase, and he allowed her to storm through from the bedroom to the front room and to slam the door in a way that caused old Mrs Staslovski upstairs to pound on the floor. From the window he watched Mary hail a cab and fling her suitcases into the back seat, and then he went into the bedroom and finally changed the sheets.

Simone arrived again at the end of April. They'd managed to organise it via letters sent to and from New York and Pennsylvania, she asking him to come to New York City, he insisting she come back to Chicago, until eventually she found three days she could rearrange to spend with him alone. The snow had melted, and the temperature had risen to an almost tolerable degree. This time she didn't pull up in a limo; a cab dropped her in front of the building on Wabansia and she pressed the button for the bell.

Her Chicago man was waiting. He had seen the cab pull up and was already halfway down the stairs by the time the doorbell sounded. He opened the door and she dropped her bags to embrace him, then followed him up the stairs into the little apartment.

It was neater than two months ago. She could see the floor – it wasn't strewn with newspapers – and the air wasn't permeated with the fug of old stew. A yellow flower stood in a vase on the little kitchenette table. She took all this in as he led her by the hand through to the bedroom, where they removed each other's clothes.

They went to the Tug and she told him about visiting her friend in California, and the University of Pennsylvania, where she'd given lectures and mostly been bored. He didn't tell her about the visit from Mary G. He'd mostly just been writing, he told her, and it was true. She looked around as they talked, and she recognised some of the other drinkers: the one-legged man and the skinny poker player sat talking together at the bar, and Barusz the bartender she remembered as well. It didn't quite feel familiar, but nor was it as strange and overwhelming as it had been two months previously. She imagined her earlier self sitting here in this same booth with this same man, and thought how different that woman was from this present-tense one, despite how little of her had changed. She'd wished without trying for another brief affair in California, and the New York one had fallen through, but here she sat in Chicago, feeling glad for all that, feeling glad to have Nelson Algren as her only American man.

He took her to a baseball game and explained the rules while she pretended to understand, and he took her to the zoo and they laughed at the monkeys. He took her to Maxwell Street and they looked through the conglomeration of radios, both stolen and repaired, clothes, kitchenware, numerous other things for sale, while they ate Polish sausage from a place called Jim's and musicians sang and played blues music on electric guitars. She'd never heard music like this – it wasn't the same as the jazz records she listened to in Paris, or what she heard Boris Vian and others playing in the clubs. Together they walked around his neighbourhood, both in the daytime and at night, and it grew less strange, and less intimidating. Even the basement dive bars and walk-up brothels, always with a cigarette-smoking or toothpick-chewing youth standing at the door, became familiar landmarks.

He'd received a grant from the American Academy of Arts and Letters, and Simone persuaded him to spend some of the money on a flight to New York so they could be there together – she'd already had to go back. Now here he was, sweating it out in a window seat of a big silver airplane, flying for the first time, just to be in New York with a crazy Frenchwoman. For most of the flight he kept his eyes shut and listened to the throb of the engines, or watched the hemlines of the stewardesses as they paced up and down the aisles serving cocktails and food. He hadn't thought to wear anything different, and so, as he sat surrounded by people in suits and dresses, wearing his checked shirt, flannel trousers and leather suspenders, he amused himself by imagining he was a podunk prairie boy on his way to the Big City, a local youth on his way to be corrupted by the wiles of the New Yorkers.

She met him at the bus terminal, her hair as always up, and still wearing the navy blue dress, despite the warm and sunny springtime weather.

'Do you even own another dress?' he asked, tugging on its sleeve after they'd kissed.

Simone looked down at the blue wool. 'What is wrong with this dress?'

'I just wonder what you wear when you wash it.'

She held out her arm and looked at the sleeve, then back at him, and she shrugged. They both started laughing.

'Let's take a cab,' she said.

They rode to Greenwich Village, to the Brevoort Hotel, which she'd booked just for them to stay in, away from where she'd been before, away from where people knew how to find her. She didn't want secrecy – she didn't care if these Americans knew what she was doing, or with whom – but she was jealous of the privacy, of the time she could have with Nelson. She'd been invited to other parties, she'd been invited to dinner, but she turned them down, as she did another speaking engagement. She would've enjoyed seeing Fernando and Stepha, Richard and Ellen, but she wanted her time to belong to her and Nelson only, and on their terms. Two weeks suddenly felt a short time, in the back seat of this cab, almost as though she could already feel herself riding the reverse journey, hotel to bus terminal, but without her hand, as it was now, in his, without the soft hum of the airline bourbon on his breath.

The hotel room had a chest of drawers, a small nightstand, a chair and twin beds spaced about a foot apart. He dropped his suitcase next to the chest of drawers and she pulled him by the waist to one of the beds. It had only been two weeks since she'd been in Chicago, and she'd been busy in New York – more lectures, more parties, and yes, after all, a little fling – but now with him on top of her the time felt longer, it felt as if those two weeks had been two months, empty and boring, or not even existent at all, a stretch of purgatory, of waiting for Nelson Algren to appear at the bus terminal. He too, afterwards, pressed against her in the skinny bed, his leg between hers, her arm across his shoulder, knew that he hadn't just blown his money and endured the flight for adventure, to play the local youth. He wouldn't have done this for Amanda, no, and certainly not for Mary.

'Do people call you a nickname?' She tried to shift so she could see his eyes, but it was impossible in the tiny bed.

'They've only ever called me Nelson,' he said.

'In my time at university, my friends, they began to call me "Castor",' she said. 'The animal with the flat tail and building things that block a river. Because I was always working.'

'A beaver,' he said.

'Yes, a beaver.'

'Busy like a beaver. It's an expression.'

33

'Perhaps you would like to call me Castor, too. None of my friends calls me Simone.'

He looked at the ceiling and laughed. 'I'm not going to call you a – ' He thought better of it. 'I always think of you as my frog.'

'Oh, ha ha.' She traced her finger along his lips. 'That first night in Chicago I thought of you as a strange man with the crooked smile of a crocodile.'

He kissed her. 'Let's go get something to eat.'

Chicago was his city, but New York, even if it wasn't the same thing, was hers. She'd walked all over Manhattan during the month before she left for Chicago. Richard and Ellen had taken her to jazz clubs in Harlem, and she'd walked the Bowery alone, because none of the dinner and party guests she'd met would go there. She'd been to Times Square and all the way to the bottom of Broadway to look out into the bay at the Statue of Liberty, that tenuous connection between her home city and America. Her hosts had taken her to expensive restaurants and to cocktail bars, but she didn't want to take Nelson to places like that. He'd shown her the Tug and a burlesque and Maxwell Street and brothels and diners: she wanted to impress him with what she knew of these types of places in New York.

That first night she took him on the subway to Harlem, and they listened to jazz and drank whisky. She told him on the way that Richard and Ellen had brought her to this club a few times, and the music was always very good. Richard was a writer too, she told him, and had also been in Chicago, and he smiled and listened, and didn't say that he knew that, that Richard had been his friend. Nor did she ask if they'd known each other. They listened to and watched the quartet – a

34

trumpet, a drummer, bass and guitar – and between songs she told him about the jazz clubs in Paris. They were always full of Americans, both on the stage and in the audience, she said. But they were full of French, bohemians like her, too. That was the word she used, bohemians. But the Americans always stuck to themselves. She had a friend, a young trumpet player, Boris, he was very good and played crazy things, but she had trouble describing it – not music like this, and not better, but different. He was beginning to understand what it must have been like for her that first night in Chicago, sitting in strange places and listening to a steamroller of words.

They took a cab back to the Brevoort and tried the other bed, and at some point they fell asleep. She awoke before him in the morning and let him sleep while she sat in the little chair reading and writing letters. When he opened his eyes the first thing he saw, hazily at first, was Simone, the cap of the red fountain pen between her teeth, and he heard the scratching of the nib on the paper. She was dressed, and her hair was braided atop her head.

'You do own other dresses, right?' He raised himself to his elbows.

She smiled, and removed the cap from her teeth. 'It is the best one I own, the most comfortable, and durable. Everyone is always making fun of it. I do not understand. But yes, good morning, Mr Algren.'

He slid naked to the end of the bed and leaned forward to kiss her on the forehead. 'Good morning.'

She continued to write while he showered and dressed, and when he was standing between the beds, flannel trousers, checked shirt, suspenders, she put down her pen. 'And Mr Algren, he also only ever wears the same clothing, yes?'

He grinned.

'Not always. I have different shirts. I just wanted to match you.'

'Oh, what a gentleman! But always these awful suspenders.'

He pulled with his thumbs on the leather straps. 'I like these.'

'They are ridiculous. You look like a farmer, not a Chicago man.'

He stepped over to her chair and put a hand under her jaw. 'A prairie lad is all I am. They'll write about me in the newspapers back home: "Local Youth Travels to Big Apple".'

She laughed, and stood and kissed him. 'Maybe the local youth would like to farm some food for his local girl. It is almost noon and I've had nothing to eat.'

They walked up Fifth Avenue to Broadway, and all the way to Times Square. It was thirty blocks and took almost an hour, passing by diners and drugstores. He pointed at each one they passed and suggested the hash browns there were just as good, the eggs in that one just as scrambled, but she insisted, and so they kept walking. On Times Square she steered him to a small drugstore, its neon RX sign blinking feebly in the sunlight.

'Special place,' he said, holding the door open for her.

She ignored him and marched directly to the sandwich corner on the left of the store. Two Formica-topped tables and a cluster of chairs crowded the space between counter and window. Already – and it pleased her – she was learning to gauge his sarcasm, and to decide how she wanted to respond to it. It was a part of the lovers' game, and it was a part she enjoyed playing.

He followed in her wake, but she was already ordering in the few seconds between the door swinging shut and his hand touching her waist. The woman knows what she likes, he thought, and ordered a Reuben on rye.

'Here is where I ate my first lunch in New York City.' She said it proudly, and straightened her back. 'It is, perhaps, my favourite thing in America: bacon, lettuce, tomato and orange juice in a drugstore.'

'I thought I was your favourite thing in America.'

She rolled her eyes. 'My second-favourite thing in America is Mr Nelson Algren. My true love is bacon and lettuce and tomato. You would never find such a place in France. The whole time I was here, before, I tried always to eat in drugstores.'

They took a long and meandering route back to the hotel, holding hands for a lap of Times Square, then down and over to Penn Station, across to Union Square and around the park, before winding through Greenwich Village back to the Brevoort. She talked the whole way, trying to point out interesting things she'd seen before – buildings, spots where she'd seen particular types of people – and she was conscious that she was trying to live up to his tour of Chicago, to show him things he wouldn't know.

But he didn't know New York City anyhow, and so he listened and nodded and asked her questions, and he was entertained both by the city and her knowledge of it, this always curious little French dynamo, no longer the overwhelmed tourist he'd taken to Wabansia in February, but a whole different creature. He loved that she was trying to meet his expectations – he could see her trying to impress him with New York's grubbiness – and he loved her non-stop rattle of garbly and accented English, which moved from overly formal to tentative slang in a single sentence, though she never spoke in single sentences.

37

He laughed and she stopped walking. They were halfway down Greene Street, brick buildings on either side.

'What is funny?'

'I was just thinking that, instead of walking around with you in your dress and me in my suspenders, I'd rather be back in one of those tiny beds.'

She turned and pulled his hand in the other direction, heading as straight a route as she could remember back to the Brevoort, to their floor, to their room, to their bed.

She'd gone to the Pan Am office as soon as she knew he was coming, to move her flight back, but now the day was arriving – tomorrow – and she wished she'd been able to make it longer. She'd written to Sartre, of course, and told him she was staying longer, that he probably wanted a little more time with Dolores – Dolores, who had sat across from her at a little cocktail bar table back in January, staring at her, making her feel as though she – she, Castor, Sartre's Castor – was somehow an interloper – but she had said nothing of Nelson Algren. That could remain a secret until she was back in Paris. Years ago, she and Sartre had made their pact: their relationship was inviolable. Their emotional bond, their intellectual work together, stood at the centre of their life – their one, shared life – and any other men and women who came into it would be contingent on this life. Sartre gave more to his contingent loves than she to hers, however, and she'd sat in New York City in January with Dolores days away from joining Sartre in Paris, wishing it could be she who would return, wishing that she'd never come to this stupid country, wondering who in all of America and its millions of people could ever want her. And there had been those few and mostly dull men, though they'd seemed interesting enough at the time. Then she arrived in Chicago, and with Chicago arrived Nelson Algren, from Chicago. And she couldn't stand that now she had to leave him, to Paris, to Chicago.

They went again to the drugstore on Times Square, so her first lunch could be her last lunch. She ate the BLT and drank the orange juice and stared out of the window at the cars, the buses, the pedestrians. Her quietness saddened him, because he knew it signalled the end, and it was hard to gauge what that end meant, here at what really felt like a beginning. Each time she turned from the window to look at him she would smile half-heartedly and turn away, either to her sandwich or the window. When her plate was empty he reached across the table and thumbed a spot of mayonnaise from the corner of her mouth. She smiled again and he saw she was trying not to cry. He slid his hand down to hers and as they stood he pulled some dollars from his pocket and tossed them on the table.

Out on Times Square it was sunny and warm, and she kept saying I'm sorry as she sniffled and cried and he kept telling her not to be. She, too, thought the air and the noise of traffic would push her tears away, but it wasn't really working. They walked slowly around Times Square and he rubbed her back between her shoulderblades, he thought of jokes and pointed out people and made them into characters to amuse her. It made it better and worse. She would smile and laugh and then she would think of how much she would miss him after tomorrow.

'I wish I could change my flight again,' she said. 'But it's too late, and also, we have our work to do in Paris.' They were waiting to cross at a traffic light.

'I'll be leaving tomorrow anyway,' he said. 'I wouldn't want you walking around New York City all alone. Or with somebody else. Or without me, at least.'

The light changed and they stepped into the street. 'Perhaps I could travel again to Chicago to see you, later in the year or early in the next.'

'I would like you to.'

He let go of her hand. 'Keep going. Wait on the corner. I'll be back.'

He ran back to the sidewalk they'd just left, and she, baffled, followed his instructions, looking back when she got to the other side, but unable to find him behind the traffic of taxis and buses. She couldn't feel upset, but only bewildered, alone on the corner. She watched the drugstore, assuming he'd left something behind, but no, it was taking too long for that. Somebody knocked her with a briefcase, but she didn't see who and it didn't matter. She was still watching across the street. Another bus blocked her view as it passed, but then a minute later there was Nelson; he waved across at her and she lifted her hand quickly – nervously? – in return. She felt like a child, watching him from the corner, waiting for the light to change, waiting for him to cross.

'Here.' He took hold of her left hand and slipped something on the middle finger, past the purple nail varnish, down over the knuckle to the base, and lifted the hand to her eye level. It now wore a silver ring, a wide band with a complicated decoration. 'I saw it in a window back there. I want you to have it.'

'I won't take it off,' she said, and kissed him.

'I love you,' he said, and surprised himself with the words, and with the sense that they were true.

'I love you also,' she said, and surprised herself as well.

They kissed again, and he took her ringed hand and together they walked the thirty blocks down to the Brevoort, and didn't leave their room until the next day, when it was for good.

She'd wanted to say goodbye in the room, where they'd slept together, made love together, eaten room service and talked about themselves to each other. But he insisted on at least seeing her to the taxi. He sat in the chair and watched her as she packed her suitcases. When she was ready he handed her a small brown paper package and told her to open it once she was in the air, then picked up her luggage and carried it down the carpeted corridor. She leaned her head against his shoulder as the elevator carried them down to the ground floor. He tipped the elevator operator but waved off the bellboy, and she linked her arm under his for the walk across the lobby. They had met in a hotel bar and now they would say goodbye in a lobby. She wanted to look up at his face but knew it would upset her, so she focused on the door until she had to drop his arm to rotate through it and on to the pavement.

The doorman hailed a cab and now it was becoming too real. The trunk popped open and the luggage was going in, Nelson was handing a dollar to him and telling the cabbie her destination, and now he was turning to her, his lips pressed together in a reluctant smile. She began to cry.

'Goodbye, crazy frog,' he said, and kissed her, first on the forehead, next on the lips.

She pressed her fingernails into his back as she kissed him. The doorman swung open the back door of the cab. She kissed Nelson one final time and stepped in. The door shut behind her and she thought of the doors in the Cook County Jail in February, and tried to laugh at her own ridiculousness. She put her hand to the window, and watched him raise his in return, the other resting in his trouser pocket. She looked at the plaid shirt, the awful leather suspenders, his crooked smile and messy hair, until seconds later the cab had pulled around the crescent hotel drive and out into the Fifth Avenue traffic.

Yougonnabeawayfromyourhusbandalongtime?

She looked away from the window and saw the cabbie's eyes in the rear-view mirror. She hadn't understood a word, and asked him to say it again. Are you gonna be away for a long time? he repeated. From your husband?

My husband? She looked again to the window. A few blocks behind her perhaps he was still standing outside the hotel pretending he could see the cab. Yes, a long time.

Chapter Three

ON THE PLANE she tried to keep from crying, but she couldn't manage the job very well. She sat with her head leaning against the window and watched the suitcases being loaded into the luggage hold. The package wrapped in brown paper sat on her lap. Still watching the baggage-handlers, she ran her finger along the edge, feeling the corner of what she knew was a book inside, and across its top, somehow soft and rough at once. The last suitcases were in, though she hadn't spotted her own, and the plane shuddered as the cargo doors thumped shut. Soon they would be in the air, flying away from New York, towards Paris, further away from Chicago. She wiped the corners of her eyes with the heels of her hands and sat back, waiting for take-off.

The machine lifted into the air, and over the ocean, and banked to the left, and she could pretend she would plummet into the sound. When it flattened its course towards Canada she pushed her fingernail into the knotted string to loosen it and opened the brown paper package from Nelson: his two novels. She'd suspected as much, but just seeing his name on the covers made her start to cry again. One was *Somebody in Boots* and the other was *Never Come Morning*, and inside this second he had written:

I send this book with you
That it may pass
Where you shall pass:
Down murmurous evening light
Of storied streets
In your own France
Simone, I send this poem there, too
That part of me may go with you.

She rested her head against the window and looked at the clouds, the ocean, the shoreline and cried until the creamed chicken was served. She wanted to ask someone what 'storied streets' meant but she didn't want to share her poem with anyone. She recalled – strangely at first, but then, no, with obvious connection – 1929, when she had first come to know Sartre, when they had spent hours studying together for the exam, and – although perhaps only in retrospect – she felt a mark, a shift: her life as Simone had during those days and nights become new, or not new but different; she had become, not Simone, but Castor, that nickname René had given her and which everyone had called her ever since; but also, she had ceased during those days to be Simone alone, and had moved, even if it wasn't until some months later that she and he really came to acknowledge it – came to seal their pact together – had moved from Simone to Castor to Castor and Sartre. And now she was looking down at this poem and this empty plate of airborne dinner and this small glass of whisky and she was feeling another such shift, which she wanted to both embrace and deny at once. He was the local Chicago youth, and the taxi driver had called him husband and talked of distance and Paris, and her youth with his crooked crocodile grin had called her crazy frog, or maybe with capital letters, and she knew she loved him, and wanted to love him more. But here she was in an aeroplane bound for Canada, and Paris: home and Sartre. With other men and women, no matter the intensity, it was easy to see their contingency, to imagine telling Sartre about it, to imagine its end, and enjoy the end as the emotion as much as the rest; but it wasn't easy now, with Nelson, to see that, to see any of that. It was something new.

The plane circled a Venn diagram of ocean and pine trees and nosed downwards to Newfoundland. Simone took paper and pen and filled her two hours on the ground with writing, beginning, not *Dear Nelson Algren*, but *My own nice, wonderful and beloved local youth*.

Nelson sat at the bar in the Tug with a beer and a whisky and an old copy of *The New Yorker* he'd found lying around the apartment. He hadn't read any of it, and wasn't even sure why he'd bought it in the first place, but as he was heading out this afternoon he'd seen it and thought it might be an amusing way to pass some time in the Tug. The cover had a drawing of some high-class snob in a top hat holding a monocle towards a butterfly. He turned to the 'Talk of the Town' and started laughing. There was a feature on Simone de Beauvoir.

What's funny? Barusz asked, wiping a spot on the bar with an already dirty rag before coming over.

Nelson tapped the magazine. You remember that woman I brought in here?

Barusz did. The French lady.

Nelson turned the magazine around. Turns out she's some kind of big shot.

Barusz picked it up and read aloud. *Mlle de B is the prettiest Existentialist you ever saw; also eager, gentle, modest and as pleased as a Midwesterner with the two weeks she spent in New York.*

Not as pleased as she was with the Midwesterner she spent two days with in Chicago, Nelson said.

Barusz asked what an Existentialist was supposed be.

Nelson shrugged. A frog that thinks it's a lizard.

Barusz handed the magazine back and told him there was a poker game starting upstairs in a little while if he wanted in. Studs, Pharaoh and a couple of others. Nelson read the 'Talk of the Town' article again, and again, and looked again at the cover: 22 February 1947. Officially, it had been published while Simone was in his apartment on Wabansia.

She arrived in the middle of Paris on a Sunday. The streets were empty, the sky was grey, and she had nowhere to go but home, though she didn't want to go anywhere else anyway. She looked at her ring, held it up in front of her, and smiled, and touched it with her right index finger and thumb. She had something to carry with her.

It felt important to have something to carry with her these first several days. She could be alone, because nobody knew when she was coming back, though eventually she'd be spotted in Café de Flore and the old life would return. She wanted it to return, but she also wanted to grasp at the American life, at the Chicago life, the Nelson Algren life. She needed to grasp at that life for now, because she couldn't see Sartre, who knew she was back. Dolores was still here in Paris, and, until she left, Simone couldn't – didn't want to – see Sartre. Dolores again. She could meet her on New York ground, but she wouldn't give that woman the satisfaction of thinking she was part of their life in Paris. Let others talk of Castor around her; let others remind her of the contingent nature of her stay in Paris, of her stay in Sartre's life.

But of course, Nelson: she hadn't told Sartre yet. She examined again her silver ring. It suddenly made her feel a sharp sting of – of – a sharp sting. She knew that if she were to be faithful the way she wanted Sartre to be – the way she knew, in the end, he would be – that no matter what with Nelson, she would never give herself entirely to the local Chicago youth. She smiled at the thought of his own nickname for himself. Could she? What betrayals that would involve. What betrayals everything involved.

In June she threw a party at a cellar bar in a hotel, welcoming herself back to Paris – welcoming herself away from America, she told him – and it was awful, the band too drunk to play, Boris unable to blow his horn even, everybody passing out, vomiting in the toilets or in the corners, the young men arguing with the young women and each other, the records good but not loud enough, but the party nonetheless pressing on until five o'clock in the morning and everybody the next day saying they had fun. She walked home drunk through the empty morning streets and passed out thinking of Nelson, and what he would be doing at that moment, all those hours earlier – she could never keep straight how many – in Chicago, drinking maybe at the Tug or watching the line-up, or was he going around the burlesque shows with another woman?

In July she couldn't stand it any longer and wrote to him that she'd like to come and visit for maybe two or three weeks around September. She waited for a response, but couldn't wait longer, so wrote to him again, and told him what dates she'd like to come, and that he could work, and she could work, and they could go to the Tug, and they could make love in his bed, and they could eat pancakes in Wabansia, and she wouldn't even be in the way, and a week after that letter she received a telegram: LOCAL YOUTH PREPARES FOR ADVERTISED ARRIVAL OF CRAZY FROG.

Chapter Four

THE PLANE TOOK OFF from Paris, and landed in Shannon, then lifted off of the Irish island and flew towards the Azores. The plane was old, an engine blew, and so they turned in a wide, slow, anxious arc back towards Shannon, for hours the passengers paralysed and unable to eat with the fear of an Atlantic grave until the Irish shore finally appeared and the plane landed. They sat in the airport for another two hours while the machine received its repairs, Simone unable to read, only to write, and only to write about the fear, incoherently, and to wish she were only already in Wabansia Avenue, safe in the nest, in the arms of the local Chicago youth. Again the plane lifted off, and the anxiety was no better, wondering about this stitched-together engine that ferried them to the archipelago, where on landing – of course – the tyre exploded, and again the passengers waited in the airport of a foreign island, staring in helpless fear at the unreliable machine that would take them to the American continent or die trying. For eighteen hours – she couldn't sleep – she imagined Nelson, sitting in the apartment in his flannel trousers and checked shirt – at least he'd given up the suspenders – or grey bathrobe, wondering if his frog had hopped elsewhere. She sat in a state oscillating between anxiety and panic, feeling the itch and sweat of – yes – the blue wool dress, and tried not to daydream of Chicago.

But eventually she landed at Orchard Field Airport, and climbed into the back of a yellow cab and rode east towards Wabansia Avenue. Two weeks already seemed too short.

She didn't need to ring the bell. The taxi drove slowly up Wabansia, Simone keeping an eye out for something to remind her of exactly which house was his, and she saw the billboard, SCHLITZ – THE BEER THAT MADE MILWAUKEE FAMOUS! and said, Stop! and the cabbie stepped on the brakes, so she had to excuse herself, overexcited – It's just on the next block, she told him, and yes, there outside 1523, standing on the porch, checked shirt, flannel trousers, belt, no suspenders, crooked smile, round glasses, Local Chicago Youth Nelson Algren. He bounded down the steps and paid the driver before she could get out. She fumbled with the door – it was ridiculous, her hands were shaking – while he pulled her suitcase from the trunk. She slammed the door behind her, the cab made a U-turn and she pressed her head against Nelson's chest, his arms around her shoulders, her suitcase on the kerb. Arm in arm they went up the steps, but he had to trot back for the luggage. Once inside the apartment he dropped the case at the door and took her straight to the bedroom. Neither had yet said a word, and she didn't even have the time or attention to notice that he'd cleaned the place for her arrival.

Afterwards they smoked and talked, half-covered by the Mexican blanket he used as a quilt. They knew from each other's letters what they'd been doing these past months, so they could talk about other things: books they'd read, ideas, small anecdotes they'd saved for telling instead of writing. They didn't go out that night. Nelson cooked a lasagne and after they ate they spent the night in bed. Simone, exhausted long before she'd arrived, fell asleep before Nelson, and he watched her and listened to the sound of her breathing, spluttering into the occasional snore, before he too eventually closed his eyes and slept.

She awoke to the sound of his typewriter, and listened to it, smiling, for several minutes before she opened her eyes. She could see into the other room, but not to the corner where his writing table stood. The keys would clack and clatter until the bell, the scraping slide back across, clatter and clack, sometimes through three bells and then a pause, a long pause, and she realised she was holding her breath during these pauses, until his fingers again pressed the keys, and the letters clacked on to the page.

He looked up and saw her leaning, naked, against the doorframe. She'd been there for five minutes, and goosepimples stood out on her arms and breasts. He rose and crossed the small room to her. His bathrobe was tied loosely at his waist. He kissed her, first on the forehead, then on the lips, and put his arms around her.

'Are you hungry?' he asked, and she nodded in reply.

He shrugged out of his bathrobe and wrapped it around her, sliding the sleeves over her arms and rolling them up, and walked naked into the bedroom. She moved to the window and looked down on Wabansia Avenue. Leaves had begun to fall off the few skinny trees along the sidewalk. A man with no legs pushed himself along on a platform with wheels.

Nelson came back dressed and mixed pancakes, and after they ate they went out to the public baths, and spent what was left of the morning walking around, Nelson pointing out the places she'd seen on her first time in Chicago, reminding her of the snow that had been falling then, asking her what she'd thought at the time, and what she saw in it now. Late in the afternoon they stopped at a diner and she ordered a BLT – her old New York favourite – and he ate boiled chicken.

'This cannot be a good idea,' she said, watching him bite into the chicken bones. 'Do all Americans eat chicken bones? Nobody in France would do it.'

He nodded as he chewed, and, once he'd swallowed, said, 'Only your courageous Chicago Man eats the chicken's bones.'

'I think my Chicago Man is more foolish than courageous in that case.'

He shrugged, and smiled, and ate the rest of the bone.

The afternoon was sunny but cold, the weather a herald of the end of the summer, the beginning of the autumn, and the promise that, any brief Indian summer notwithstanding, the winter would arrive in only a couple more months. None of this touched them as they walked the Near North streets of Chicago, her arm linked under his elbow. She talked a little of her book, 'The woman essay' as she still called it, and of the translation of his novel into French, and he listened. She told him of some publicity she'd received, and complained that nobody ever called her a writer, only a woman writer, as though the distinction said something important.

'But, if you're writing about women, then it does say something important.'

'Perhaps. But I'm writing about women now, and they're talking about other things – about women, yes, but about men, about people. And they don't mean it usefully. They only point it out.'

On Rush Street they passed a small shop front, Seven Stairs Bookshop, and Nelson stopped. 'Let's say hello to Stuart,' he said.

The shop was small, and heated by a wood-burning stove. An enormous salami hung from a rafter behind the counter.

A man looked up from a shelf in the corner. 'Nelson!' He put a handful of books on the floor and strode over. Simone followed as Nelson walked to meet him, and the two shook hands. The man was a little shorter than Nelson, and had a large head, and dark black hair. He wore a shirt and tie, but no jacket.

'Simone,' Nelson placed a hand on her arm, 'This is Stuart. Stuart, Simone.' She shook the man's hand, and Nelson added, 'Simone is a woman writer.'

She glared at him, and he laughed, and she bit her lip to keep her own laugh from slipping out.

'Of course,' Stuart said. 'Mademoiselle Beauvoir! It's a pleasure.'

'If he'd known you were coming, he'd be forcing you to do a reading for his customers.'

'Not fair, my friend.' Stuart adjusted some books on the nearby shelf. 'But yes, fair. Nelson tells me you're translating *Never Come Morning*.'

'Not personally,' she answered. 'But I am keeping an eye on the man who is doing the work.'

'It's a terrific book,' Stuart said. 'I wonder what the French will think, though?'

Simone began to answer and Nelson walked to another corner of the shop, taking an apple from a barrel by the door. He browsed the books and listened to the sound of their conversation, but not the words. After a few minutes he wandered back over with a couple of books.

'Simone wants to buy these,' he said, and popped the last of the apple core into his mouth.

'You eat the apple core too?' She turned to Stuart. 'This man eats all of everything. At lunch he eats the chicken bones, the only man in the world who eats the chicken bones.'

Stuart laughed, and took the books behind the counter. 'Everybody eats the chicken bones when they've been boiled for long enough.'

He wrapped the books in paper and Simone paid him. She took an apple for herself as they left, and once on the street, punched him in the arm. 'Only you eat the chicken bones?'

He scratched his head. 'I might have fibbed.'

They walked around the corner to the Allerton Hotel, and rode the elevator up to the Tip Top Tap for a cocktail with a view. Another swanky hotel bar, like where they'd first met, though not as fancy as the one at the Palmer House, Simone decided, and nicer for it. They amused themselves by pretending they could see Nelson's house, and by making up stories about the people at other tables. The whole time they held hands, his much larger than hers, his finger occasionally stroking the silver ring.

The next morning, after apple pancakes and coffee, they worked, he clacking the typewriter in the front room, she on the bed in the other, reading and taking notes. They stopped for lunch and continued working through the afternoon. Around three or four, the clacking stopped and Nelson came to the bedroom. 'Let's go have a drink,' he said.

'Let's.'

They walked back through the apartment but he stopped at the door. 'Hold on.' He went over to the record player, shuffled through a pile of records next to it, selected one, placed it and dropped the needle. After a second or two of blank rotation, Marlene Dietrich began singing 'Lili Marlene' and Nelson came back across the room, took Simone by the hand and waist, and they danced for the three minutes of the song, liltingly and laughing, at odds with the melancholy of the music.

'Now I'm ready for the drink,' he said, and they left.

The pool table was unoccupied at the Tug, so after chatting to Barusz for a few minutes they set up the balls and played. Nelson pretended to be not very good, but Simone was awful. The cue would glance off the ball, or, if she caught it cleanly, it would careen in the wrong direction. She managed to pocket only a single ball by the time he'd sunk the eight, and he suggested they move back to the bar before they destroyed the felt.

A pair of youngish guys came in and nodded in recognition towards Nelson and Simone, and as they set up the balls at the pool table he explained who they were – guys he knew from the horse track. Barusz set a couple of beers on the bar, and, while one of them broke, the other came over and picked up the beers, replacing them with two quarters.

Various other regular and semi-regular customers came in over the next hour or so, and Nelson seemed to know every single one, if not by name, then by sight. Simone remained the only woman, but she expected that about the Tug now, and in a way she would have found strange anywhere else it made her feel at home. The television above the bar was on but silent and nobody was feeding the jukebox, so the only sounds were the balls on the pool table and murmurs of conversations.

They'd already had a couple of whiskies and Simone suggested a beer before they went. She ordered and paid the fifty cents, and they touched glasses and drank. A few minutes later the door opened and a man, dressed in a suit – not expensive, but nicer than the usual cut seen in the Tug – came through and perched on a bar stool further along from them, nodding at Nelson like all the others. He ordered, and Barusz put a beer in front of him and asked for thirty-five cents.

'Expensive beers in this tavern,' the man said as he handed over a quarter and dime.

Barusz said nothing, but pointed at the sign listing the prices. Simone asked Nelson if he knew the man. He didn't.

'Why does he get charged thirty-five cents, when we pay twenty-five?'

Nelson brushed his thumb across her temple. 'Because nobody knows him. Or, more importantly, Barusz doesn't know him. The people who aren't known pay the posted price, and the rest of us pay the regular price.'

'Even the mayor is a criminal in Chicago,' she said, quoting him from the night they'd first met.

'I wouldn't say it's criminal,' he said. 'Just the rules of the game.'

'Not a very nice game, then.'

'Maybe not. The rules are always rigged in the games around here, but, when they're rigged in your favour, you don't tend to complain.'

So the pattern continued: working by day, to the Tug or another bar or burlesque or jazz club in the evening, the work day broken up in the bedroom and in long walks around the streets of the neighbourhood and into other parts of the city. Nelson became grumpy when his work wasn't going well, or when he was ready to go out and Simone was still reading, but the dark mood never lasted long, and she understood it as part of his personality, his restlessness. As the first days turned into the end of the first week, and became the middle of the second – as her time in Chicago began to point closer and closer to its end – she realised that, although parting would once again be painful, and although it was necessary, they could continue this relationship – yes, this marriage of its unique kind – and continue it well. The commitment to Sartre didn't mean – and this was the worry she'd harboured since that bewildering February night in Chicago, since their New York farewell and during the Paris time in between – didn't mean she couldn't have Nelson, her Chicago husband, too. She could see how it worked, she could see it continuing to work, the way these thirteen days – now almost past – had worked, with love. They would visit one another every six months, and they'd hatched a plan to travel next spring, down the Mississippi River, and to Mexico, and already – before she'd even left Chicago, before she'd left his arms – she was looking ahead to it, to the months together instead of mere days, to seeing thihgs that neither of them had seen, an equal footing for their partnership, and yes, it was, after all, a partnership, she could feel that – not the simple affair she'd been afraid it might turn into, but a real, a lasting relationship, despite the complications.

They were eating dinner in a pizzeria several blocks from Wabansia. They'd drunk most of a bottle of chianti, and as he emptied the remainder into their glasses Nelson signalled the waiter for another half-bottle. She was smiling at him, already thinking she might suggest they just go home after this, and listen to some records, or skip the records and go straight to bed.

He used the last piece of crust to sweep up some cheese that had fallen to the plate. 'It's made me happy, having you here,' he said.

'Yes.' She continued to smile at him. 'It has made me very happy as well. Such a short time! Soon I will be on the aeroplane and we will be speaking of it in the past tense.'

'Yes,' he said. 'Writing of it in the past tense in letters. But even that's better than nothing at all.'

'And it is only a short half-year until the Mississippi River and Mexico.'

'A long half-year.'

'I suppose it is.' She stretched her hand across the table and rubbed his with her ringed finger. 'More than six months. But not much. And less than a year. And there is always excitement in the planning.'

'Maybe,' he said, taking hold of her hand, 'you could plan to stay after the trip. For good.'

'Nelson – '

'I know. But think about it. If not for good, for a year. You'll have work to do, I'll have work to do – I can find a bigger place if that helps.'

'Oh, it all helps and sounds so nice, but Nelson – ' She couldn't tell him what he wouldn't understand. 'There are just too many things in Paris that require me. And that I require.'

He nodded, and poured wine from the carafe into each of their glasses, starting with hers. They were silent while they drank the wine. She couldn't read him, and it scared her, a little. She didn't want their last few days to be silent and strange. She didn't want to end this way, just as she was beginning to feel the real possibilities.

But out on the sidewalk the first thing he did was kiss her. 'Really, won't you come for a year?'

'Nelson!' She stepped back, but checked her volume. 'Nelson. I can't. I've told you. I need to be in Paris.'

'Yes, but you can work, you can write here – look what you've done the past two weeks. You can always turn it around: make the short trips back there, and the home here in Chicago.'

'I can't. It isn't just Paris, it isn't just me – there is also Sartre to think about.'

He felt his throat tighten. The dread of what he'd half-expected but managed to push out of his mind to the point that it seemed less and less possible. She'd written to him about her commitment to Sartre, and he'd written back that he understood, but he didn't. Her explanations didn't really make sense.

'I'm no replacement for him, I suppose.'

'No. That is the point. There is no replacing. You don't need to replace him. You are my Chicago husband, and he is Sartre.'

'Some husband, when he has to put up with that. You'll stow me in your Chicago drawer for a rainy day.'

Simone put a hand on his waist. 'Nelson, you aren't understanding. With Sartre it is nothing like us. Sartre and I are not a couple; we are not a husband and a wife. We are Sartre and Castor – a partnership, only the two of us, but us as one thing that cannot be divided. I need him, and he needs me, and we need the work that we do together, and that is all, but that is also everything. It is our life.'

'So our life can be divided by it.'

Her hand left his waist and pressed itself against her own cheek. 'It is not so simple, Nelson. I love you, and what we have is love. But we have to recognise how our love will work, and how it can work. Working and loving in the Wabansia nest is wonderful, and means very much to me. But it cannot mean everything – there is too much in Paris that needs me.'

'There is Sartre in Paris that needs you.'

'Yes!' She stamped her foot. 'There is Sartre in Paris that needs me! But this is not – are you listening at all to what I am saying? This is not what you think, or what you are making it. I am only loving you, am only making love to you, am only in Paris crying about you. And when I am in Chicago loving you I also think of the work that Sartre and I have to do. That work is inescapable. Necessary. And of a very different kind. Please, Nelson: understand this.'

'I'm trying hard to "understand this" –' he copied her inflection ' – but it's not as easy as you might think, with it all thought out for yourself.'

'Nelson, when you stop loving me – '

'I will not stop loving you.'

'When you stop loving me, you'll stop. But please at least love me now, because right now I love you and need you and want that love and need it to last as long as possible, in both of us.'

They stood on the dark Chicago sidewalk, the restaurant sign stuttering neon light across their faces. He kissed her, and put his arm around her shoulder, and they walked back to Wabansia Avenue, stopping several times to kiss again, and once inside the apartment there was no question, and no talking into the bedroom, into the bed, and she knew he loved her and she loved him, on the terms that they would have to take for their love.

She wouldn't let him go with her to the airport, so once again they said their goodbyes outside a waiting taxi. Her suitcase was heavier than when she'd arrived, laden with the books he'd made her buy, a couple of bottles of whisky, gifts for Sartre, for Bost and others. She tried her best not to cry, and even in the cab kept herself together, talking to the driver a little as they passed the funeral home, the pizzeria where they'd been only a few nights earlier, and then turning into streets that were strange to her, west towards the airport.

He stood out on Wabansia for several minutes after the taxi had disappeared around the corner. He would've asked her again to stay right now forever, if he'd thought she would do it. In the pizzeria he'd asked what seemed more reasonable, or more plausible, or more – well, it seemed like the option that involved a compromise. But maybe it didn't. It made for a strange relief, looking down empty Wabansia Avenue. If she wouldn't stay, then it was better now she was gone. No, not really. But the last days, knowing he would put her suitcase in a taxi and watch it disappear, watch her disappear for eight months when they could be working together in the apartment all that time, going out, staying in and listening to records. It was true – he felt more in love with her, more of a marriage with her than he ever had with Amanda, whom he'd loved, and with whom he'd failed. Here was the woman he could hold on to forever, he knew. Or there she went, anyway, to the airport, to Paris. He went inside and poured himself a drink.

She'd arrived at the airport early – too early – and sat in the waiting area with her eyes closed, not wanting to watch the people, not wanting especially to watch people wishing each other farewell, or the couples travelling together. She listened to the sounds of footsteps, of chatter, faraway and nearby, of announcements being made over the public address system. It kept repeating things, two three four times, and it took several repetitions before she realised this particular announcement included her name. She opened her eyes and listened to the voice again. It was calling her to the information desk, so she took her suitcase and sought it out, and announced herself as Simone de Beauvoir. The man handed her a small box and told her she must have friends in Chicago. Inside was an elaborate corsage, an arrangement of white flowers. She lifted the box to her nose and smelled them, and then thanked the man and took the box back to the waiting area. She smelled the flowers once more and pinned them to her dress.

Chapter Five

WITHOUT HER, and with nothing else to do but wait for spring, when she'd finally return and they'd be on the river and in Mexico, he got to work. He rose early and went to the Y and skipped rope and worked the heavy bag, then showered and came home and wrote. Every day, the same pattern. He made a stew and kept it going all week, and every Sunday made a new one. He stayed out of the Tug except once in a while on a Friday or Saturday, and he stayed out of the upstairs room. No vices, he told himself, just work. Work as well as he could so when Simone came back and they travelled he'd have nothing else.

He ran into Jack one Friday in the Tug, and they had some beers and played a few frames of pool, but not for money. He'd known Jack for years, a guy he sometimes played some cards with, though he didn't know him well. Jack was the kind of guy Simone would've described – it made him smile to think it – as 'The real Chicago', that night they first met. A couple other people came in later, and Jack introduced them: his girl, Patty, and her ex-husband, Karl. They all sat at a table drinking beers until Barusz closed up, and then walked the neighbourhood looking for a place that was still open, drank a few more beers there and, when it shut down, trawled for another. He hadn't been out in a few weeks, and they were good company. Bar-hopping could be better than work, maybe, to hold back the creeping loneliness. Eventually they ran out of bars but they were around the corner from the place where Jack and Patty and Karl lived so they went up the stairs and sat around with a few more bottles of beer and a jazz record he didn't recognise. Karl was a drummer and he tapped along on his knees, and Patty sat in a chair next to Nelson, who slouched on a sofa, resting the beer bottle on his thigh, his eyes heavy and only half-open. Jack got up and went behind a curtain and Nelson, only kind of half-aware, watched the silhouette of his arm pumping up and down, hand tightening into a fist and opening out again, tightening, opening. Patty said something about Jack having trouble and Karl grunted or mumbled something – a series of sounds to Nelson in the brain-haze of beers. A few minutes later Jack came back and flopped next to Nelson, and whatever trouble he'd been having was forgotten.

He was keeping his work schedule – the rope and boxing in the morning, and back home to the typewriter – but now Jack or Patty or Karl would stop by sometimes in the afternoon or at night, one of them or two or all three. They'd show up unannounced and hang out for a while, then take off again. He didn't mind. It kept him from becoming a complete hermit, and he liked talking to Karl about music. Whenever they came one of them would be carrying a cigar box, and wouldn't let it go. Sometimes one of them would disappear into the other room with it, and come back, and it wasn't long before Nelson shook the naïveté and put things together. He wasn't sure he minded. Or maybe he did, but it was because they were acting like they weren't doing it, like they were pulling the wool or something, and that was a kind of bullshit. Jack sheepishly offered him some one time, and Nelson said maybe he didn't need to, and Jack giggled and said yeah, no, it wasn't a good idea, he didn't want the monkey, but he asked if Nelson wanted to watch how it was done. Nelson wondered if Simone would want to watch, eager for what she'd call a real experience. He didn't want to gawp at people shoving needles into their arms, doing whatever else – he didn't know – but Jack stayed and shot up anyway, sitting on the Mexican blanket on the bed in the other room, out of sight.

Nelson was up late one night, drinking scotch and listening to a couple of new jazz records he'd bought, when Karl and Patty banged on his door and pleaded for help. Jack was pale and sweating and they said they had to score now and he had to help them. What the hell he had to do with it he didn't know, but there he was, putting on a coat and following them into the still-waiting cab. Jack was shaking, with Karl and Patty sitting either side, Nelson pressed against the door because the cabbie wouldn't let anybody sit in the front. Karl said an address. Patty was stroking Jack's sweaty hair. A few blocks later the cab stopped and Karl told the driver to wait and Nelson to come with him and Patty and Jack stayed put. Nelson trailed behind Karl through the snow on an uncleared sidewalk, up some steps into a fleabag hotel. What necessary part he was playing, he wasn't sure. Karl said some things to the fat guy behind the reception desk, and the guy rang a bell. A minute later a slouchy kid came down the stairs and fat man told them to follow him. In a room on the third floor there was a guy sitting on a bare mattress, and another who blocked the doorway once they were in. The slouchy kid stayed in the hallway. They were given a paper bag. Karl looked in it and handed it to Nelson. Karl didn't have enough money and Nelson had to cough up the difference. The slouchy kid led them downstairs and they were back in the cab, Jack now crying, his arms smacking across the back seat, only the scrum of friends keeping him contained. The cabbie was none too pleased. Neither was Nelson, when they stopped in the middle of Wabansia outside his place and he was paying for the round trip. Patty and Karl had to pretty much carry Jack upstairs and Nelson went into the bedroom, listening while they helped Jack tie off and shoot up. The crying stopped and Nelson came back in and Jack was sitting there with a vague smile on his face. It's not a big thing, he said to Nelson, but sometimes it seems like one, and he thanked him. They stayed for a while chatting, but Nelson wasn't really participating. He wanted them to leave but didn't want to make an argument out of it. Even though he wasn't, he felt like he was being conned. He knew he was really just the only reliable person they knew.

Somehow Castor and Sartre found themselves one night in a Russian restaurant with Arthur – miserable, reactionary Arthur. How or why they remained friends, or some approximation of friends, she could no longer say. But here they were, she and Sartre, Arthur and also Albert. The last time she'd seen Albert it was the morning after her return from Chicago, and she'd looked so worn and puffy from travel – and, yes, from separation – that he'd asked her if she was pregnant. He sat next to Sartre, and she sat next to Arthur, which at least meant she didn't have to look at him the whole time, and could more or less ignore him, eat her golubci and watch the people at other tables.

They were on to a second bottle of vodka. Arthur was getting belligerent by steps, and of course Sartre and Albert were rising to it. They couldn't help it. Arthur leaned over, palms flat on the table, swaying in miniature loops, and asked Sartre if the accusations were true. Sartre deliberately misunderstood and Albert told Arthur to shut up. Arthur sneered. He wouldn't put it past the little man, he said, watching Sartre but speaking of him in the third person. The good Existentialist has to look after his own existence first, and he was never a real Communist anyway. Albert told him enough, but Arthur didn't stop. He knew, Arthur said, that the Résistance never trusted Sartre. All this anti-De Gaulle rhetoric, it was just a vehement smokescreen. Arthur didn't even care that much. He just needed to show he wasn't so right-wing he could be a collaborator.

Castor sucked in air and glared at her empty plate. Sartre told Arthur to fuck himself. Arthur grabbed a glass and flung it at Sartre. It glanced off his shoulder and smashed on the floor. Albert half-stood, leaning across the table, but before he could do anything Arthur had plunged a fist into his eye. The cutlery danced as all three stood, banging knees and thighs against the table. Castor didn't move. Albert walked straight to the door, but Sartre and Arthur were arguing and shoving and it would've been funny to watch, little Sartre trying to physically intimidate the much taller Arthur, if it didn't make her sick. Now they were outside, visible in the window, shoving and yelling, and the other people watched and laughed and started the gossiping already, and Castor waited until they'd disappeared from view before she paid and left in the opposite direction.

She stopped in a basement jazz club and watched some American musicians play to a mostly American audience, and drank whisky. It was twice the price here as in Chicago. She tried to imagine the crooked smile of Nelson Algren but her head was too full of mouthy arrogant Arthur. She drank a second whisky and could feel herself wanting to cry, so she left.

Nelson was at a party at the Seven Stairs, leaning against a bookshelf, drinking a beer and eating some salami on a slice of bread. There'd been a reading, some poet he'd never heard of but Stuart liked. It'd been okay, not great. Nelson watched the guy as he talked to a group of two men and a few women, and Stuart near the potbellied stove holding court with some regular customers. Stuart pointed over at Nelson and a young woman separated herself from the group to join him. She introduced herself as a student at DePaul, and told him that Stuart had said he was Nelson Algren, the author. Stuart's no liar, he told her, and she laughed, and told him that she particularly liked his short stories. She was drinking red wine. She was short, with brown hair and brown eyes. She continued to talk about what she liked about his stories, even though he hadn't asked, and she talked about her studies. He asked her what she thought of the poetry reading, and she said it was good, but maybe too much like Sandburg, not original enough, not in Chicago anyway. She touched his arm when she talked. He would've – a year ago, he would've – taken her out and taken her home. But he'd promised himself he wouldn't betray Simone. He'd stay faithful to Simone like a husband, like a good husband should. He excused himself and said goodbye to Stuart and left, taking an apple from the barrel on the way out. He ate the apple as he walked from Rush Street to the El. He watched the streets as he rode, but there wasn't much to see, at least not at speed. Back in the neighbourhood he stopped at the Tug. He drank a whisky and watched the pool players and chatted idly to Barusz. After another whisky he went home and slept.

Sartre and Castor were in Berlin, February Berlin, which was like February Chicago, cold and snow and wind, but no Wabansia Avenue, no Tug, no basement burlesque, or at least not that the French Embassy chaperones would be showing her. Sartre's play was on, and he had a lecture, and the two Existentialist heroes had to be taken on tour after tour, and never go anywhere without a chaperone: French sector, British sector, American sector, Russian sector. All that lay ahead. Here now they were barely landed at the American sector airport and already seated in the French Embassy at a large table and a formal dinner. The way things changed. You're the most hated man and woman in France and calling the president ugly and a Fascist, and then you're in a foreign city at a formal table with ambassadors and generals and businessmen of types it was hard to construe, plus all their wives, the dangling-jewelleried, single-occasion-dress-wearing bourgeois foreign cohort. She and Sartre had to sit among these smiling and hateful idiots and pretend to be part of it, pretend to be like them, and of course pretend to like them.

At dinner she was seated next to an American man. He mentioned Mary G., and said he thought they'd known each other. So she spoke politely of New York City, and asked what Mary was doing now, and the man said he was engaged to marry her. He talked around mouthfuls of steak about some novels he'd read recently, and she named Nelson Algren. He'd read the stories, he said, and one of the novels. He said some literary things about them, vague things about style that didn't really mean much, but she said anyway that she knew him, and the man responded by saying she must have met Algren after Mary's affair with him.

She felt slapped but she hid it well. Yes, it must've been after. The man laughed in an unpleasant way, as though he knew something she didn't, as though he was superior to her, and waved a hand and said it wasn't really anything, that Mary was always falling in love with one writer or another, and for a while there a year or so ago it had been Algren. She smiled and made some kind of reply. Yes, it must've been after. She couldn't care, after all, shouldn't care, before or after: her Chicago husband was free to do what he wished. But he'd never said anything about it. This man beside her continued to talk and she gave the appearance of paying attention, making small comments where necessary, but really she'd lost interest.

May was getting close, and they both felt it. His letters couldn't stop mentioning it, and hers couldn't either. Each day, each letter brought them closer together. Each one made their love seem more real, and each day that passed on the calendar meant one fewer day to wait. He worked harder to make the time pass more quickly, and to make his mind more clear for her arrival. She tried to work, but as May got closer she found it impossible, her mind so agitated with the plans for travel, with the anticipation of the flight, of driving up Wabansia Avenue in a taxi. She went to a dentist and had her missing tooth – lost long ago in a cycling accident – replaced so she would look nice for Nelson, Nelson who wrote that from May to September, in Chicago, on the Mississippi River, in Mexico and Guatemala, in New York and back in Chicago, wherever he would go, to be able to go with his frog wife would make it the happiest summer, the happiest five months he could imagine.

She was happy too, but had already changed her flights. She would be back in Paris by July. She could never tell Nelson why, and she wouldn't tell him at all yet. She would have to find the moment. Sartre had told her that Dolores – again, Dolores – wouldn't be in Paris after all. She didn't have to avoid Dolores. Without Dolores, Sartre would need her. She could compromise on the time. She would simply have to find the right way to tell Nelson, and the right time to tell Nelson. It would all be okay. He was her loving husband, after all. The reasoning seemed sound to her, but a decision built on a partial truth is essentially a lie. She was lying to Nelson, and she was lying to herself.

Chapter Six

THE PLANE LANDED in New York – this time, the flight had been routine – and she sent Nelson a telegram from the airport announcing her return to the Home of the Brave. In only a few more days she would arrive on Wabansia Avenue, but first she would visit Stepha and see to something important. She was terrified, and she'd written to Nelson to discuss it, that five months – she still called it five months, a small but necessary lie – could be risky, if they didn't use some kind of contraception – it had been foolish before, but at least they'd been at home, whereas now they'd be in countries foreign to them both – and she felt bewilderingly stupid, because of France, because of Catholic, backward France, not quite knowing what to do.

Stepha had made an appointment for her. They ate dinner at home with Fernando and the baby, the night of her arrival, and caught up on things they hadn't written in their letters, and early the next afternoon they walked up through the lunchtime Manhattan sidewalks, past suited businessmen on their way to steakhouses, groups of secretaries in long thin skirts moving towards the diners and lunch counters, to a doctor's office. The physician was a woman, and spoke French, and told her how honoured she was to meet her, and it made her all the more embarrassed, to be treated, as at home in Paris, as in London or Berlin, as an intellectual, as an eminent guest, and yet to be sitting bottomless on this examination table with her legs open and her vagina calipered and scrutinised and assessed and fitted.

She and Stepha rode an elevator down to the ground floor and walked back out on to Seventy-Eighth Street. She carried the diaphragm in a brown paper bag, and it could have been a sandwich, or a toy. She laughed at how ridiculous she felt, and said to Stepha as they walked that it made her feel almost like a schoolgirl, or like when she'd been in love – or thought she'd been in love – with her cousin, Jacques. But not like that at all, because this was an adult love, an intellectual connection and – she looked down at and waved the brown paper bag – physically unlike any other she'd known. It was a womanly love, and the love he returned was manly. He'd told her of things she hadn't considered, showed her new perspectives on things she had already thought through, and opened her eyes to things right in front of her that she hadn't seen, she told Stepha. The charge he'd given her essay, now growing and growing, the books and ideas he fed into it, from even across the ocean and half a continent in his Chicago apartment – and the jokes he told her; the sensitivity of his own feelings towards himself as well as towards her, and when they were in each other's arms – oh, she'd cried for days after their last parting, she told Stepha, and spent all too many hours thinking about him and writing to him and waiting waiting waiting for his letters to arrive on their yellow paper. He is an honest husband, she told Stepha, and without noticing raised her silver-ringed finger against her cheek; a man unlike those of Paris, a man whom she could follow around the dirtiest corners of Chicago, and who followed her through these same streets of New York, a man who drank beer and whisky in the most run-down bars in the most run-down neighbourhood, but talked to her of Dostoevsky and Faulkner and Gunnar Myrdal and the Chicago White Sox.

Stepha stopped. They'd been walking the wrong way, and neither had noticed. She stepped out towards the street to hail a taxi, but Simone held her arm and said they should walk back down, so she could save the fare to spend in Mexico. Stepha told her that was ridiculous. She wouldn't walk fifty blocks all the way back through Manhattan. She'd pay for the taxi if that was what it took.

Another taxi in another city – that other city – now carried her along Wabansia Avenue, closer and closer to her local youth. But the street seemed unfamiliar to her, and her mind so full of the image of Nelson, of being embraced by Nelson, she couldn't concentrate, and couldn't think of the number, that number she'd written on countless envelopes, twice a week for months, for more than a year now. One easy number. They passed an alley sentried by half a dozen metal trash cans and she recognised it and called for the driver to stop, and paid him, and he popped the trunk and got out to help her with the suitcases. She kept expecting Nelson to gallop down the stairs to the sidewalk, but he didn't appear. The taxi made a U-turn and sped westward. She looked up at the house and realised it was the wrong one.

She looked back the way she'd come, and forward. It must be forward. She couldn't have passed it without realising. She picked up her bags and started up the street, wobbling with the weight of the luggage. She had to stop three times, but two blocks later she saw the sign, SCHLITZ – THE BEER THAT MADE MILWAUKEE FAMOUS! and realised her mistake, and now knew exactly where to go. She looked up and yes, Nelson was coming down the stairs of the front porch, and she could already see his smile and he was waving and she dropped her bag to return the wave, and she didn't know whether to keep going or just to drop her things and wait, but now she was in his arms and he in hers, his lips on her neck, now her mouth, and that outstretched accordion of months compressed back together and felt now, in each other's arms, like nothing, or like seconds, and he'd spent a couple of hours at the window, pretending to listen to records but waiting and watching for a taxi to appear, for the taxi to appear, for Simone to appear, and she didn't, and didn't, and he looked enough times at the street and at his watch to decide to do something, or anything, and pacing the street seemed the best option so down he went and out on to the porch and then saw that little Frenchwoman, hauling two bags up Wabansia Avenue and staring at the Schlitz billboard and at once he knew she'd gotten lost so he broke into a trot to be here quicker, now, her face against his chest, his arms around her, crazy frog wife, to be here now together for five months that could accordion out, now, as slowly as possible, now that they could love not from across the ocean but together as one.

He picked up her bags and carried them the half-block and up the stairs and into the apartment. She was trying half-successfully not to cry. He poured a whisky for each of them and put 'Lili Marlene' on the record player. She smiled, then laughed, and lifted her glass.

'It began to feel as though these months would never arrive,' Simone said.

'They arrived. You arrived.'

She smiled, and felt her eyes trying to keep the tear ducts closed. 'Yes. Here in the Wabansia nest.'

He put on a new record, Blind Willie Johnson singing 'Nobody's Fault But Mine', and refilled the whiskies, and when they'd drunk them, and Simone was just beginning to think about how hungry she felt, he announced that he had some people he wanted her to meet. Her coat was on, they were out the door and down the stairs and out on to the sidewalk, she was trotting as quickly as she could in his wake and he was talking with excitement and fast about these people, but she could only catch half of it. They passed a little restaurant she knew, and the pizzeria where she'd eaten her last Chicago meal, and where she wished she were eating her next one, but Nelson strode past, yammering still, and she knew she wouldn't be eating for a while. They arrived at a house not much different from the building Nelson lived in and climbed the stairs.

A young woman, long brown hair, answered the door and Simone thought oh so here is a test, some little whore he's been seeing, and she suddenly saw the man in Berlin laughing at her about Mary G. But no, she thought, no, she remembered, he hadn't, he'd told her he'd been faithful and anyway so who was this woman?

Nelson introduced Patty, and they entered the small apartment, a room divided by a curtain and, she was told, another room behind a door behind the curtain. Karl was the man sitting on the sofa, which had a tear on one armrest, the stuffing crawling out of it. There's also Jack, Nelson said, but Jack, Karl added, was in the other room just now. He said it looking at the floor, and Simone understood that, whatever Nelson had been telling her on the way over, it was information she was missing now, that she needed now to make sense of this shabby place, these pale and shabby people.

They stayed for about an hour but it was long enough or maybe too long for Simone, who wasn't exactly uncomfortable, but really didn't understand why she had to meet these people, and meet them so urgently. They struck her as pleasant but vague, and not the kinds of fast-talkers or hustlers that Nelson was usually telling her about in his letters. It had started raining while they were there, so instead of walking they took a streetcar back towards Wabansia, getting out a few blocks short to go – finally! she decided not to say – to a restaurant.

Back in the apartment there was no music, no whisky, only a straight path to the bedroom, the multicoloured blanket and his hands sliding from her cheek to her neck to her shoulders and over her breasts, down her sides to her hips, and her mouth found his, her hands found him, his chest, his back. But before they went further she had to excuse herself, and it felt silly, almost formal, like a social blunder, but he just laughed and called her his funny frog, and she went into the toilet and carefully followed the New York doctor's instructions. When she stepped back into the bedroom and lay down on the blanket, she was ready and he was ready and she pressed her lips against his and they found each other once more.

When she awoke in the morning there were only two days before they'd be leaving for the Mississippi River and Nelson was in the other room preparing breakfast. She could smell the coffee and the potatoes and the ridiculous crispy American bacon that she could never quite decide whether she liked or not unless it was between bread with lettuce and tomato. She opened her eyes and a minute or two later Nelson appeared with a mug of coffee.

'The rest will have to be taken at the table.' He used an overly formal voice. 'Chez Algren does not have a tray for breakfast in bed.'

After breakfast she sat on the sofa reading a book from his shelf while he worked. He spent a couple of hours rewriting a part of the novel, and another couple writing letters. She watched him for a while as he wrote, using a red fountain pen like the one he'd given her, writing on the same yellow paper on which he wrote his letters to her. A childish twinge of jealousy pinched her heart, as though this paper were precious and should be reserved only for her. She laughed at herself, silently, or not as silently as she'd thought, because Nelson glanced up and, seeing her watching him, winked, and laughed himself.

'Perhaps I will go out and buy some things for lunch.' She draped the book over the armrest. 'And you can keep working.'

'You're a good little wife.'

She moved to the desk, and ran her fingers through his hair. 'Don't become too comfortable with it,' she said, and kissed the top of his head.

He watched her step on to the sidewalk, his palm flat against the window pane, and he continued watching as she disappeared to the west, but where she thought she was going to find lunch that way he didn't know, so he kept watching the street, and a minute later there came the little French lady back in the other direction, and he slapped his hand against the glass. She glanced up and, seeing him, shrugged and hit the heel of her hand against her forehead in an exaggerated gesture. He shook his head and laughed and went back to his writing desk.

He took a small box from the bottom drawer, set it on the blotter and removed the lid. A picture of Amanda lay on the top of the stack inside. She was standing on Oak Street Beach, one hand pressing her skirt to her thigh, the other clutching a wide-brimmed hat, despite which she was squinting. The shoreline stretched southward behind her. Beneath that photo was one of Mary G. sitting at a nightclub table, trying to look sophisticated by letting cigarette smoke leak slowly from her pouted lips. There was another one of Lucy in New Orleans, long enough ago. There was another of Amanda, in her wedding dress, and one of Marita, in his old room on Rush Street. And there were a few others, one of a girl whose name he couldn't remember any longer, and a handful more of Amanda. He collected them back into the box, re-lidded it, and placed it back in the drawer. His only photo of Simone stood in a frame next to the typewriter. He picked it up and laughed – she wore the blue dress in it. He ran his finger along the edge between the glass and frame, and then along her outline, from hair to the bottom of the picture. Don't let this one end up in the box. He replaced it next to the typewriter and moved to the window to watch for her return.

Their trip began with a two-day train journey to Cincinnati, from where the boat departed along the Ohio River through Louisville, where Nelson told Simone about the Kentucky Derby, which had been won a week earlier by Citation, a horse with a legit shot at the Triple Crown – and he explained the Triple Crown. The day after Louisville they celebrated what they'd decided was their anniversary: not that snowy February night of the phone calls and meeting in the Leetle Café, but the New York May afternoon when he'd slipped the silver ring on to her middle finger, this ring that she held in front of her eyes now, and that he touched with his own middle finger. They had dinner in the fancy dining room, and drank a bottle of real champagne, and after the meal they walked slowly along the rail, listening to the paddles churning the water and watching the dark river, the occasional star that flickered through a break in the clouds, until they reached their cabin – they skipped the bar this evening – and Simone made Nelson close his eyes while she fitted the diaphragm. He didn't cheat, and so with closed eyes he felt her move towards him and her hands on his shirt buttons. She hadn't said you can look, so he kept his eyes shut and she moved down his chest to his belly, full of catfish and fried potatoes, and when the shirt was off she started on the trousers, and when he too was naked she pressed herself on top of him and they celebrated their marriage as husband and wife, the steamboat paddles seemingly dictating their rhythm, the river pulling them along.

The boat travelled through Owensboro and Evansville, and Nelson made up facts about them, at first plausible, then, testing her credulity, increasingly ridiculous until she broke, laughing and punching him in the arms, demanding to know which things were actually true. They watched from the deck as the rivers joined at Cairo – the western frontier of the Egyptian Empire – and they sat in the bar drinking bourbon as they floated past what Nelson assured her was the Spanish colony of New Madrid. In Memphis they left the boat for the day and walked streets that offered little of interest to either of them. They went to a bar with live country music, but it left Simone cold. New Orleans jazz was the only music she had an ear for right now, but that city was still three hundred and fifty miles downriver.

'Three hundred and fifty miles means nothing to me,' she said as they meandered back towards the marina where the boat was docked.

'It better mean something,' he said, 'because that's the distance between you and your Dixieland jazz and turtle soup.'

She curled her lip in a sneer of disgust. 'I do not want to eat turtle soup. But I mean that I don't know how long a mile is.'

'Six hundred kilometres to the Big Easy,' he said. 'We'll find you some music in Natchez.'

The morning before they arrived in Natchez Nelson awoke and Simone was already moving around the cabin. She was dressed and pulling clothes out of her suitcase – no, pulling clothes out of his suitcase. He raised himself on to his elbows and forearms and asked her what the hell she was doing.

'I am looking for clothes that are not a shirt with checks and holes or wool trousers with holes. A battalion of moths must base themselves near the clothes of Nelson Algren.'

'It's not called a battalion in the air force.'

'I don't care what it's not called where,' she said, laughing. 'You need to buy some new clothes in Natchez or New Orleans.'

Nelson got out of bed and took the grey trousers from her and put them on. 'Not so many holes.' He patted the thighs. 'And only small ones.'

She rolled her eyes. 'I am going to eat breakfast.'

The boat arrived in Natchez in the late morning and they spent the day walking the streets and watching the people. From a gazebo in a park they could look over the wide river to Vidalia on the other side. They ate sandwiches and drank whisky in a bar for lunch. Afterwards Simone dragged Nelson to a store and bought him a new shirt, yellow and linen, despite his protests: it was no kind of garment for a Chicago man, he said, but she told him it was just the thing for a local youth on vacation.

'Don't expect it to last beyond that,' he grumbled, but she didn't catch it so he said, 'Let's go to a bar.'

After a few beers and whiskies in a bar that had three patrons and a jukebox filled exclusively with records by local singers they staggered back to the boat. Simone carried Nelson's new yellow shirt in a paper bag tucked under one arm, and her other arm was stretched across his waist. They stumbled up the ramp, Simone leaning against Nelson, Nelson steadying himself against the rail. Safely in their cabin, they dropped to the bed.

'Maybe one whisky too many,' Simone said, her arm draped across her eyes.

'Maybe one, maybe two. Or let's blame the beer.'

'Yes, the beer is to blame.' She still carried the bag wedged between her arm and ribs, but now she flung it towards the chair and suitcases. 'Your new shirt,' she said.

'What about it?'

'There it is, with the old ones. They don't deserve it.'

Nelson laughed. 'If you say so.'

'No.' She shifted to try to face him. 'They don't.'

She rolled over and stood and moved to the suitcase. For the second time he watched from the bed as she flung his shirts around the small cabin. Some she threw left, others she threw right. She picked some from the left pile and put them in the right, then moved them back. There must be a logic, but damned if he knew what it was.

'Leave the poor shirts alone.'

'No, I have this work to do.' She picked up two pairs of trousers and tossed them on to the right-hand pile.

'Leave the shirts and pants alone and come lie down with me.'

She made no reply, but scooped up the pile she'd made and moved towards the door. One of the shirts dropped as she stepped out on to the deck, and now Nelson realised what was going on here and shouted something, and jumped up, banging his shoulder against the doorframe as he followed, already too late: one shirt – the grey checked one – fluttered down towards the Mississippi River. The boat had pulled out of Natchez, and from their side Vidalia was already close to disappearing around the bend. The next shirt fluttered down, followed by a pair of trousers. Simone was giggling and Nelson trying to wrestle the remaining clothes from her; he was angry, and her giggling made it worse, but in the struggle two shirts and one pair of trousers tumbled over the rail and into the water. The trousers caught the rail below, but only for a moment before sliding down and under.

'I hope there wasn't anything in the pockets.'

'There wasn't. I checked.'

As she said it, someone's head peeked out and up from the deck below. They jumped back, and ran into their cabin, Simone still giggling, and now Nelson was laughing too. He sat in the chair next to his upturned suitcase and the bag with his new shirt.

'I guess I'll have to get used to yellow,' he said. 'What would you do if I threw the blue dress into the river?'

Her giggling stopped short. 'You would never behave so shamefully,' she said, in as serious a voice she could muster. 'But do not do it. Or I will go to Mexico without you.'

New Orleans was his town. He'd lived there for a short time, and still remembered it with a mixture of excitement and nostalgia and terror. He charged around town in his yellow linen shirt feeling like a kid, eager and excited and desperate to show Simone every single corner that he could remember, and several that he didn't. He took her to the market and showed her the buckets of turtles and the man who hacked their heads off with a cleaver. He dragged her along past rows of brothels and talked rapidly – she sometimes made him repeat himself several times – about the scams they pulled inside. They ate Cajun and Creole food – spicy gumbo, blackened catfish, boudin, turtle soup – though Simone avoided the turtle soup. They spent a night trawling jazz clubs, but always they were crowded, and too hot – even at night, Simone was red-faced and constantly sweating – and in the heat, pressed up to a table or against a bar or against other people, the lilting horns or vamping banjo would mutate into only noise, the reedy clarinet like a mosquito in the ear, and with whisky in the blood, straight to the brain, it became too much, and Simone shouted close to Nelson's ear that they should go, could they please go home. His face showed the disappointment – he'd been nodding and tapping, eyes on the band – but he too was overheated, his shirt darker yellow under the arms and across his back, and so they pushed out on to the only relatively cooler street and walked to their hotel and slept.

The heat rose again early, and so did they. Simone woke first, a film of sweat and dirt already covering her, and spent ten minutes under the shower, the cool water a temporary respite from the horrible thick air of this uninhabitable city. At breakfast she drank as much water and juice as she could. Nelson put away bacon, toast, eggs and sausages, and drank what seemed to her like a litre of coffee, but Simone could only push the food around her plate and eat some fruit and a slice of toast. Most of the breakfast she spent tearing small pieces of bread and rolling them into balls while she tried to enjoy watching all these Americans eating their oppressive breakfasts. When Nelson finally had drunk the last of his coffee her plate was littered with tiny doughy hailstones.

Tomorrow they would fly to Mérida, and Nelson had a plan of final New Orleans things he wanted to see, more things he insisted Simone needed to see, but as he outlined them in the hotel room he could see in her face that doing anything more than sitting around would not be entertained. They went to the City Park and strolled under the trees until Simone decided even the shade was too hot for walking. They sat in the grass. Nelson went off and returned with sodas and po' boys, but Simone could barely eat. One piece of the bread and a slice of meat, and the rest she fed to the pigeons.

They lay in bed, the light filtering through the curtains from the street, the ceiling fan throbbing lazily and creating more shadow than breeze. God, this heat. Simone wondered if Mexico would be as bad, or possibly worse. Another good reason to be leaving earlier, and she could use it as her excuse. It would be true. Better than trying to explain again about Sartre, their work, their life – a thing only she and Sartre could understand. But it would still make for a miserable journey, and they might have to end it even earlier. She didn't want to leave Nelson any earlier. And Nelson, he stared at the fan, trying to feel the breeze, trying to imagine it was cool, and wondered whether it was just disappointment, or maybe the trip had been a mistake. They should've gone someplace more suited to her. But how could he have known anyway? Mérida would be just as bad, but at least there wouldn't be his agenda to follow, so she couldn't just scowl at him. The Mexico part of the trip was her deal. Though that could make it worse. Anyway, it was a change.

Next morning they lifted off from New Orleans, their unspoken but nonetheless clear disappointments and apprehensions translating into a new conversation: as the silver machine hurtled down the runway and lifted, vibrating, into the air, they created a scenario, leaning in like conspirators to hear one another over the roar of the engines, of the plane crashing into the Gulf of Mexico. Simone started with a detail and Nelson added another. They created characters, and imagined the atrocious ways in which each would behave as the plane ditched into the sea. They created predatory animals, both real and fantastic, and gleefully narrated the savaging of their fellow passengers as the relatives of the sea turtles Simone hadn't eaten in New Orleans carried them – or perhaps only her – safely to the Mexican shore. Meanwhile the plane flew due south from New Orleans, landing, despite the best efforts of the imaginations of the writers aboard, safely. In Mérida the wind, for the moment, anyway, was blowing in from the not too distant sea, bringing a cooling air that offered them a chance to forget about how miserable New Orleans had been.

Simone collected mail from the post office and they spent a day looking around Mérida, and the second day took a bus for an overnight trip to the temple at Chichén Itzá. The man at the hotel in Mérida had tried to talk them out of the bus and into a taxi, explaining that the bus would take too long, and that the taxi driver could serve as a guide for a special rate, if they stayed at a particular hotel, the Mayaland Hotel, that this was the way it would be done; this was the way the Americans usually did it. But Nelson knew a tourist trap when he saw one, and had found out about another hotel. He explained in broken Spanish that it was fine for the Americans to travel that way, but his wife here was French, and he was from Chicago. The hotel man didn't seem to understand the joke, but he wasn't sure he'd said it correctly anyway. They took the bus. Nelson took a photograph of Simone standing in its doorway, the uninterested faces of their fellow passengers profiled in the windows.

Chichén Itzá was further inland, more or less in the middle of the Yucatán, and the drive there, at least to Nelson, was dull: a single straight road, lined with trees and shrubs and nothing much to look at. He watched other passengers, and stared at the passing landscape until he dozed. Simone watched out of the window for the entire journey: the trees, the shrubs, the flowers of various colours, varieties she'd never seen. The open windows created a hot breeze that only seemed to grow hotter, but she didn't mind. It wasn't like the oppressive and humid New Orleans. She felt a rising optimism about Mexico already, before even the first temple.

Taxi drivers in the temple parking lot all shouted Mayaland Hotel at them when they stepped off the bus. They were the only gringos who had taken this bus journey and so were the focus of attention. Nelson talked to one of them, and told him the hotel they wanted, but the driver just shook his head.

'*Ustedes no quieren hospedarse allí,*' he said. '*Mayaland.*'

In the end they walked, carrying the suitcases in the heat. The entrance to the Mayaland complex was only a five-minute walk, and they congratulated themselves on not falling for the taxi scam, for not staying in this luxury. But their hotel wasn't so easy to locate. Eventually they found it: a hundred yards from the far wall of Mayaland was a gate, with a wooden sign and pigs and chickens in the yard.

'Here!' Nelson exclaimed, and dropped his suitcase.

'This is a farm,' said Simone. 'We can't stay on a farm.'

'No, this is the hotel. I'm sure.'

She waited outside the gate, and watched him navigate through the animals to the small building. After five minutes he reappeared at the door and waved her in.

'They have beds, and a small dining room,' he said. 'I told you it was the hotel.'

They ate beans and tortillas and drank lukewarm beers in their little hotel and spent the night in narrow single beds with hay mattresses, covered by mosquito netting. They were close enough to the Mayaland to hear chatter and laughter from the bungalows on the other side of the wall.

'I'm glad we're staying on this farm,' Simone said, 'and not with those people. It must be dreadful.'

'They're not my kind,' Nelson said. 'Tourists. Here we can be visitors, instead of tourists.'

They drank some whisky before sleeping, passing the bottle quickly from beneath the mosquito netting, back and forth, being careful to tuck the net back under the mattress each time. Eventually Simone made ready to pass the half-empty bottle back across but realised Nelson was snoring, so she recorked it and set it on the floor. It was only a few minutes, listening to the mixture of Nelson Algren snoring and rich American babble from the other side of the Mayaland wall, before she too floated into sleep.

The man who ran the little hotel served them eggs and bacon and tortillas for breakfast, cooked by his wife in a small kitchen while they watched from the dining room with the one other guest, a middle-aged Mexican man. They drank a pot of coffee and, after Nelson collected his camera from their room, walked through the little yard and back towards the entrance to the national park. The chickens scattered as they walked through, but the pigs ignored them. Nelson asked Simone which pig she thought they'd be eating tomorrow morning. She punched him on the arm as reply. He took a photo of the pigs, and said it was the final portrait of one of them.

Chichén Itzá was a network of roads and stone buildings: temples, a bath house, an enormous ball court, columns that had once supported roofs; and at the centre was the main thing: El Castillo, the Mayan pyramid, rising almost eighty feet. Archaeologists had excavated new parts of it only ten years earlier, and plenty of work was still being done. Groups of Americans from the Mayaland gathered around their Mexican guides, listening to various stories, and Nelson surreptitiously photographed them, pretending to be lining up angles on the temple.

The sun beat down on the stones, on the ancient roads, and there was nothing resembling shade apart from the shadows cast by the temple. Simone was already sweaty and red, and Nelson took a photo of her standing at the bottom of the steps, smiling, strands of hair sticking to her face. As soon as she heard the clatter of the shutter she turned and started to climb. Nelson recapped the lens and followed after. She was already six steps up by the time he hit the first. There were ninety-one on each side, they'd overheard one of the guides telling his Mayaland tourists, and, if you counted the temple platform as one, that made three hundred and sixty-five total, one for each day. Already they were warm to the touch. Simone charged up like a mountain goat, pausing every so often to turn and admire the view, shading her eyes with her hand, before waving at Nelson and continuing, always charging ahead before he caught up. The second time she stopped he stood ready with the camera below her and snapped two photographs of his mountain goat frog before taking up the chase again.

From the top she could see the entire complex, and kilometre after kilometre of jungle: a green canopy stretching all the way to the horizon. She walked along the edge, staring out across the trees, feeling the sun on the back of her neck, her pulse still high from the climb and excitement. Now Nelson was at the top, just one step to go, and he lifted the camera and pointed it at her and she smiled and he clicked the shutter. This one would be a partial silhouette, the sun just slightly behind her, a thin corona along her partially profiled face. He climbed the final step and she reached out and touched his shoulder. He pushed his hand through his sweaty hair and smiled.

'Make a photograph of the view.' Simone swept her arm towards the horizon.

'Those never come out right. They just look flat and pointless.'

'Oh, don't be like that. Try anyway.'

He shrugged, and lifted the camera to his eye. He focused on a point somewhere halfway across the jungle, figuring that might be the trick, though he was pretty sure it wasn't, and this wouldn't work. He pressed the shutter. It would come out as an abstract series of grey blotches, he was sure: the dark grey blotch of the jungle, the thin and less dark nearer blotch of the grass, the light blotch of sky with the vague blotch of the single cloud. He could mail her this photo when she was back in Paris and ask her and she wouldn't have any idea what it was.

They walked a complete lap of the edge of the temple. Simone tried to convince Nelson that she could see Mérida, and that she could see the sea, but in the end she didn't even believe it herself. She felt astonished that this had been built a thousand years ago. Nelson pointed out that it wasn't that much older than Chartres cathedral.

'Yes, but they spent so much time building it. And even if not, it's so much more. It has more mystery.'

'I don't know,' he said. 'It's just a less familiar myth.'

She shook her head. 'This is more. All these buildings. And even if it was just this temple – I read that the sun strikes it during the equinox and makes a serpent in the light and shadow. Nobody ever thought of that at Chartres.'

He conceded that. 'I still say it's got nothing on the Tug of Chicago, though.'

She punched his arm. 'That makes me wish we'd brought our whisky bottle.'

'Water would've served us better.'

'Yes, water would have been smart.'

He put his arm across her shoulders. 'What a stupid husband and wife we make.'

'If we die of dehydration on the way down, we will be the first human sacrifices here for hundreds of years.'

'That's not the way I'd like to make my name.'

The descent proved as hard work as the climb. They had to keep their balance on the uneven steps, and the heat of the noon sun pushed their thirst. They would pause to look out at the jungle occasionally, but while they walked they had to keep their eyes on the stones and their feet. Two-thirds of the way down, when the view no longer seemed worthwhile, Nelson sat down to rest. Simone remained standing a step above him, arms akimbo. A few tourists were beginning their climb, and one or two nodded in greeting as they passed, their bright smiles showing how far they had yet to climb. One had a canteen in a canvas carrier slung over his shoulder. Nelson leaned his forearms on his knees and dropped his head, trying to feel cooler. An ant was scurrying along the step to the right of his foot. In fact, there were several, a whole line of them, small brown ants. The first ones were climbing vertically on the step behind him, and the end of the trail was still climbing the one below. He pointed them out to Simone.

'Do you think they're going all the way to the top?' She crouched to look at them more closely.

He shrugged. 'They're pretty stubborn ants if they are.'

'They're like the people who built this,' she said, 'climbing each step with the load of stones for the next one.'

The thought was a load itself. 'Slaves.'

She put her hand on his head.

'Slaves,' he repeated. 'Like these ants. Imagine climbing up and down these steps every day in this sun with a belly half-full of tortillas and not enough water. Everything like this was just built on the backs of the poor. It makes me want to crush these stupid ants, to put them out of their misery.'

'Come on.' She smoothed his hair and rubbed the back of his neck. 'Let's get down to the bottom and find some water and lunch. The ants don't have feelings anyway. Let them climb their stubborn route to the top.'

It was no good, though. Nelson was shot. He couldn't stop thinking about all those bastards, too poor to even call them poor, carrying rocks for some king. He sat in the growing shade of the eastern side of El Castillo while Simone walked around with his camera looking at other parts of the temple complex. One of the strange features of this pyramid was that people at the top could talk in normal voices and be heard clearly at the bottom, and so he was forced to listen to his fellow Americans at the top, who spoke in voices several decibels above normal to begin with: Oh my, what a view! Will you look at that, Gordon! It was a tough climb, but the view sure is swell! Imagine the pride they must have felt, building this temple to their pagan gods! Pride didn't come into it, he wanted to shout at them. It'd almost be worth climbing back up just to grab each of them by the collar, one by one, and explain what building this place was really about. All these rich bastards, running around Chichén Itzá, running around the Mayaland, sitting down to five-course meals served by the descendants of the builders of this temple, basically scratching out the same kind of living from the same damn stones. This heat. How Simone could suddenly run around in it when in New Orleans it had driven her into the ground. Another battalion of ants was running around in this shade, some of them carrying pieces of leaf or little pebbles of something. The ants, the waiters in the Mayaland, the taxi drivers and tour guides, the whores who were no doubt lurking someplace not too far away. And then there were the Mexicans back in Chicago – not to mention the Poles and Lithuanians – chopping their fingers off in the packing houses, burning themselves in the steel mills, collecting diseases in the whorehouses. So Frederick Prince and Joseph Kennedy and Martin Kennelly could live in mansions and stay in five-star hotels and eat bigger meals and make more money. So Nelson Algren and Simone de Beauvoir could take boats down the Mississippi and planes to Mexico and watch ants marching up the steps of El Castillo.

Simone came back after an hour. He watched her march across from the direction of the Temple of the Tables, holding his camera in her right hand, and waving to him with her left.

'I ran out of film,' she said. 'I'm afraid I took too many and not very good pictures. But there was so much! And so beautiful! Amazing!'

It was like listening to the temple-top conversations but with a foreign accent. 'Let's go back to the hotel and have some lunch.'

'Yes. You poor thing. Are you feeling any better?'

'Not really.'

'Poor Nelson.'

Back in their little farm of a hotel, the owner served a lunch of meat and beans and cheese and tortillas, and water and coffee. The food improved Nelson's mood, at least a little, and they spent what remained of the afternoon under their mosquito nets, joking together about the gee-whizz voices of the Americans that drifted over the wall from the Mayaland.

They travelled by bus back through Mérida, and then south to more Mayan ruins at Uxmal. It was the same set-up, with taxi drivers offering unnecessary rides, a hotel for the gringo tourists – though not as elaborate as the Mayaland – and a smaller guest house for regular people. Simone was disappointed that no chickens or pigs seemed to live at this hotel. How would she know what her breakfast looked like? As before, they slept beneath mosquito nets in side-by-side beds, and this time were served breakfast in the kitchen, Nelson chatting and laughing with the owner while Simone tried unsuccessfully to follow what they were saying. The only word she could understand for sure was Chicago.

Uxmal didn't have the same disheartening effect on Nelson as Chichén Itzá. He'd been looking forward to seeing this place because he'd seen it before. He'd seen a fake of it before. When the World's Fair returned to Chicago in 1933, one exhibition had been plaster casts of the façade of the nunnery at Uxmal. He remembered seeing the mosaic designs, and he'd also read about Uxmal in the book by John Lloyd Stephens. He'd been anticipating telling Simone of the legend of the pyramid like a kid waiting for Christmas. As they walked around the base of it, he told her it was the Pyramid of the Magician, but that it was built by a dwarf. An old witch tended an iguana egg until it hatched a little boy, who grew only to dwarf-size. When he was old enough, she sent her son – she considered the dwarf her son – to the king to challenge him. After a series of trials of strength, all of which the dwarf completed, the king told him to build overnight a building taller than any other in Uxmal. The short guy went home to his mother, and the witch told him not to worry, but to go to sleep. The next day, this pyramid, all hundred-odd feet of it, with the rectangular building on top, had appeared. The king and the whole city were amazed, but now the king was angry, too, so he set one final task for the dwarf. He had to go and find two bundles of strong wood. The king would break one bundle over the dwarf's head, and then the dwarf could break the other over the king's. The dwarf went to his mother again, and she put a magic tortilla on his head and told him not to worry. The king smashed the bundle over the dwarf's head, but it didn't hurt him. The king tried to chicken out of the bargain, but he had to go through with it, and the dwarf smashed his skull to pieces, killing him right there in front of all the men of the town. And the dwarf became king.

Nelson laughed and shaded his eyes as he looked from Simone back up to the top of the temple. 'There's a good story for the people at the Mayaland Hotel.'

'The stubborn ants will have their revenge,' Simone said.

'The stubborn ants will have their day.' He lifted the camera to his eye and snapped a photo of the temple, and another of Simone looking up its steps, her hand across her forehead like a visor. He kissed her and took her hand. 'We have to see this nunnery. They threw away the plaster version after the Fair. I would've lived inside if they'd let me.'

From Uxmal they bussed down through the Yucatán, into Chiapas and across the border into Guatemala, and finally to

Guatemala City. Nelson was happy to see the end, for now, of Mayan temples. Even the curiosity of seeing the actual Uxmal and the fun of retelling the legend hadn't really erased the black smudge inside him. Simone had noticed, and so was glad to move on, too. The days of travel and landscape, the border crossing and arrival into a city would pick him back up.

The hotel in Guatemala City was the same one the other gringos stayed in. There was no choice. They walked through the long street from their hotel, and it was like being in a shabby imitation of New York City – or, no, like a shabby imitation of what someone had been told New York City was: the wooden hand-painted signs named the bars as Big Apple Bar, Broadway Bar, Harlem Jazz Club. Nelson insisted on going into this last one to satisfy his curiosity. There was no music or dancefloor. Wooden tables stood in lines like a cafeteria, and in the corner a slot machine only accepted American nickels and dimes. They left without taking a drink. Simone wondered aloud whether it wasn't really a bar but a brothel. Nelson pointed out that a brothel would have had music, and more importantly girls, though he didn't rule out the possibility it was a funeral home.

The streets in and near the markets were sticky with the sugary smells of frying foods: sausage, chicken, bananas, dough, corn fritters. They walked past stalls with fresh fruits stacked in wooden crates, unsure apart from the bananas what most of them were: small wrinkly green things, bright pink and green cactus-like ones, dark purplish almost heart-shaped things the size of apples, berries of various sizes and colours. Other stalls sold woven rugs, bolts of brightly coloured cloth, clothing, a variety of leatherwork and basketry. Almost everything grabbed Simone's attention. She wanted to buy the first bolt of cloth she saw, but Nelson persuaded her to look around, and maybe buy something tomorrow. She bought two of the dark purple fruits and they bit through the skin to find whitish and juicy flesh.

All these things were sold by women and children, and women were frying the food at the grills around the markets' edges. As they wandered the streets further away from the markets, the stone and wooden buildings gave way to mud huts, and children, too small to sell anything to gringos, running around with filthy faces. Here was the real thing, actual existence for the same type of people – no, the same people, really, the direct descendants of the slaves who built the temples and fed the kings. These people seemed barely a decade removed from that life. Simone suggested they find a bar before Nelson could spend too much time dwelling on it.

'Anyway,' she said, 'we are not the kinds of tourists who come and gawp at the beautiful dirty children of poverty. We are not tourists.'

In an undefined – to them – area between these mud huts and the markets they found a small bar with live music, a trio of musicians – one strumming a guitar, another playing a marimba made of gourds, the third shaking maracas and singing. A small group of men clustered at the bar, and a pair were playing cards at another table. None paid the visitors much attention, but the barman appeared at their table with two cold beers. Nelson asked for two whiskies also.

'*¿No cervezas?*' The man leaned back, his hand still holding the two bottlenecks.

'*Sí, sí, y también dos whiskies,*' Nelson said.

'*Ah, bueno.*' The man smiled beneath his moustache and placed a beer before each of them.

They touched the bottle necks and drank. The beer was too cold to taste, and Nelson thought maybe that was for the best.

'It is important,' Simone said after her second mouthful of beer, 'when one travels, to be aware of not being a tourist. To travel and pay attention and see the things and visit the places that regular tourists don't, and to be aware of how people actually live.'

'And to avoid getting hoodwinked in the tourist traps.'

'Hoodwinked?'

Nelson reached across and covered her eyes with his hand. 'Blinded. Duped. Conned. Tricked. Hornswoggled.'

'Hornswoggled?'

'It's a good American word.'

'But it means – ?'

'Same as the others: hoodwinked. What we're always trying to avoid, in Guatemala, in Chicago, in Paris, in life.'

'Is that all? Life is to avoid being – hornswoggled?'

'Maybe.' Nelson finished his beer and signalled to the barman for another round. 'That's what those men at the bar are doing, and the card players, and that's what those little dusty-faced kids are trying to do.'

'And you and me?'

'Us too.'

'We too.'

Nelson lifted his whisky and laughed. 'Is the frog giving her husband lessons in American grammar?'

She laughed too and raised her own glass. 'She doesn't want the language to hoodwink him.'

The barman set down new beers and whiskies and cleared the empties. Nelson stood. 'I'll be back in a few minutes,' he said, and leaned over to kiss the top of her head before darting out of the door into the sunlight.

The men at the bar had paid them little attention apart from when they walked in, and now they glanced to the door

96

as Nelson left, but, seeing Simone placid and sipping her beer at the table, they quickly returned to their conversation. Hoodwinked. She said the words aloud. Hornswoggled. Sartre would like these words. She would have to remember to tell them to him. Or write, but no – it would be more fun to tell them to him, fresh. But she did need to write to him, tomorrow maybe. And check at the post office for letters. She wanted to know how he was, what he was doing, what work needed her attention. At least there was no Dolores to worry about this time. And she would be going back sooner. Though breaking this news to Nelson was a storm that had yet to announce its presence on the horizon; or maybe was just now announcing itself, to her anyhow. But she would save it for when they went back through Mexico.

The door darkened and re-brightened as Nelson came back through it, a blue bundle in the crook of his arm. He sat back down, grinning like a child who'd stolen an extra cookie, but said nothing.

'What have you done?' Simone returned his grin with a squint of confusion.

'I bought you this.' He unfurled his bundle. It was a cotton jacket, medium length, dragging for now on the tabletop, with large brown wooden buttons and wide lapels. He was still grinning at her, above the collar. It was simple and lovely.

'It's beautiful,' she said.

'What about me?'

'And so are you.' She rolled her eyes, and took the jacket to try it on. It fitted well, maybe a little too big but actually not very much. 'Thank you,' she said. 'Did you get hornswindled?'

'Hornswoggled.'

She slapped her forehead.

'Hornswoggled. Or hood...winked. Did you?'

He kissed his teeth, loudly. 'Of course not. Your local youth knows what he's doing.'

'Ah,' she said, 'but he is not local to this particular city.'

'No, but his local city rhymes with this one.'

She dismissed him with a buzzing sound. 'Gua-te-ma-la.'

'Chi-ca-go. You see? Perfect.'

'I think you are trying to hoodwink me.'

'Never.'

'But perhaps.'

They drank a third round. No one came or went before they left, and the card players continued their game. When the beers and whiskies were empty Nelson went to the bar and paid, and they walked from the cool dark bar into the bright and hot street, unaware that they'd been charged triple the locals' prices.

First thing in the morning they found the post office so Simone could check for mail. There was a letter from her mother, and another from Sartre, but neither imparted anything of more than regular interest. From the post office they went to the almost brand-new National Palace and the Metropolitan Cathedral next to it. The cathedral was enormous, but inside there was little in the way of decoration, apart from the prayer candles lining the sides and carpeting the area in front of the main altar, and the altars themselves. There were only a dozen or so people in the cathedral, and of those, all apart from Nelson and Simone were bowed in the pews, praying, clutching rosaries or touching new candles to lit ones.

'I am going to light a candle,' Simone whispered.

'Why?' He felt a twinge of genuine surprise.

'I don't know. I feel like I want to.'

'You're a good little bourgeois Catholic girl, aren't you?' He'd meant it to sound joking, but it didn't quite come off and she looked hurt. 'I don't mean that.'

'Then I won't.'

'No, go ahead.' All his words now sounded sarcastic and he knew he couldn't retrieve the situation, and yet he tried. 'I'll wait outside.'

She followed him back on to the square. A large fountain spat several streams of water. It was getting close to noon and the sun was bright and hot.

'Look, I'm sorry,' Nelson said. 'I didn't mean to be a jerk.'

She placed her hand between his shoulder blades and rubbed. 'No, it's okay. You were right. It is a foolish affectation. And a lie.'

'You can take the girl out of the church,' he said.

She stopped rubbing. 'I don't understand.'

'But you can't take the Church out of the girl. It's a saying. Kind of. Once a Catholic, always a Catholic. No matter how hard you try.'

'I suppose,' she said, 'but I don't like it that way. I don't have any belief.'

'But you still want to do the rituals.'

'I don't even – that is why you were right. I don't know why I even thought to do it. Foolish.'

'Let's forget it,' he said, 'Let's go back to the markets.'

Simone bought several yards of cloth that she could have made into a dress in Paris, and Nelson bought a blanket. At the hotel they arranged for their purchases to be sent to Wabansia Avenue. They found a restaurant and spent the entire night there, eating and getting drunk. Nelson was in a good mood – too good – and the drunker he got, the more he entertained himself – and Simone – by singing ridiculous songs, making up characters who would speak to her in a variety of voices and accents, and letting his hands wander across her thighs, her stomach, her breasts. She tried to keep his hands away, but the drunker she got, the less inclined she was to resist, regardless of the spectacle they might be making. Eventually they paid their bill and stumbled into the night, taking a meandering route past the mud huts, the now empty market stalls and eventually to the street where the hotel stood, through the fake New York where the voices of tourists competed with one another inside the bars, and Nelson stopped and shouted, 'The frog and her local Chicago husband will outdrink you all!' before Simone dragged him by the hand into the lobby, up the stairs to the first floor and into their bed.

The next morning they left, hungover, for Chichicastenango, fifty miles north and mostly west. After they found their hotel they went to a small bar and nursed their hangovers with chicken and cold beers, and spent the rest of the afternoon quietly, Simone writing letters to Sartre and to her mother, Nelson reading one of the novels he'd brought along.

The hotel arranged a guide for them and their second night was spent in a small hut on top of a mountain several miles outside of Chichicastenango. A man arrived in a pickup truck at seven o'clock in the morning and drove them through the town, all three of them side by side in the cab, out into the jungle and over a small mountain to a wide valley, where he left them outside a small cluster of wooden buildings. They leaned against the truck bed while the man went from one building to the next, calling a name that neither of them could quite catch. He disappeared around the back of one, and after a few minutes returned, a small, middle-aged woman trailing behind him. She was Olga Maria, and would take them up the mountain, he told them. Simone gave him some cash and he drove back down the dirt path towards the Chichicastenango highway. Olga Maria pointed towards the mountain, turned without saying anything and started walking towards it. They followed. Whether she thought they wouldn't understand her language, or whether she simply didn't want to talk, Olga Maria was mostly silent as she led them across the valley, where sheep grazed on dark green grass, and into the trees that marked the beginning of the climb. She told them she was a shepherdess, but otherwise communicated only by pointing at obstacles, at trees, at birds and lizards and insects and spiders. She might have been pointing them out as items of interest or danger; they had no way of telling.

In the early afternoon they reached their destination: not the peak of the mountain, which rose another hundred or more feet above them, but a plateau and clearing, the trees sloping down to the valley below them, grass as tall as their knees, a small lake and, near it, the one-room hut where they would spend the night. They shared with Olga Maria a lunch of bread, chicken, spicy sausage, avocado and other fruits they didn't know the names of. Simone paid her half the money and she left; she would return around the same time the next day to guide them back down.

They dozed for a while in the afternoon sun, Simone resting her head on Nelson's belly, occasionally opening their eyes to watch the handful of cumulus clouds drift past, or to stare across the valley, dotted with the cumulus sheep, to Chichicastenango. Simone untucked Nelson's shirt and lifted it to kiss his belly, and as her lips moved upwards his hands moved along her ribs, her waist, her hips, and he lifted her dress and soon they were both naked in the tall grass, the mountain rising above them, the breeze tickling across their bodies as they pressed themselves to one another.

Afterwards they swam in the mountain lake. They stepped in tentatively, Nelson sucking air when the cold water reached above his knees, Simone squealing almost as soon as she set foot in it. Eventually Nelson found the courage to dive in, and the water pressed a pleasant ache into his muscles and his face as he kicked down several feet. When he resurfaced, Simone was still standing knee-deep, her arms crossed beneath her breasts.

'Swim out,' he called, treading water.

She shook her head. 'I am fine here.'

He flipped and swam a handful of strokes until his feet could find the sand and pebbles. He reached a hand towards her as he waded in.

'Come on, let's swim together.'

She took his hand with her fingertips, but looked down. 'I would rather stay here.'

'You don't want to swim with me?'

She shook her head. 'Not like that. I am not good at swimming. I am not confident.'

Nelson laughed and tugged gently on her hand. 'Come on, we'll swim together until you are confident. All the girls of Chicago were made confident swimmers by your local youth.'

She smiled. 'With such a resumé, I suppose I can put my faith in him.'

They waded out until Nelson was waist-deep. He held his hands beneath her back and shoulders as she floated, and gradually let them drop away, slowly enough that she wouldn't notice, until she was floating entirely on her own. She could feel the sun warming her face, her body lightly numb in the water, his hands beneath her. She felt safe. She felt as close to nothing as she'd ever felt. Slowly she brought her legs out and pushed into the water, only now realising that Nelson had let go of her and was floating alongside. She moved her arms in unison with her legs for the next push, and her body glided through the chilly water, small drops of water tickling her face. She opened her eyes to squint at the bright sky, and found she could open them further, now the sun was dropping to the other side of the mountain. She could lift her head a little – though it was difficult to keep it lifted for too long – and, while swimming, look out across the valley. Nelson glided beside her, parallel. Together they floated, pulling their arms and legs through the water nearly in unison, and from above, from a distance, they might have looked almost like one creature moving slowly across the surface.

They swam the short distance back to the shore together, Nelson diving down to the bed once, and popping up several feet ahead of Simone. The air was still warm, but they shivered nonetheless as they emerged from the water. Nelson wrapped his arms around her and they held each other close to drive the cold away. After several minutes he kissed her forehead – his lips felt warm against her still-cold skin – and took hold of her hand, and placed something warm and smooth in her palm. She opened it and saw a dark stone, black with a few reddish and white lines running through it. The stone was more or less an oval shape and it glistened.

'I picked it off the bottom of the lake,' he said.

The hut contained a grass mattress covered in two grey wool blankets and a fireplace, nothing more. Nelson built a fire and, once the flames were crackling, Simone spread one of the blankets in front of it. They ate their supper on the blanket, the same chicken, sausage, bread and fruit meal they'd shared with Olga Maria for lunch. Their clothes remained where they'd left them in the clearing outside. After they'd eaten Nelson put another log on the fire, and they opened a pint of whisky they'd brought with them and drank it slowly while he made up some long story based loosely on when he'd run a gas station in Texas and been conned out of everything by his partner. As he talked he watched her face, noticing the way her cheeks creased when she laughed, and the widening of her eyes as he pushed her credulity. He finished the story and drank a little more whisky, and passed the bottle to Simone.

'I've never been as happy as I am right now,' he said.

She took the bottle. 'Neither have I,' she said, and the jolt she felt on hearing his words and her own and knowing they were the truth astonished her. She drank some whisky and said it again, for comfort. 'I've never been so happy.'

Olga Maria returned early the next afternoon and guided them silently back down the mountain, where after a short wait the man returned with his truck to ferry them back to Chichicastenango. The following morning they were up early and boarding another bus, their eventual destination Mexico City, with various stops in between. They tried to read, but the bumpy roads made them both queasy, and writing was impossible too, so they spent the time watching the landscape and nodding off to sleep.

The bus crested the final mountain and as it wound through the switchbacks on the way down they caught glimpses of the sprawling Mexican capital city. Simone had booked the hotel here, and it was fancy – not quite the Palmer House, but fancy – and, although normally this kind of place would have given Nelson the creeps, he was too content to think about it much at all. They arrived late, so treated themselves by ordering room service and spending their first night in Mexico City in bed. They rose early the next morning and spent the entire day walking the city, ducking into a bar or restaurant when intermittent showers dumped cold rain on to the hot streets. They found markets with fruit and vegetables, and others with textiles, not all that different from Guatemala City, and they also found the sprawling slums with their filthy children playing in the streets, and, on the edge of the tourist district, where the slums gradually dissipated, rows of seedy bars and whorehouses.

Before they set off the next morning they sought out the main post office so Simone could check for general delivery mail, and arrange for any further letters to be forwarded to the hotel. Nelson sat on the steps outside and smoked a cigarette while she went inside. She emerged after almost an hour, shuffling through a clutch of letters from various correspondents: one from her mother, two from Sartre, another from Bost, from her sister, and from Stepha in New York.

'A day's worth of letters to read,' Nelson said as they walked along the sidewalk.

She tucked them into her bag and took hold of his hand. 'Most of them I can probably read later.'

'Even from Sartre?' he asked, and, sensing his own jealous tone, added, 'Even from your mother? What a terrible daughter.'

'I think I was always a terrible daughter, apart from being good at school. Why didn't you give a forwarding address?'

'To whom? Nobody has anything to write to me that can't wait.'

'You really don't think you might miss out?'

'No. The poker players can live with winning somebody else's money for a while, and I don't think the junkies would write for help.'

'But publishers? Or magazines?'

'There's not much I'd be able to do about anything from here, even if I wanted to, which I doubt I do.'

'You're a strange kind of local youth.' Simone squeezed his hand.

In Xochimilco they found San Cristóbal and together with a gaggle of tourists rode through the canals in a colourful *trajinera* called the *Santa Maria*. Nelson said he wished they were travelling with the *Niña* and the *Pinta*, and had to explain his joke; it wasn't funny even after he had, and probably wouldn't have been even if he hadn't needed to, but she humoured him by laughing nonetheless. Part-way along the journey another *trajinera*, the *Lupita*, pulled next to theirs and a mariachi band – guitar, *vihuela*, *guitarrón*, fiddle, trumpet and maracas – began playing. They played 'Mal Hombre' and 'El Capotín' before launching into a lilting rendition of 'Yankee Doodle', to which Nelson – alone among the tourists – sang along heartily, even though the band sang it entirely in Spanish, 'Yanquí Doodle'. Afterwards a sombrero was passed through the *trajinera*. Coins and dollar bills filled it by the time it reached the musicians.

In the late afternoon they went to the Plaza de Toros and watched a bullfight. They'd talked about this several times – neither had ever seen one, though Nelson had seen them on television in the Tug a couple of times, only half paying attention, and both had read the Hemingway stories, and *Death in the Afternoon*. Nelson had sent Simone a copy of the book so she could read it before the trip. So they felt prepared, and felt they knew something, as their anticipation mounted watching the bulls paraded into the ring, watching the *cuadrilla* enter, the mounted *picadores*, the *banderilleros* and *torero*. They leaned in, from their distant seats in this enormous arena, as though they could get closer to the event, get on top of it, as the *torero* entered with his large cape and the bull was guided through a series of passes, *verónica* after *verónica*, and the *picadores* rode in and jabbed at the muscle behind the bull's neck, next the *banderilleros* hooking the *banderillas* and finally the *torero* returned with his small cape and sword and, after another series of passes, drove the sword through the bull's shoulders, killing it. Even from the back half of the seats they felt the drama, moved and cheered and applauded with the crowd, squeezing one another's hand as the *banderilleros* attempted their manoeuvres, dropping back against their seats, half-exhausted, when the *estocada* had been successfully completed.

'He is right, Hemingway,' Simone said later when they were eating in a nearby restaurant. 'It is not at all a sport. It is tragedy. Real theatre.'

'Not so many steps away from the Mayans,' Nelson said.

'The Mayans?'

'Chichén Itzá. Uxmal. The human sacrifices, the ball games. It's the same order of killing and blood and sacrifice.'

She reached her hand to his cheek. 'Don't brood on it, Nelson.'

'No.' He took hold of her hand and rested it on the table, still enclosed in his. 'I'm beyond it depressing me. Anyway, the bullfight didn't.'

They ordered a series of small dishes: pork tacos, chicken tacos, *huitlacoche* quesadillas and cactus quesadillas, and they drank rounds of beer and tequila, eventually ordering more tacos – marinated beef and more cactus – and more tequila.

They'd seen axolotls, large and white or grey, swimming in the canals and debated ordering that, too, but in the end couldn't bring themselves to do it. Juice and sauce from the tacos ran down their arms, and Nelson's napkin became saturated beyond use. Before he thought to ask for another he began using his trousers. Simone's face grew red and redder from the spicy salsa that she nonetheless continued to pile on top of each taco and quesadilla, which she washed down with more and larger slugs of beer and tequila. Their conversation focused almost exclusively, and repetitively, on the deliciousness and heat of the food.

'It's spicier than in Guatemala,' Simone said, finishing her third or fourth beer.

That was a good one. 'I remember a half-day lost to your reaction to the Guatemalan chilli peppers.'

Simone waved a taco at him. 'No, you misremember. It was not so bad.'

'It was last week. I remember each detail. A frog, bent on the bed and moaning and clutching her belly, a frog moaning from behind the door of the bathroom. "Oh, Nelson, aye kant bear ze shillis!"'

She grabbed the empty beer bottle and waved it at him like a weapon, but laughing. 'Do not tell such terrible lies!'

'Don't shoot!' He raised his hands as though it were a stick-up.

The waiter arrived, having seen the hands, so they ordered more drink and more tacos.

'And besides,' Nelson pointed at the dishes of salsa on the table, 'you're in charge of the spicing here. Only yourself to blame if you overheat.'

'But it's delicious.' Simone laughed at herself. 'And painful. Delicious and painful.'

The new platter of tacos and the fresh beer and tequila arrived. They picked up the tequila and toasted themselves, and Nelson had an idea. He picked up a taco and reached across the table and, before Simone had any idea what he was doing, it was atop her head, warm and yes now wet and Nelson was saying, 'A magic tortilla. Not to protect the Uxmal dwarf from the king's faggot, but to protect the Existentialist frog from the Mexican's chipotle.'

She dipped her head forward and the taco flopped upside down on to the tablecloth. They both exploded in drunken laughter.

He'd been thinking about it all through Guatemala and around Mexico City. A few days later as they sat in the hotel room, he flipping through a magazine, she writing a letter, he asked her.

'After this trip,' he said, 'why don't you go back to Paris and pack your things and send them and yourself to Chicago for good?'

She stopped writing mid-sentence but couldn't look up. 'Nelson – '

'Come live with me in Chicago.'

She put down the red pen. 'Nelson, I can't, you know I can't.'

'I don't; I don't know that you can't. You can.'

'I can't, Nelson. My work is in Paris, and – '

'You can work in Chicago.' He slid to the end of the bed and sat on its edge. 'We have paper, we have pens, we have libraries. We have me.'

'If it were just that simple,' she said, and picked up the sheaf of envelopes from the table. 'Nelson, I want so much to connect my working life in Paris to my life with you in the

Wabansia apartment, in our lovely nest, but I just can't; too much of my life is in Paris.'

'You just won't,' he said. 'Not can't. You could.'

She tapped the envelopes against her shoulder. 'I wish it were so simple. There are too many things in Paris that need me to be there, too many people who rely on me to be there.'

She decided to avoid saying Sartre's name, and hoped Nelson wouldn't mention him.

He didn't. 'You could still go there. We could go there. But together. We could live together. We've been so happy these past weeks, and we could have that all the time.'

She walked to the bed and cradled his face with her hands. 'Nelson, I would love nothing more. I love no one more. But it is not so simple as all that.'

'It could be,' he said.

'I wish it was.' She kissed him.

He took hold of both her hands, still cradling his face, and they remained still and silent for several minutes, each thinking what the other wouldn't say.

They stayed another week in Mexico City, mostly spending their days walking around different neighbourhoods, which never seemed to run out of variety and interest to them. They went to the Ballet Folklórico and saw a performance of traditional and new Mexican dances. They went to the cinema and saw *The Kid from Brooklyn,* starring Danny Kaye as a milkman who becomes a boxer in fixed fights. The boxing scenes were ridiculous, but Nelson thought it was funny enough, though Simone wasn't all that entertained. There were more Mayan pyramids for Simone to drag him to, and they made day trips to Taxco, Cholula and Pueblo. After two weeks of Mexico City and its surroundings, they boarded yet another bus, this one bound for Morelia.

Simone, as always, had spent breakfast tearing small pieces from her bread and rolling them into tiny balls. Now on the bus, in lieu of bread, she was rolling the cloth of her skirt between her fingers. She watched the farmland out of the window, cows grazing and cornfields, and occasionally glanced from the corner of her eye to Nelson. He was reading. She'd banished the conflict from her mind, but it was too close now not to tell him. Probably she should have told him earlier, or before they left, but that might have risked the whole trip. She knew him well enough to know that. He was stubborn enough. Now at least they'd had a wonderful time, even if he ruined it now. But she had to tell him. She laughed silently at a bitter thought: if that temperamental clown Dolores had simply been able to keep to her schedule, she wouldn't have to be doing this. Dolores could be as far from her mind as Paris was from Mexico.

The bus arrived in Zitácuaro. A handful of passengers got off, and another handful boarded, scattering to the free seats. When the bus had left the depot and was leaving the edge of the town, heading back into farmland, Simone put her hand on Nelson's shoulder and smoothed it along his arm to his hand. He turned from his book and smiled. It was the last smile she would see in Mexico.

'Nelson, I have to tell you – '

He took off his glasses and folded them into his pocket.

'When we fly back to New York on Monday, after our days there, I will have to return to Paris.'

'What happened?' His innocence was genuine. 'Is everything okay there?'

'Yes – no. Nothing happened. I don't know.'

111

She began to cry, already. It wasn't what she wanted. He put his hand around her shoulder but didn't say anything. 'Nelson – I have to go. There is work I have to do. You see – '

He removed his arm. 'I see.'

She looked to him, but his eyes stared at his lap, and his jaw was set.

'There is a film script assignment.' This was not an entire lie, but it was less than truthful. 'Sartre needs my help to finish it before the deadline. It is very important work. Important.'

The repetition clanged in his ears. He said nothing, his teeth pressed together, and breathed slowly through his nose, his eyes focused on his knees, his hands between them.

'It cannot be done without my help,' she said after his silence had continued too long. 'So I must return to Paris early. I would love to come back to Chicago, to Wabansia Avenue, but – there is simply too much to do. You understand, Nelson? I need to be in Paris for the work. You understand, honey?' She touched his forearm, but took her hand away when she felt the hard, tense muscles. 'Nelson? I want to discuss this. I want to stay. I just cannot – the work. There is no choice. Nelson.' She rubbed his arm, but it didn't soften the muscles. 'Please.'

He stared at his thumbs, along the edge to the first knuckle, down to the second, single curl of hair just below where it joined his hand. There is no choice. She has a choice. Whatever promises she makes in Chicago, in Guatemala, in Mexico, the promises made in Paris matter more. Even if she doesn't make them. It was clear now. She could say to Nelson Algren that she loved him or that she'd never been happier, and it might even be true for that moment, in the absence of Paris, in the absence of – yes, Sartre. But she would always come running when the call came from the other side of the ocean. And never the reverse. She could stop rubbing her damn hand along his arm, but he didn't want to move it away. Didn't want to give her the satisfaction of a reaction beyond silence. You have your priorities, Simone de Beauvoir, and love is not one of them.

He still had not spoken when the bus reached Morelia and they found their suitcases and carried them along to the hotel. She'd given up trying to coax a word from him when the bus left Hidalgo, and instead turned her attention to the landscape, to try to keep it in focus and the tears buried. She followed him from the Morelia depot to the hotel, and when they reached their room she suggested they go for a short walk around and then find a restaurant with magic tortillas for their heads. He didn't smile at her joke. He didn't move from the bed, his hands once more clasped in his lap. She tried to keep her voice from breaking into something hysterical as she announced to him – or to the room, at least – that she would go walking on her own, in that case. She was calling his bluff, but it was no bluff, and she walked into the corridor and out on to the evening Morelia street alone, biting into her lip, frog wife with no husband.

He wouldn't pretend. If she was already looking back towards Paris, she could do it without him by her side, without the pretence that they were still leading their lives together. Her mind had already travelled elsewhere, regardless of where she claimed her heart to be. He stood and opened the window to allow the breeze into the room, then stretched back out on to the bed. He wasn't hungry, anyway. He would lie in the darkening room, and imagine himself alone, and content with that aloneness, a different feeling from loneliness.

Although the air was beginning to cool, heat still rose from the streets and her feet quickly grew hot. She walked with no pattern, no attention to where she was going or how she might return, not looking at what she passed: the vegetable stalls being packed up until tomorrow, the noise just beginning to rise from the bars that during the daytime were quiet with card games and checkers. The street urchins who sold trinkets on every corner of the area around the hotels were all tripping home, and paid her as little attention as she did them. She used deep breaths to keep the tears from her eyes. This was how it would end: separate in the streets of Morelia, Mexico, the calm, warm love of the Chichicastenangan mountain hut as dead as the volcano that had made their little lake. Was it really only a moment? No, it must last longer than that. This, too, was a moment, and it would pass, and those moments of love would return. He would see. He would stop being stubborn, on this. For the good of – when he saw the reasons, when he saw that it hurt her too, when he saw that arrangements couldn't be helped, when he saw that it didn't change her love for him and shouldn't change his for her. That some work was too important. That her life in Paris with Sartre must sometimes dictate other compromises. That those compromises didn't mean an end or a lessening of her love. Had she not made these things clear? She had. She had, she had. He would always be her husband, her local Chicago youth husband, and she would be his frog wife. But there were other things, there was Sartre – inviolable. There was the Paris life, and then their – me and you, Nelson! Me and you! – lives in Chicago, or on the Mississippi River, or at Chichén Itzá, Uxmal, Guatemala City, Chichicastenango, with a tortilla on my head in Mexico City, wherever we go. That does not mean there are not other things, and other things do not mean there

114

is not you! They are just not always together! It cannot revolve around a single point. It cannot. I cannot.

She did not know where she was, nor was she aware that some of these thoughts had sputtered aloud from her mouth, muttered and a few of them shouted into the Mexican evening. The light stretching pain of hunger prickled her stomach, but she was too agitated to eat. She stopped in a bar and drank a dark brown tequila, slowly, and then another more quickly. She would go home – back to the hotel. She would find her way back to the hotel and talk to Nelson once more. He would see. He would understand. There was love.

The room and the night outside were both dark when she arrived back. She whispered his name, unsure of whether he was there or not, and repeated it twice more, each time more loudly. Closer to the bed, she realised he was there, but he was asleep. She took off her clothes, folded them and placed them on the small chair and slipped beneath the sheet and next to him. Tomorrow would be better. Tomorrow he would see. Tomorrow he would show her his love once more.

Nelson lay on his side, staring from the dark room through the open window at the dark night. Eventually he would sleep.

The morning was no different. She awoke when the sun became too warm through the uncurtained window. Nelson was already awake and reading a book. He'd moved her clothing to the empty half of the bed and the chair to the corner by the door.

'Good morning, Chicago husband,' she said, stretching her arms above her head. Nelson glanced up from his book but said nothing, so she added, 'Are you going to ignore me all day today as well?'

'I haven't decided.' He didn't look up from his book.

'Shall we go to breakfast?'

'I already did. While you were still sleeping.'

She took her clothes from the space next to her, stood up and began dressing. He continued to read. When she was dressed and her hair tied back in a bun she went downstairs for breakfast without another word. She was very hungry, having skipped dinner the night before, and ate two eggs, bacon and sausage and several slices of bread, leaving only a few rolled up balls of dough on her plate. She felt anxious climbing the stairs back to their floor. Would he have used her breakfast as an excuse to leave, to abandon her for the day? Maybe that would be better than his reproachful silence, the accusing picture of him sitting on a chair in the corner reading a book instead of holding her hand as they walked through the slums, through the markets, as they sat in the bars.

She opened the door slowly at first, then tried to recover by opening it more quickly, to show that she was behaving normally. He had moved to the bed, his legs outstretched and crossed at the ankles, and was still reading. He didn't look up.

'Will you come with me to the market?'

She looked to him for an answer; she needed an answer, even if he only said no, as long as he said it. But he simply shrugged. She looked through her suitcase and found the blue jacket, the one he'd raced out of the bar in Guatemala City to buy. It would be too warm for it later – it might be too warm for it already now – but maybe he would see her in it and change his mind. Change his heart. Nelson, please. He glanced up and she smiled, her hands rising slightly, as though about to strike a pose, but her wrists never left her hips. His face remained placid. No, not placid; it remained neutral. Nothing. It was damning. Even anger would be a relief.

'I am going to visit the markets.' She pulled at the hem of her jacket. 'If you would not like to join me, then I will return at dinner time and perhaps we can eat together, here on our last night in Mexico, Nelson. At least we can do that.'

She left, through the door, along the corridor, down the stairs, through the lobby and out into the street, his silence trailing behind her like a wake. She looked up at their window as she passed, but could see only the glare of the sunlight shining at the pane. Nelson watched hidden behind the glare, and saw her turn towards the window, knowing that she couldn't see him. A few minutes later, he too left the hotel, and set out in the opposite direction, away from the market and restaurants. He could choose to live without her, just as easily as she could choose to abandon him. He could choose to be alone, at least for a day, for a morning, for an afternoon. Whatever he told himself as he walked towards the edge of town wasn't the truth, though. A husband can't be a husband without his wife.

She walked through Morelia in the morning sun, paying more mind to the places she saw, the streets she navigated. In the market she bought several blouses, brightly coloured, being charged more than she would have if Nelson had been there to help her barter. She ate her lunch alone at a table outside a small restaurant, and despite herself she couldn't stop watching the street for his blond head, expecting all the time to see his wire-rimmed glasses, his crooked grin, to hear him say all was forgiven, he understood, let's drink beer and tequila and eat tacos.

She didn't see those things. She didn't see Nelson Algren, and when she returned in the late afternoon to the hotel he was no longer in their room, either. She packed away her blouses and sat on the edge of the bed, then moved to the chair, then back to the other side of the bed, from where she could look out the window to the street below, as though watching would bring him back more quickly. His absence now seemed worse than his silent presence. He would not come back until late, and she would have to sit here waiting and not knowing, once again feeling hunger stretch across her stomach. But there he was now, and he glanced up at the window. She waved, a nervous, involuntary wave, just the hand, before she even realised she was doing it and he smiled, she thought, she saw him smile, yes, that one-sided smile, the eyes creasing, and maybe it would be okay.

A few minutes later he was at the door of the room. 'Are we going for dinner?'

To her it sounded almost like I love you.

The plane touched down in New York, and they took a cab to the Brevoort. From the hotel Simone went to the airline office to move her flight back another week. There were too many things to do, and one more week with her husband seemed necessary now. They spent the afternoon walking, around Greenwich Village and over to Astor Place. They had a couple of drinks and crackers and onions in McSorley's. They sat in Washington Square Park. Simone recalled her first time in New York, walking these places and others alone, and the second time, with Nelson, as now, sharing drugstore sandwiches, benches in the park, his dash across the street at Times Square, and his return with this ring, which she could not and would not ever remove.

Nelson sat on the bench recalling that time as well, though it sunk him a little, to know it couldn't be recaptured. This woman next to him, her hand with its silver ring that he'd placed on it, held in his, Simone, was the same Simone as a year ago, and he was the same Nelson as a year ago, and this bench was probably the same bench. Knowledge was different, though. His knowledge that she would always slip away, away from him, away to Paris, away, and her knowledge too that she would always slip away, that she could always slip away, that she would never risk anything for the possibility of their happiness together. In the bus for Morelia the realisation had struck him hard and sharp on the nose, but that surprise and anger had now sunk to melancholy, a dull but insistent bruise.

Even at night the heat and humidity pressed into them, a steady reminder of those horrible mismatched days in New Orleans, and Simone insisted they go to a French restaurant she'd been to on her first trip, because it was air-conditioned. He had to wear a jacket and a tie, and on top of that it would cost more than about three days' worth of food in Mexico. But he did it. He went. They ate. Simone praised the food, and she talked about her various appointments, and that tomorrow they would have dinner with Stepha and Fernando, and asked him about his appointments, and said it would be nice, to ease from a vacation life together to a kind of working life together. Nelson gave one-word answers to keep himself from pointing out that there was very little 'together' when she was leaving. They took a taxi to the hotel, and while Simone read he lay on his side next to her, and when she had finished and stroked her arm along his shoulder, his ribs, his thigh, he pretended to be asleep.

They had dinner with Stepha and Fernando. They both called her Castor, and Nelson felt as though he was talking a foreign language when he addressed her as Simone, but otherwise it was nice, a sense of things being normal. They dined and talked among friends, though Stepha was plenty more interesting than Fernando. Nelson felt himself returning, if just a little. He touched Simone's arm as he talked, his hand was on her thigh beneath the table, he studied her face as she spoke. Back in the hotel it was like the beginning again, a year ago and love was something they were just beginning to feel.

The next day she had people to see and he had his appointments, so they met in the late afternoon and ate, then went to Madison Square Garden to see a fight. The day after was the same, with a film instead of a fight, and the day after that they saw a baseball game. They ate hot dogs and drank beer and watched the Yankees lose to the Senators in twelve innings, Masterson and Byrne both going the distance, Byrne the better of the two but losing anyway, the unfairness of baseball, all of this lost on Simone, who thought the box score was the cumulative score – millions of runs – but enjoyed the spectacle nonetheless, and spent more time watching the other fans than she did watching the game. That evening Simone would have liked to go to another film but Nelson only wanted to drink so they went bar-hopping around the dives on the Bowery, and, though they started out having a good time, the drunker he got, the more surly Nelson became at the idea of Simone's leaving, and he brooded in silence over his whisky.

And after two weeks of keeping themselves afloat by watching films and boxing and drinking and gambling on horses and even a game of poker, at which Simone was disastrous, Simone walked down the corridor of the Brevoort alone, travelled down in the elevator alone, walked across the lobby alone, and got into a taxi alone, and Nelson sat on the bed, elbows on his knees, chin in his hands. An hour earlier he'd asked her one last time to stay here, or, if not to stay here, then to come back right away, with all her things, to live with him in Chicago. He'd said it three times, each time watching her work harder and harder to keep the tears that were rising from falling. He knew he was hurting her, but she didn't seem to realise that he was hurting himself, too: he wasn't just saying these things knowing the answers were preordained, just saying them to cut the wound wider, he wasn't just saying them at all. She saved her tears and managed to make it to the airport. She called the hotel and asked for his room – their room – and spoke down the line to him, and listened to his voice, and now she started to cry, and he ended the call and said I love you, and she replied that she loved him too – despite all the pain it causes us both, I love you, Nelson. And how it costs us.

Chapter Seven

SIMONE LANDED in Paris after the familiar stops and delays
– though this time, at least, nothing important or terrifying –
from New York to Gander to Shannon to Paris, and a taxi ride
to her front door and sleep. She'd brought a tin can of pickled
cactus back from Mexico, and when she awoke the next
morning she opened it and ate half of it for breakfast with
several cups of coffee. The lingering tiredness of the travel
and time change and separation from Nelson – Nelson, now
alone for two more days in their Brevoort room – mingled
with the sharp vinegary and sticky glucose cactus, already
a nostalgic taste on her tongue. The taste made her think of
Chichén Itzá, the photographs he'd taken of her at the bottom
of the temple, on the steps, at the top, of the stubborn ants.
She thought of the little dwarf of Uxmal, of the Mexico City
bullfight and most of all of their little volcano lake outside
Chichicastenango. Though she tried not to, she had to think of
the bus to Morelia, the hotel in Morelia, alone in the markets
of Morelia, but then also of their laughing and playful dinner
on the last night, of the sometimes joyful sometimes painful
days and nights in New York. And the terrible, silent goodbye.
Even on the phone at the airport. Stepha had said to her how
clear it was, how obvious that Nelson loved her. They were

almost like schoolgirls whispering about it in the next room while Fernando and Nelson talked over their drinks. And she was clear that she loved him – but why couldn't he see that? – oh the complications we make! Nelson, stubborn as the ants climbing the temple! She'd tried to write already on the aeroplane, and would finish the letter today, explaining herself better, but never, no never well enough. But he would see, she would make him see.

Approaching noon she went to Café de Flore to finish her letter and await Sartre, who would arrive sooner or later, if he wasn't already there. She wore one of her Morelia blouses, her blue Guatemalan jacket and a Mexican skirt. Bost came by and greeted her and commented on her new clothes, and that odious man Arthur passed her table and simply raised his eyebrows; she scowled at his back when he'd passed. She shared a few words with Colette, mostly about the long colourful skirt and the blouse and jacket. After these brief conversations she returned to her letter to Nelson, trying to make clear that her love was still real, was still love, even when it caused pain for both of them, hers no less than his, even across – especially across the ocean.

She heard his voice exclaiming her name across the room, Castor, and looked up to see him, hair plastered on his head, the round glasses, pipe dangling from his mouth, gambolling across the Flore. She rose and they embraced and kissed and he flopped into the chair opposite her and almost immediately she realised that something was not as it should be. She told him to come straight out with it, and he did.

The film script had fallen through, at least temporarily, he told her, but this wasn't exactly news. He'd said in his letter it was precarious. He was drawing circles with his finger on the tablecloth. He looked up at her. He looked down at the tablecloth, and across the room. Back to her. He told her: Dolores was in town after all.

Dolores. Her face – her whole body – tightened at the name. She folded her hands on the table and tried to maintain an outward picture of calm, while inside she felt only turmoil. Sartre was silent, guiltily, for a moment but then started explaining. She listened with apparent but not real patience. A month that woman would be here, interfering in everything. Even if Castor never saw her, she'd have to make an effort not to see her. She would have to avoid certain places. She would demand the Flore, though. He had to give her that. He could go to whatever clubs and bars, as long as he kept Dolores out of the Flore. Or perhaps she should just leave Paris. Go to the countryside for a month. Or – yes: go to Chicago. Wouldn't it make Nelson happy – wouldn't it make her happy – to have his frog wife landing once more in the Wabansia nest?

She sent a telegram a few days later, after she knew he would be back home, and waited anxiously for a reply, which eventually came: NO TO MUCH WORK. Not too much work. They could be together after all. She immediately sent another, outlining her plan for departure, but soon after that received a second from Nelson: DONT COME. MUST WORK. She'd misread the first. She felt stupid. Rejected. Sartre didn't want her here. Nelson didn't want her there. The second hurt her more. He hadn't wanted her to leave in the first place, but now she was gone – and now she was proposing exactly what he'd wanted – he didn't want it. Didn't want her. Not exactly what he'd wanted, okay, but a version of it. A month together working and loving. She wouldn't have it. They wouldn't have it.

He threw her telegram into the wastebasket. It was hard to say what made him angrier – sadder and angrier: her

124

presumption or his own rejection. Something must be up in Paris, he decided. It wasn't just his own cynicism. I must go to Paris, Sartre needs me, there's so much work; but now she wants to show up because she has time after all. As though he didn't have his own work. Well. He wasn't going to put himself through that again. If she couldn't decide: that was a kind of decision. She couldn't just toss his heart around on her own whims. If their love was real, it was also fragile; but so was his pride, and he was determined to protect that too. She was always saying and writing that she loved him truly and loved him deeply, and he didn't doubt that. But she also had conditions, and they were her conditions, always her conditions and not his. These telegrams showed that clearly enough. She couldn't drop anything – even something across the ocean in Paris – for the sake of their being together, but he was expected to do exactly that if she didn't have anything else going and wanted to be with him. He knew it wasn't true, but it felt as if he played a role of space-filler. Time-killer. The human equivalent of a movie like *The Kid from Brooklyn*. No, that wasn't true; but it still hurt.

It was the truth that he had work, and close enough to true that it was too much work. He set himself a schedule. Up every morning, breakfast, to the Y for a workout, usually just punching the heavy bag and maybe a swim, shower, then back home to start work. It was mostly rewriting now, and adding passages, and it felt good to be knocking a shape into this thing, finally getting it to look like a novel. He was going to stay away from the track and the poker room until this thing was finished, he'd promised himself that, and he rarely dropped in at the Tug or anywhere else. He'd take a break most afternoons to run errands, but that was about it.

The first week back he took his rolls of film to the camera shop for developing. A dozen rolls in all: Mississippi riverboat, sweltering New Orleans, Mérida, Chichén Itzá and the horrible temple, Uxmal, Guatemala City and Chichicastenango, Mexico City, the bullfight, even a few of Morelia. Photograph after photograph of Simone. A couple of days later he went back to pick them up but when he entered the shop the owner looked dismayed. None of them had come out. Not a single photo. His camera, apparently, was broken. Or the film had gotten spoiled somehow. It was hard to tell. An undeveloped photo is an undeveloped photo.

Stuart threw a New Year's Eve party at the Seven Stairs, and persuaded Nelson to come along. Nelson hadn't wanted to, but what else was he going to do, Stuart asked him. He wasn't going to sit at home on New Year's Eve. The barrel, usually full of apples, was full of ice and beer bottles, and the shelves had been slid against the walls to make more space. Stuart had laid out food: salami, bread, cheese, cold cuts; and there was a makeshift bar set up next to the cash register. Nelson knew a few of the people – Studs was there, and a couple of Stuart's friends he'd met at Seven Stairs poetry readings – and there were a lot of strangers too. None of the junkies, though. A record player churned out some anonymous jazz, and Studs was arguing with Stuart about putting on the radio instead.

He refilled his whisky out of a different bottle from the one he'd brought – somebody else obviously had better taste or more money than he did – and dropped an ice cube from the barrel into it. A woman was pulling out a beer at the same time so he handed her the opener, which hung on a string along the side. He asked her how she knew Stuart, and she said he'd done some work for the Wallace campaign. So had he, Nelson told her. She asked him what sort of thing, and he said he'd given a couple of speeches at meetings. Not full-time work. She'd worked on it, too, but behind the scenes, handling finances. She was going back to work at a bank now that it was over, but hoped there was some future for the campaign. Was he staying involved? she asked. He shrugged. It depends on what happens with Truman, and what Wallace does, he told her. He had a lot of other work too. She asked and he told her he was a writer. She introduced herself, and he told her his name was Nelson. Oh – Nelson Algren, she said, half as a question, half statement, that writer, of course. He told her he hoped by that writer she didn't mean it like most people did, like it was a swear word. She laughed. She'd read a few of his stories. They chatted about books and about Wallace and about themselves. She told him she was divorced; so was he. Later, when Studs had talked Stuart into submission and the radio was playing what Studs went around telling everyone was the real stuff, she and Nelson danced. Towards midnight he found her standing next to him and they counted down with everyone, all of them holding hands to see 1949 arrive, and on the stroke of the new year she turned to him and he kissed her, and they held it just a little longer than they needed to. At three or four they were stumbling through the snow and icy sidewalks back to Wabansia Avenue together, arm in arm. And why not?

On the ninth of January Simone turned forty-one. For a birthday present she went to Gallimard and handed in the full manuscript of her book. It should have made her feel better than it did, though she felt a certain, if only small, joy at having reached the first stage. She missed out on the Flore and went straight back home and looked at herself in the mirror. Her eyes were puffy. Her cheeks were puffy. Her stomach was puffy. She took hold of it and jiggled it. Too much alcohol, too many pills to keep herself going, too much bad food because there was no time, too much work. She took off the blue jacket, she took off her blouse and skirt and underclothes and looked at herself naked in the full-length mirror. *Quarante-et-un*, she pronounced to herself, aloud but in a whisper. An old lady. She turned to the side, and then to the back, glancing over her shoulder at herself. A blue mark stretched across her neck. She'd known it was there. It was a wonder that Guatemalan jacket had any dye left in it at all. Nelson's jacket. As though Nelson had left a permanent blue mark on her neck. It would go away eventually, of course. So would Nelson. Self-pity was so pathetic. Especially on one's birthday.

A telegram from Nelson arrived in the afternoon, FROG BIRTHDAY WISHES FROM WABANSIA NEST. A few weeks from now he'd write to her about the woman from the party. They'd seen each other a few more times in the week since the new year and over the next month it would turn into a steady and solid and fond affair. Fond; Nelson couldn't bring himself to call it love, and it wasn't. But it did draw him closer to the thought, which he finally articulated to himself in a letter to Simone, that he wanted to get married again. He wanted – needed – that stability, that companionship. A child was something in his mind somewhere, too. But after three months the affair had slipped away, without animosity though not without tears, and he was writing to Simone that as soon as he could get a passport he wanted to come to Paris.

Part Two

May 1949–October 1951

Part Two

Chapter Eight

HIS BOAT DOCKED at Le Havre and he piled all of his luggage on to the Paris train. He'd spent a couple of days in New York visiting people – he'd even seen Stepha and Fernando, like a warm-up for seeing Simone – and then he'd floated for two pretty tedious weeks at sea, but now the train would take only a few hours to Paris, to Gare Saint-Lazare, to Simone. The train trundled through Rouen, and passed through French countryside in which he had no interest, or was too tired to take an interest. It slowed at the outskirts of Paris and he watched out of the window as the buildings clustered closer and closer together, and he could see the Eiffel Tower, and not too many minutes later the train pulled under the roof of the station, slowing to a stop along the platform.

She'd thought about going to Le Havre to meet his boat but eventually that seemed stupid, schoolgirlish and a waste of money and time, so now she stood outside the platform watching the passengers coming down, many of them Americans from the boat dragging large trunks behind them, and also small groups of students from Rouen with day bags. Every American accent made her jump, but each belonged to someone other than Nelson. She craned to try to pick out his messed blond hair, his round glasses, his crooked teeth as he smiled at his anxiously waiting frog: here, here I am on the concourse waiting for my Chicago husband, waiting for you, Nelson. But the flow of passengers dissipated to a trickle and then there was none and still Nelson hadn't appeared. He couldn't have missed the boat – he would have wired. Maybe he'd missed this train and was waiting in Le Havre for the next. She should have made the journey. She tried to stand still as several more minutes and only another couple of passengers passed by, and then she walked home to wait, after consulting the timetable to find when the next Le Havre train would arrive.

He finally piled all of the bags and boxes off the train and on to a trolley with the help of a porter who spoke no more English than Nelson did French. It took over half an hour; first he had to let everyone else push past and collect their luggage, and then haul each thing one by one off the train. He'd gotten most of them off when the porter started waving his arms and saying French things at him. I'm not trying to cause trouble, he'd said, and the porter just said something else incomprehensible, so he added, look, I'll be finished in a minute just leave me alone, and it seemed to work: the porter left. A minute later though he was back, and pushing a trolley and waving as Nelson tried to figure out how to carry everything at once. Speaking at a regular clip, the porter piled the boxes on the bottom, the suitcases on top of that, and *Non, non*, brushed Nelson's hands away when he tried to push. They walked the length of the platform together, the porter talking all the while, and laughing at his own jokes, Nelson laughing along to be polite. A lap of the waiting hall didn't turn up Simone so the porter helped him pile everything into a taxi, and Nelson tipped him and told the cabbie to drive to *Un-Un Rue de la Bûcherie*.

She tried to read while waiting, but couldn't concentrate. It was stupid that he'd missed his train, and stupid that she hadn't simply gone to Le Havre. It would be even stupider if he'd gotten on the wrong train. How long would it take him to realise? But he couldn't have. Paris was the end station, she'd told him that. He couldn't speak French but he wasn't actually stupid. She walked around the apartment and listened to the music from the Arab café below, and listened to the Arab men talking and laughing as they played backgammon, sighing at the window as she looked over the Seine to Notre-Dame as though a vague and insincere prayer at the cathedral would bring him closer, pouring herself a short whisky and flopping into the chair as the men began to argue, and argue louder, and now it was a commotion unlike the usual so she went to the window and saw a taxi, and a driver tossing a suitcase, and then a box, on to the pavement, and there he was, there was Nelson, yelling at the driver. One of the Arabs was gesturing towards the driver from his chair at the café. Nelson looked up, and she waved, though she knew he didn't see, he wasn't really looking, only exasperated. She knocked back her whisky and hurried down the stairs and out into the street to greet her arrived-at-last Chicago husband.

'They all want to meet you,' she told him a couple of hours later, after they'd taken all of the luggage up the stairs, after they'd drunk a whisky together, after they'd gone to bed together.

'They?' He raised an eyebrow.

'Everybody. Bost, Boris, Michelle, Jean – the others – Sartre, everybody.'

Sartre. He'd consciously stopped himself from thinking about meeting Sartre, and she'd certainly consciously said his name last. What were they going to do? Measure each other up and glare across the table at one another, probably. As long as he got to sit next to Simone. He was here to see her, had crossed the damn ocean to see her, and the philosopher would just have to go philosophise for a few months. Anyway, now they were walking to meet him – to meet them, everybody – Simone holding Nelson's hand, and now she was waving at a short little man standing outside a café, his hair swept over his head, squinting behind round glasses, wearing a shabby suit and with a pipe between his teeth, and the little man was waving back.

'Who's that?' he asked as they approached, still hand in hand.

'That's Sartre!' Simone exclaimed and she felt Nelson's hand tense against hers.

'Castor!' Sartre said, removing the pipe from his mouth, and with this half-greeting out of the way turned and said, '*Et Monsieur Nelson Algren!*' and slammed his hand against the small of Nelson's back and practically pushed him into the café. Nelson let go of Simone's hand and tried to follow what this little Frenchman was saying, but it seemed to be some mixture of French and English, *bonjour* hello *comment* how are you *je suis* I am pleased to meet you sit *ici*, a blur of jumbled words, he didn't stop talking as he guided Nelson to a table, Simone in their wake. There were several people there already, and Sartre announced '*Monsieur Nelson Algren*' and said all their names, though Nelson caught none of it. He was planted next to a pretty blonde woman and wondered briefly if this was Sartre's ploy, but no, it didn't seem to be, Simone sat on the other side and took hold of his hand again, Sartre across the table and still talking talking talking. A waiter appeared and drinks were ordered, Nelson had no idea

134

what, but drinks, anyway, and everybody was saying things, he heard that man over there say something about Henry Wallace – were they really talking about Henry Wallace in Paris? – but the drinks arrived and now everybody went silent as Sartre banged against his glass with a fork, and raised it in the air. 'To arrival of Algren!' he said, and everyone repeated him: 'To arrival of Algren!' and all turned to the new guest.

Nelson raised his glass and looked at this assembly of French strangers: the man who knew who Henry Wallace was, next to him the nemesis-no-longer Sartre, a woman whose name he missed, an Algerian who'd been introduced as a singer, the blonde next to him, and lastly Simone. 'To arrival of Algren!' he said, and downed his drink – it turned out to be whisky – in one. They all laughed and applauded and a party began. She watched anxiously as her Chicago husband and her Paris – her Sartre – began to talk, but that anxiety dropped away as Nelson joked and Sartre laughed, as they leaned towards one another, and as Nelson clapped a hand on Sartre's arm. She could hold both this husband and this Sartre in the same life. She told herself this.

He had no idea what was happening most of the time. Drinks arrived, more people stopped by. The blonde turned out to be someone called Michelle. She spoke perfect English – better than Simone's – and translated things for him when she deemed it necessary. Her husband was also a writer, she said, and a trumpet player, and he remembered, yes, Simone had told him about these people before. A picture started to fill in. Sartre made him tell stories of Chicago, and he had the impression that the little philosopher was struggling heroically to understand as everybody else laughed at the jokes he threw into embellished stories of mostly what other people had done. Nelson liked him all the more for it.

They awoke late the next morning hungover next to one another in her Paris apartment. It seemed remarkable, historical. Here he was: in Paris. The tension and dismay that had marked the end of the Mexico trip, the longing and loneliness of the ten months in between, it all vanished when she ran out of the door, into the street, into his arms, and it stayed away through the hours in the café with all those people, her ersatz family, coming and going and drinking and smoking and talking and laughing, and it stayed away as he lay here awake, frog wife Simone still sleeping next to him, her arm across his waist.

Later they went to a local café, Les Gargouilles, named for the gargoyles on the nearby cathedral, and ate a large lunch: bread, meat, green beans, cheese, coffee, wine. They strolled around the neighbourhood afterwards, and over to Notre-Dame. The cathedral hummed with the noise of tourists and performers and beggars. The tourists pointed and took pictures of themselves, of the cathedral, and of the performers, and the performers strummed guitars or bowed violins or clacked and pulled at accordions, and of course the mimes made no noise at all, while the beggars sat in various places on the plaza, against the cathedral, on the bridges, holding out filthy hands or tin cups or hats. They had grey faces like the gargoyles on the cathedral, said Nelson to Simone.

'Yes, there are too many little gargoyles in this neighbourhood, and in Paris, everywhere. The government doesn't seem to care.'

'Governments never care about the gargoyles,' he said.

'Oh, but let's not spoil our reunion talking about that.' Simone squeezed his hand. 'We don't want to talk of the slaves and ants of Chichén Itzá or the gargoyles of Paris. Tomorrow is our anniversary, Chicago husband. Let's talk of ourselves.'

So they did, and walked over the bridge and along the Seine, from Notre-Dame to the Tuileries Gardens, and around the park. They stopped and sat on a bench beneath a tree and watched people passing by. They played their old game of making up stories, and crossed back over the Seine to walk home along the Rive Gauche, stopping in one café for a beer, in another for a rum, eventually eating a meal and returning home.

They spent their anniversary day walking in the sunshine in the Jardin du Luxembourg. They watched children pushing small sailboats with sticks in the fountain, and the Guignol puppet show, children squealing and shrieking at the story and the dancing marionettes. Later they walked up to Montparnasse and around the cemetery there. They looked at the gravestone of Charles Baudelaire, shared with other family members. From Montparnasse they walked back through St Germain and stopped at the Deux Magots. It excited Nelson to be in Hemingway's café, and Simone shared the enthusiasm, though she'd never thought of it as Hemingway's before. She'd reread some of the stories and *The Sun Also Rises*, in English this time, after Nelson had sent them. They were better in English, of course. They made more sense as American books.

'You never saw them?' Nelson stirred sugar into his tiny coffee.

Simone shrugged. 'We must have seen them, but I was only young then and so full of studying, I'm sure I didn't care.'

'They were nobodies then anyway. Maybe not Joyce or Pound. The rest of them.'

'American nobodies.'

'Not Joyce.'

'No, not Joyce, Nelson. But we didn't have anything to do with the Americans and English – '

'Irish.'

She rolled her eyes. 'Nelson!'

'Accuracy matters.'

'Nelson!' She punched him on the arm and giggled. 'But we didn't. They were their own important circle. Important to themselves, I suppose. We didn't know anything of or about them.'

'Like your own circle?'

'Our circle is different.' She scowled as he raised his eyebrows. 'It is. We are French, and we are involved in France, in the things that matter in France. In shaping France. Politically. We are not just *flaneur* expatriates.'

'Just *flaneurs*?' He jerked his thumb over his shoulder. 'Like Baudelaire.'

She dropped her coffee cup into its saucer, too hard. 'No! *Les Temps Modernes* is addressing things; Sartre and Merleau-Ponty and Bost, they are working hard to engage with the life of this country, the direction – they are publishing extracts of my essay, and we are – '

Nelson had been biting into his lip but now he was laughing out loud, and wiping his eyes. Simone glared and folded her arms across her chest. After a few seconds she began laughing too.

'It's almost too easy to be a sport.' He touched her elbow.

'You're a mean Chicago husband,' she said, trying to control her laughter, 'Coming all the way to Paris to hassle your poor wife on her anniversary day.'

May and the beginning of June passed in a kind of lazy whirl: daytime walking through Paris, going to the cinema to see films that Nelson could watch but not listen to, drunken evenings in various bars and cafés with Sartre, Bost and Olga, Michelle and Boris, Michel and Zette and various others. They went to basement dives where Americans played jazz, and a few times to places where Boris was playing trumpet, or they sat around a large table at the Flore, Nelson getting drunk and bewildered in the babble of French, Michelle or Olga always sitting nearby to translate when they thought it was important, Nelson making up Chicago gangster and huckster stories to entertain Bost, or talking in a ridiculous version of English and translation to Sartre, the little philosopher always pulling on a pipe or cigarette, and slapping each other on the back as they laughed over their half-communicated jokes and stories. Simone's book – *The Second Sex*, the essay on women, which Nelson, after all, had encouraged her to make longer and longer, no mere essay but a book, and which Nelson had fed with books he bought and sent from America – was published and selling in the thousands, and the excerpts in *Les Temps Modernes* were, as Simone said, 'no joke of Nelson Algren': publicity was crackling everywhere, in the papers and on the radio and in the magazines, and not only the intellectual titles and programmes, and it made them all giddy.

Arthur approached their table at the Flore one evening. The drinking family tonight was Nelson, Simone, Sartre, Olga, Bost and Michelle. Simone had seen him come through the door, and scowled, hoping he'd go to another corner, but knowing that, even if he did, it would be by a path past their table. And so it was. 'Mademoiselle Beauvoir,' he said as he approached, his face composed as usual in a smirk.

'Monsieur Koestler,' she replied, more to shut him up than anything. Sartre, his back to Arthur, rolled his eyes. The others half-heartedly tried to continue a semblance of conversation, but it was killed.

Arthur placed a hand on his cheek. 'Congratulations. I see your book and your magazine have created – ' he lifted his hand from his cheek and made a twirling motion ' – quite a stir.' The word stir came out as a sneer.

Simone kept her voice calm. 'My work has achieved some notice, yes, and I am pleased, thank you.'

Arthur returned his hand to his cheek. 'Yes, yes. I am sure in time all of France will be grateful for the, ah, political and cultural, ah, changes – ' again he turned a word into a sneer ' – you will have wrought with your pen and your vagina.'

Sartre rolled his eyes again and bit into his lip to stifle laughter. Simone glared, her mouth tightening. The others were silent, save Michelle, who whispered a translation to Nelson. Bost found his voice and told Arthur to fuck off, but Arthur had already turned on his heel and left the café.

'Should I go punch him in the face?' Nelson said.

Sartre lost control and started laughing, hard. So did Bost, followed by Olga and Michelle.

'Yes!' said Bost. 'Send Algren to punch his nose!'

'Send Algren!' yelled Sartre. People at other tables turned to look.

Nelson began to stand, but Simone took hold of his arm. 'Sit down, Nelson. Nobody needs to punch Koestler.'

'Send Algren!' said Sartre again.

Now Simone, too began to laugh. 'We'll send you to punch somebody's nose when the nose belongs to somebody important.'

A few days later Simone and Nelson went to watch the crowds at the ceremonies for the renaming of the Avenue d'Orléans. She wanted to show him what a crowd in Paris looked like, the kinds of people who populated it. He wasn't sure he wanted to stand around with a bunch of *tricolore*-waving patriots and listen to jingoistic speeches about Leclerc's glorious liberation of Paris, speeches he couldn't understand in the first place.

'Besides,' he said, spreading jam across a torn-open croissant at the breakfast table, 'every fool knows that Hemingway liberated Paris. Leclerc was just the Frenchman closest to hand, so Papa threw a tunic on him and let him walk in ahead.'

Some of the crowd were people on their way to work, dressed in overalls or uniforms of various kinds. Groups of war veterans in ill-fitting and worn-out uniforms, some complete, others missing various elements, had also gathered. The majority of people seemed to be regular Parisians who had come out for the occasion, and dressed for it too: three-piece suits and ties, women in formal but sober dresses.

'People who lived out the war in Paris,' Simone said, 'and rejoiced like hell when freedom finally came. People like me.'

Nelson looked at the people immediately around him, all of whom had either fought in the war or endured a Nazi occupation. 'It's impossible to understand to those of us who lived the war second-hand.'

'But you had your own first-hand, in the army.'

He laughed. 'No, sitting around a camp in Wales and going to Marseille just long enough to be demobbed isn't really fighting the good fight to topple Hitler. Private Algren was a little below average on the softball field in Swansea and a little above average on the black market in Marseille, and no more or less.'

They meandered through the crowd towards the stage that had been set up at the north end of the avenue. Nearly everyone clutched a small paper flag; someone must have been distributing them somewhere. A brass band was playing indistinguishable martial music that floated just above the collective chatter. Simone's progress snagged as someone grabbed her arm, briefly but firm enough to make her stop. A man glared at her. She didn't know him. '*Tu n'as pas le droit d'être là.*' He spat at her feet. '*Sale putain de lesbienne.*' She braced herself for a slap, but it didn't come. The man and his paper flag pushed back into the crowd.

'Another fan?' Nelson asked.

Simone unclenched her tight-set jaw. 'You could say that. I am a lesbian whore with no right to be here.'

'Your vagina seems to grow in power and range with each passing day,' he said. 'And contradiction.'

'Let's leave it there,' she said, though she smiled.

The ceremony over, the street successfully renamed to honour the General, they found the most direct way out of the crowd and to the Flore for a drink. After an hour or so Sartre came by. They watched his approach from their terrace table, an excited and comical half-walk-half-run.

'*Vingt mille*,' he said before he'd sat down, and repeated it in English for Nelson's sake. 'Twenty thousand. I was just speaking to Gallimard. They've sold twenty thousand copies of your book, Castor. Twenty thousand!'

Nelson whistled. 'It's having its effect, too,' he said. 'It's making enemies.'

Sartre waved his hand as though he was shooing a fly. 'Koestler is nothing. Not a new enemy, or a real enemy. An old antagonist.'

'Not just Koestler,' Simone said, and she briefly described what had happened at the Avenue d'Orléans.

'Hmm,' said Sartre when she'd finished, and took out his pipe and began filling it. Once he'd packed it he stuck it in his mouth and took out a box of matches. 'Did you send Algren to punch his nose?'

Simone laughed.

Nelson lifted his hands from the table. 'I was too slow, too slow.'

'A shame.' Sartre struck a match and put it to the tobacco. 'Our American needs to sharpen his wits to protect our Castor from the reactionaries.'

'It's the fists that need sharpening.' Nelson held them up like a boxer and jabbed the air above the table. 'The wits are just fine.' He winked at Sartre and tapped his temple.

Sartre left after a few drinks to attend another appointment, and Simone and Nelson wandered up to Montparnasse to a small restaurant for dinner. When the wine had been poured, Nelson raised a toast.

'To twenty thousand copies,' he said, 'And also to the continuing angering of all the right people.'

They touched their glasses and sipped. 'It is nice to know that it's producing a reaction, but I could do without any more people telling me who I am in the streets. That wasn't a very nice situation.'

'No, but it was harmless, I suppose.'

'Harmless. But intimidating. It's conceivable that he could have punched me. And he grabbed hold of me to make me stop.'

'I'd have punched him first. I really would have.'

'My strong local youth.' She reached across the table and stroked his arm. 'But let's not talk of it any longer. There are more interesting things to talk about, surely.'

Between the first and main course a family arrived and was seated at the table next to theirs. The children were grown, or at least teenagers, and one of them pointed at their table as

143

they walked across the restaurant and said something to his sister, who giggled. Once seated, he whispered to his parents, and indicated Nelson and Simone with a tilt of his head. The parents, too, giggled, and all four whispered amongst one another giddily, and with continued giggling and snickering until their waiter arrived. Simone took a roll from the bread basket and broke it open, each movement slow and deliberate as though it required all her concentration. Nelson drummed his fingers on the table and tried to think of something he could do or say without causing a complete scene. He knew she wouldn't want him to cause a scene, though if the roles had been reversed, he in the spotlight here, that was exactly what he would've done. What she would've done, most likely, too, he thought. But not for herself.

Some reprieve arrived in the form of their main course and the family's first course; everybody had food and, just as the family fell into small talk about what they were eating, so did Simone and Nelson, though self-consciously and quietly. She felt gripped by the idea that they shouldn't – mustn't – hear her speaking English – and why? – so she spoke softly, and he followed her cue. Neither was particularly interested in talking about their meal, but it filled the air with words, and self-conscious words seemed better than self-conscious silence.

They finished the main course, and dessert and coffee, and paid the bill. Simone hurried with as much control as she could for the door, the family watching her go with their mouths and eyes wide with hilarity, while Nelson stood and slowly shrugged on his jacket. Neither Simone nor they saw the exact moment that he flicked his wrist through the cuff of the jacket and into the daughter's wine glass, and Simone was already on the street when the girl squealed in first shock, then dismay as the burgundy stain spread across the lap of her cream dress.

'What is this schoolboy's grin on the face of my husband?' Simone asked as he stepped through the door.

'Glad to be shot of that scene,' he said. 'No more.'

'What horrible people. Now you see the French bourgeoisie for what they are. Prying, gossiping shits. One cannot even enjoy a meal surrounded by these people.'

'At least your book is reaching beyond the intellectuals.' He jerked a thumb over his shoulder. 'Those are just the kinds of people you want to shock, with their bourgeois pretence.'

'Those people will never learn, though. They cower in the face of something different. Those parents were probably collaborators.'

He laughed.

'Nelson, it is not funny!'

'It is.' He took hold of her hand. 'Not everyone who disagrees with you is a Nazi sympathiser.'

'No. But those ones probably were.'

The pattern continued for the next couple of weeks: they were pointed at in cafés and restaurants, and on the street. Simone received mail, both at the publisher and at home, calling her a slut, calling her frigid, calling her a lesbian, asking if she wanted a taste of the correspondent's cock, and on and on. Further articles appeared in the newspapers and magazines. Simone de Beauvoir was famous, and not just *New Yorker* famous or French intellectual famous – movie-star famous. And hated as only a celebrity could be. Nelson shielded her from it: he joked, he distracted her, he reminded her how important and new her ideas really were – and that she didn't face these hatreds alone. Nelson could protect her like this because he was different: he was outside her Paris circle, her family. Yet his defence of her pulled them closer, and she felt it. She couldn't have faced this attention without him. Even Sartre, she realised, wouldn't have been enough.

They decided to leave town sooner than they'd at first intended. She went to the travel office and changed their flight for the end of the week, and in the middle of July they landed in Rome.

In Rome they were tourists. They went to the Colosseum, to St Peter's Basilica, to the Pantheon; they wet their hands in the Trevi fountain and gawped at the ceiling of the Sistine Chapel; they walked around the Piazza del Campidoglio, where Nelson saluted Marcus Aurelius and his horse. All over the city Nelson snapped photographs with the other Americans, occasionally mocking them and embarrassing Simone by saying 'Gee whizz!' and 'Gosh!' as he held the camera to his eye. They dined in restaurants where nobody knew who they were – where nobody knew who she was. Nobody stared, nobody pointed, nobody snickered. One evening, after stepping out of the restaurant and into the warm Roman evening, they walked two or three miles through the quiet streets, Simone's arm hooked into Nelson's elbow, and, arriving at the Trevi fountain, held hands as they each threw in a coin. Neither could remember what the coin was supposed to do for them, whether it was plain good luck or something more significant, but they did it anyway, along with other lovers, loners and tourists. A line of horse-drawn carriages stood along the Via delle Muratte and they took one home to their hotel.

'If that fountain were in Chicago,' Nelson said, watching the buildings and listening to the horse hooves, 'Thieves would come every night to plunder it.'

Simone leaned her head against his shoulder. 'Beloved Chicago husband,' she said, 'I'm sure they do in Rome as well.'

Tunis, Algiers, Fez, Marrakesh: along the African Mediterranean coast and inland once they hit Morocco. They found a man in Tunis who was driving to Algiers, and they paid him to take them with him. He couldn't believe that an American like Nelson didn't own a car, and shook his head every time he thought, aloud, about it. When it was almost dark they stopped for the night in a village the driver knew, and they paid his cousin, or a man he claimed was his cousin, anyway, to give them a bed for the night. The whole village was out celebrating the end of Ramadan, and they joined in, drinking wine, eating lamb and bread and smoking hashish. Late the next morning they were on the road again, and eventually they arrived in Algiers. They paid the final instalment to the driver and he wished them well, adding one final shake of his head at the thought of a real American who didn't own a car.

In the Algerian desert they rode camels, Nelson dressed head to toe like an Arab, and amusing the guides and Simone but mostly himself by telling stories of his grandfather, who had emigrated with his family to the Palestinian desert because it was the Holy Land. Simone photographed the prostitutes, no more than thirteen or fourteen years old, who then offered to photograph her but only took the camera and demanded ransom, which Nelson paid. Simone bought cloth for a dress in Fez and a rug in Marrakesh and arranged for them to be shipped to Paris, and after a few days they flew to Marseille.

For both of them Marseille was a kind of homecoming: Simone had spent a year in in the city working as a teacher, and Nelson had been stationed there when the war came to an end. For three months he'd been quartered on the outskirts, he told her again as they walked the hot streets, the breeze from the sea merely pushing the air around without cooling anything. He'd been taken off active duty so every day he hitched a ride into Marseille to see what trouble he could find. He bought or stole stuff from the PX – cigarettes, jackets, boots, chocolate, whatever – and went to the bars to find willing buyers.

'Algerians and Somalis were the ones doing the dealing, mostly. And they always had a scam going. They'd drop the money on the floor and take your stuff while you were picking it up, and trip you as they bolted for good measure; or they'd start yelling about the MPs raiding the place. I got to know all the tricks, but couldn't help myself from falling for them. Still, it was fun; it didn't matter.' He waved his hand, as though batting the memories away.

'The prostitutes were the saddest thing, though,' he told her. 'Worse than those cynical girls in Algeria. Younger, a lot of them, too, and selling themselves for food and getting beaten left and right by every Algerian, Somali, Egyptian and American who went up the stairs. You didn't want to be a woman in Marseille after the war.'

'Or anywhere else,' Simone said.

'Or anywhere else. But, for demobbed privates waiting for the boat like me, it was the easiest time. I didn't have any friends, I didn't have any obligations; I was just an anonymous person, doing as I pleased.'

They wandered Marseille and he tried to find some of the places he remembered – a pizzeria where he'd sat all evening drinking wine and selling army supplies, some of the seedy bars in narrow streets – but of course those places had vanished and his memory was faulty, even with only a few years' distance. 'The thing is,' he told her, 'I remember it being very African, or seeming very African, the streets, and of course the people. I thought, coming here straight from Africa, that impression would've faded.'

'But it hasn't?' she said.

'No. It seems just as African, or Franco-African, as it did then.'

The second day was Simone's turn to reminisce, starting at the train station, where she pointed out the grubby building in which she'd had her first apartment. 'I wanted to be close to the station,' she told him, 'because I hated leaving Paris, and it seemed to me that I was closer to Paris – only a train journey away – if I was as close to the station as possible.'

She'd hated Marseille, and her time in Marseille. She'd hated the other teachers, hated the heat, and hated the distance from Paris – and, yes, the distance from Sartre. Nelson's hand clenched reflexively hearing this, but he kept himself even, and had to, because she continued. It was their first real separation, she told him, and she'd known he'd be dallying around with other girls, and despite the agreements they'd made – despite their pact – it made her jealous, and lonelier than she already was. She'd first tried to write a novel in Marseille but it didn't amount to much, knowing, too, that Sartre was there in Paris, thinking and writing and full of stimulation.

'He would write letters to me about everything he did during the day. We'd agreed to be open and clear to each other, but I wasn't ready for all the details of what he did with the women he had sex with.'

She shaded her eyes and looked across the harbour. This was a slip. She shouldn't have told him that. It was between her and Sartre. And it would feed Nelson's jealousy.

It didn't feed his jealousy, but it clicked a switch. She was always, in her letters, telling him to tell her everything. It was a thought not worth following at this moment, but it was also a thought not worth forgetting entirely.

'There was nobody interesting to me in Marseille.' She picked up quickly again. 'I couldn't just go to the bars and cafés as in Paris, and wait for one of my friends to show. Oh, it was a dull time. But I started going to the mountains to walk at the weekends.'

That had been its own kind of danger, she told him, hitching a ride out or back if the buses weren't convenient, and the truck drivers sometimes trying to force themselves on her. But it was the one good thing about that year: she could go to the mountains and think about her own work, instead of what was necessary to the school, or think about nothing and just walk, and at the end of a long day, return tired and happy to Marseille and sleep.

'But then one time I went with Suzanne. Another teacher at the school. I'd started going to cafés with her occasionally, and had moved into the apartment above hers, because it was nicer than the one by the station. She was a terrible walker, insisting on going slowly like we were climbing the Alps, and not these old low mountains of Provence. It made me furious so I just marched ahead and waited for her to catch up, then marched ahead again. All day long.'

'Like a certain frog wife at Chichén Itzá.'

She rolled her eyes at him. 'When we got back to our house she grabbed hold of me and tried to kiss me, saying, "Let's not deny this any longer. I'm madly in love with you."'

'And – ?'

'And nothing – oh, you'd like that very much, wouldn't you, Nelson? But no, nothing. I was shocked. I threw her hands off me and made it clear I had no such feelings or intentions towards her. Oh, it really made me hate her! The closest thing I had to a friend!'

'But did it make you curious?' They had made their way down to the old port now, and were standing beneath the lighthouse.

She considered what she might tell him, what limit she would set, and then shook her head. 'But it certainly made me less naïve.'

They took a ferry across the harbour to the Château d'If. Nelson had loved *The Count of Monte Cristo* when he was young, and the trip across the water made him boyishly giddy. They watched from the deck both the approach of the island fortress and the shrinking of the city behind them, and as they shaded their eyes from the glare off the water he unrolled a long list of jokes about the name of the château: if our boat were a different type it would be a skiff d'If; if we make it to the château, he said, if the man in the iron mask is there, if they had marijuana they could smoke a spliff d'If; if they incarcerate your beloved crocodile, if his frog wife were to help him, if she got caught in the act, if your crocodile escapes, if he comes back for her, if they could swim back to Marseille, or if they executed him, he'd be the stiff d'If; if they composed a song would it be 'Riff d'If'; if they had a meal would it come with an aperit-if?

'Nelson, stop!' She turned her back and took a step away to try to control herself.

'Okay, the last one was a little iffy,' he said, laughing at her exasperation.

In the few hours they spent touring the fortress the weather changed: a shift in wind direction and force meant they climbed aboard a ferry that even in its moorings was bouncing like a car with bad springs. The Mediterranean had been almost glass-smooth on the way over, but now choppy whitecaps smashed into each other, even the distant ones visible. A few sailboats were tacking the route back to the Marseille harbour. Most of the other passengers headed below deck, but Nelson wanted to watch the sea.

'The waves aren't as big as on the Atlantic crossing,' he said by way of justification.

'Neither is the boat,' Simone said, but took his hand and they walked unsteadily to the front of the deck, where they leaned against the rail and watched the sea as the ferry pulled away from the island.

Some of the waves smashed against the side of the boat, and others raised it up several feet before dropping it into a trough. Simone's skirt flapped like a flag in the wind. She wrapped her arms around her ribs as a buffer.

'When we get back,' she shouted, not entirely sure he'd be able to hear over the waves, the wind, the engine, 'should we find somewhere for coffee, or just go straight to a restaurant for a full meal?'

'If we get back,' he shouted in reply.

'Nelson, don't start that again.'

'I mean it,' he said. 'If.'

Looking from the shore of Marseille to his face, she could see he meant it. He'd turned paler than she'd ever seen him. Beads of sweat decorated his forehead. His hands were no longer nonchalantly draped over the rail, but clutched it, the red creases of his knuckles a sharp contrast to the white fingers. He swallowed three times, quick, shallow swallows.

'Oh, Nelson! Are you seasick?' It was cruel, but she couldn't help laughing.

He leaned forward as the boat pitched once more and his tongue darted across his lips before they opened into a wide O and a stream of bright yellow-green bile plummeted forth to join the sea. The crosswind blew it the opposite way from Simone. He heaved once more with the same result. The third heave came up empty and he managed to reach into his pocket to pull out a handkerchief and wipe his mouth.

'Poor crocodile,' she said, and reached up to wipe his sweaty hair from his forehead. 'Shall we go below deck now?'

He nodded, handkerchief still held to his mouth, and she guided him slowly – the boat still pitching with and against the waves – and unsteadily along the deck to the stairway. She noticed the smirk on the captain's face as he glanced down at them from the tower, but thought it best to keep it a shared secret.

Back on the solid ground of Marseille, Nelson needed half an hour sitting on a bench looking silently across the much calmer waters of the harbour, trying to push away the Château d'If and the choppy waves they'd ridden from it before he'd regained his equilibrium and disposition. Once he was back on his feet he was ready for a drink and a meal.

'I thought we might drown,' he said as they walked from the water up La Canebière.

'Don't be silly,' Simone said. 'It was a little rough, but not so bad as that. You were just feeling unwell. It's normal.'

'No, I really thought that was it. That I would pitch over the side and into the Mediterranean.'

'No more crocodile.'

'No more adventures for the local Chicago youth.' He cupped his hand and waved it across the space in front of him. ' "Local Youth Dies in French Boat Tragedy". Though I'm not so sure the *Tribune* would treat me so kindly.

"Beloved Husband of Lesbian Slut Authoress Lost at Sea".
That's a better headline.'

'A little wordy,' she said.

'Yes. A little wordy. But accurate?'

'Accuracy is the main thing.'

The final day in Marseille they spent on terra firma, walking again the streets they'd both once known, investigating the present together while reminiscing about their separate pasts. They dined in a pizzeria that Nelson deemed a suitable stand-in for the one in which he'd sat for hours as a demobbed private, and drank cheap and not particularly good Chianti. Afterwards they still had one more hour to wander a lazy route to the railway station before boarding the overnight train back to Paris. They drank cocktails in the dining car and watched the city disappear as the train snaked into the mountains.

'Next time,' Nelson said, 'we should hike in these mountains. You can show me the correct frog pace.'

'I would like that. Or perhaps take bicycles. That would be fun too.' She sighed at the window. 'I never liked Marseille very much when I lived there, but I think now it is a place I would very much like to spend a lot of time with you.'

They slept in bunks in the sleeping car, Nelson on the top and Simone in the lower bed, and when they awoke it was morning and the train was crawling through the Paris suburbs. For two weeks, until the start of September, they would have the city to themselves with nearly everyone else away on vacation. They took a taxi to Rue de la Bûcherie, and the driver helped them carry their luggage up the stairs. They opened the windows to let air into the stuffy apartment. The music and chatter of the backgammon players outside the Arab café was louder without the rest of the usual street noises. They spent the day in the apartment, using the café sounds to pretend they were still in the desert of Morocco or Algeria or Tunisia. Nelson went out in the early afternoon and returned with bread and olive oil and slices of grilled lamb, which he'd bought from downstairs. It had never occurred to Simone that she could buy things from them, that they'd sell her a meal this way. Nelson shrugged and told her, 'It's Africa here.' They opened a bottle of wine and they sat on the Guatemalan carpet and ate with their fingers, telling each other stories of the things they'd done and seen on their vacation, to the accompaniment of the café music and rattle of backgammon dice.

They usually ate at home, because so many restaurants were closed for vacation, but nearly every day they spent walking in the hot August sunshine, revisiting the parks, going to a few museums and simply wandering around without a plan. Evenings they mostly spent in Rue de la Bûcherie, listening to music on the radio and drinking whisky, and sometimes listening only to the Arab café below, which they'd come to think of as a kind of companion. Eventually, in their ones and twos, Simone's friends began to drift back into Paris, first Bost and Olga, who called by and forced them out of their cocoon and to the Flore for an evening of vacation show and tell, and, a few days after them, Michelle and Boris announced their return. By the time Sartre was back so was everyone else, and Nelson only had one more week to spend in France.

They all gathered in the Flore on his last evening. Michel and Zette, Olga and Bost, Boris and Michelle, Sartre, and several others who came and went as the night moved from wine and food to round after round of whisky and cognac.

Nelson sat between Michelle, who took up her usual job of translating for him when necessary, and Sartre, who tried harder than usual to speak in his incomprehensible English. Simone sat across the table, talking and watching, trying not to take her eyes from her Chicago-bound Chicago husband, trying not to think of the months that would stretch out from tomorrow, when he would be gone, an ocean away. Trying not to think of it.

They teased Nelson, asking him who in Chicago he could practise his French with, asking him how he would get to Paris every morning for fresh bread, asking which one of them he would hide in his suitcase and take to Chicago with him.

'I don't know what we're laughing about,' said Bost as another round of whiskies was distributed. 'After tonight we have no one to send to punch noses for us.'

'No more sending Algren,' said Boris.

'We'll have to put you on standby,' Olga said. 'And call for you when we find a nose in need of punching.'

'Send for Algren!' shouted Sartre, and they all repeated after him, 'Send for Algren!'

They all laughed, Nelson too, and raised their glasses in a toast and drank. They all laughed except Simone, whose smile faded just a little as she thought that she'd have to send for her crocodile, she'd have to send for him and he might not come back. She'd felt before the loneliness and missing him and longing for him, and that would be nothing new, but now that he'd been to Paris, actually been here and sat in the Flore with her, and slept in her bed in Rue de la Bûcherie, there would be an empty space, shaped like Nelson Algren, everywhere she went. She'd have to send for him and he might not come back. She stood and walked across the café and up the stairs to the ladies'. Once the door had swung shut behind her she splashed cold water on her face and took a deep breath. Now wasn't the time to be thinking of that. She dried her hands and face and went back down to the table, pausing to tousle Nelson's hair as she passed his seat. There would be tomorrow, and in the evening he would get in a taxi to the airport and be gone.

Chapter Nine

THE FLIGHT FROM Paris to Shannon, a couple of hours in Shannon, Shannon to Gander, now several hours in Gander before New York: he knew what it was like now, why she got so bored crossing the Atlantic, strapped into the seat with nothing to do but read until you were too tired, then sit and stare and daydream about the airplane diving into the ocean. He'd survived, though, and now had to get through the four hours on this island at the edge of North America before he'd shoot down the coast to New York and stay there for a couple of weeks. Some of the passengers, having formed a kind of friendship on the flights over, sat around chatting to one another and drinking coffee, but Nelson had ignored his neighbours, so he wandered around the small terminal by himself. The newsstand had a copy of *Time*, doubtless nothing in it, but he bought it anyway and sat down near the gate and flipped through it. Louis St Laurent graced the cover along with a maple leaf and fleur-de-lis. Appropriate, he supposed. The table of contents was uninspiring; it was almost impossible to tell what an article contained from the headlines: 'COMMUNISTS: An Unfriendly Gesture'; 'INVESTIGATIONS: Friendship and Nothing More'; 'AVIATION: Rough Ride'. The book reviews were always awful, but he looked anyway, and here was one: 'Hunters and Hunted': an assessment of a World War II espionage and heroes novel, some dumb trash for Americans to remind themselves they'd won the war a few years ago. The reviewer decided that *Of its kind it is a good book*. Wow. He flipped back. The previous review was 'Is Anybody Happy?', Abner Dean cartoons that the reviewer didn't have much time for. Before that – hang on: 'The Lower Depths. *The Man with the Golden Arm* by Nelson Algren.' He looked up, as though someone might catch him in the act, and immediately felt stupid. But here it was, in *Time*. He read it through. Oh, to hell with this guy: The Man with the Golden Arm *has its specks of dross, moments when it reads like the late Damon Runyon at his slapdash, sentimental worst*. Bullshit. The sentences quoted in support didn't even live up to that. Damon Runyon could dream of writing almost that good. To hell with it. He read the review again. That was the only negative thing the guy had to say about it. He read the review again. He looked around the waiting area, and could feel his face getting sore from smiling too hard. He knew he was looking around to see if anybody else was reading *Time* and it made him feel a little stupid, but here he was, in *Time*. He read the review again. He took some writing paper from his suitcase, wrote *Gander* on the top right, the pen cap in his mouth, and one line lower, on the left, *Dear Simone*.

Castor went back to being Castor, Chicago-husbandless Castor. And now that people had arrived back from their vacations, and another section of *The Second Sex* had appeared in *Les Temps Modernes*, she also went back to being France's most hated woman. The letters arrived, and the mocking and snickering in the streets and cafés resumed. They staked out the Flore, sometimes, knowing she would be there to work, and so she would get no work done. The family of friends rallied around her, Michel or Boris or Bost telling snickerers where they could shove it, Sartre always there to talk her through her tears and her anger, or to make everyone laugh with a swift nod of his head towards a heckler and his new favourite phrase: send for Algren. It made her laugh too, but always a tinge of sadness, or longing, not exactly loneliness, would flutter inside her when he said it. If only a snap of the fingers could send for Algren. She began to fear – sitting in the Flore surrounded by her friends, and especially alone in Rue de la Bûcherie – that she would never see him again, that the view of his face, looking back through the window of the Orly-bound taxi, was her last, that she would never feel his hands on her hips or his arm on her shoulder. Alone in Rue de la Bûcherie she would sometimes cry, and find it difficult to stop, and so would drink a whisky and turn on the radio, and only make it worse. In the first days he was gone she wrote letters every day, or one long one, continually adding on. All it seemed to say was how lonely she felt without him, how much she missed him, how much she loved him and wished she could be in Wabansia with him, or that he'd never had to leave Paris. It felt like writing into a hole, because she knew it would be weeks before she got a reply, even if he wrote from New York, especially if he waited until he got back to Chicago. And how did he feel? Was he lonely and missing her, or did he have so many other things to do, girls to see – she wanted him to tell her, she wanted to know, even if she felt a jealousy she tried to hide – did all those things and girls add up to so much that there was no space left for his frog wife?

She managed to start some work. She wanted to write another novel. She had, to some extent, the idea. She wrote on the first page: *pour Nelson Algren*, in all capital letters:

POUR NELSON ALGREN. Like a schoolgirl, she wanted to decorate it with hearts, but did not.

Nelson sat at the bar in the Tug, watching Game Two of the World Series. The Yankees had won last night, Heinrich hitting a home run in the bottom of the ninth, but now it was the third inning and the Dodgers were on top, 1-0. Preacher Roe was on the mound for Brooklyn, and the Yankees had Vic Raschi pitching. Jackie Robinson had led off the inning with a double, and scored when Gil Hodges singled to left. Now the Yankees were batting with two out. Rizzuto made it to first when Pee Wee Reese kicked a ground ball, bringing up Heinrich. Rizzuto had just broken to steal second when Nelson heard a voice at the door calling for Mr *Time* Magazine. He knew it was Studs. Not just the voice, but it was the kind of thing Studs would say. He joined Nelson at the bar and ordered a beer as Heinrich gave Reese a chance to redeem himself with another ground ball, and the inning ended. Studs started warming to his theme: you want another beer, Mr *Time* Magazine? What's the score, Mr *Time* Magazine? Haven't seen you since you got back, Mr *Time* Magazine. How was France, Mr *Time* Magazine? They got *Time* magazine in France, Mr *Time* Magazine? Barusz set the beers in front of them and asked what was the deal with all the Mr *Time* Magazine. Studs jerked a thumb at Nelson, and told Barusz that Mr *Time* Magazine here was in *Time* magazine. Barusz looked to Nelson with raised eyebrows, as if to ask whether Studs was just playing around. Nelson shrugged. Jackie Robinson was stepping into the batter's box. Nelson pointed out that it wasn't really him in *Time*, just a review of his book. He wasn't in the magazine at all. Studs asked Barusz if his book had ever been reviewed in *Time* magazine. Barusz shook his head. Robinson struck out and

Hermanski stepped in. Studs said that he'd never had a book reviewed in *Time* magazine, either, and exaggerated craning his neck to look around the bar. He couldn't see anybody else in the Tug who'd had his book reviewed in *Time* magazine. A crack of the bat and they all snapped their eyes to the television, where Hermanski was rounding second, heading for third and sliding in with a triple. Nelson waved the back of his hand towards Studs and told him to knock it off. It was no big thing. But he smiled, the right corner of his mouth turning up while the left tried to stay flat to prove it was no big deal.

Bottom of the sixth, Preacher Roe was facing the top of the Yankees' order, and Stuart eased up to the bar, on the other side of Nelson from Studs, ordered a beer, and said he was honoured to be in the same tavern, let alone sitting at the bar next to Mr *Time* Magazine. Studs burst into laughter, slapping his palm on the bar. Barusz put a beer in front of Stuart and said nobody was getting another drink until someone went out and bought him a copy of *Time*. Stuart opened his satchel, flopped a copy on the bar and told Barusz to keep it. Bauer grounded out to Jorgenson to end the inning. Barusz flipped through the magazine to the back, where the reviews were, and started reading, his lips just slightly moving with the words, his head nodding in appreciation. When he'd finished reading he put down the magazine and told Nelson that he didn't realise Division Street was literature. Roy Campanella hit a flyball to left to end the top of the seventh and send it to the stretch, still 1-0. Nelson said he figured Division Street was as good for literature as Michigan Avenue.

Margo. They'd come into the Tug one late afternoon, Jack, Karl, Patty, and this pale and thin and pretty girl – she looked almost like a kid – trailing behind them. He'd slid off his stool at the bar and joined them in a booth by the door. They always sat in a booth by the door, as though they might need to make an escape. This is Margo, Karl had said, Margo, Nelson. Margo. He liked the sound of her name. He liked the look of her. There was some kind of wisdom, or no, not wisdom exactly, but he could see she'd been through things, she had the look of smarts and experience around her eyes. Margo. He asked her where she was from. Ohio, she told him, a podunk town in Ohio, but she'd been around other places for a few years now. She had a kid she never saw, looked after by her people back in Ohio. She said these things as facts. He asked her how she'd met Jack and Karl and Patty. Her upper lip curled into a wry smile. We find each other, she told him. You know how it is. He didn't, but he also didn't say that he didn't. He had an inkling.

Later on at their place Karl put on a Charlie Parker album and they drank beer and shot up. They didn't bother going behind the curtain when Nelson was around any more. Karl drummed along with Roy Haynes on his thighs until it was his turn at the needle. When he'd finished he unscrewed the needle from the syringe and took out a clean one for Margo. She offered to let Nelson go before her and he told her he wasn't on heroin. She sighed and started the routine of cooking up the powder, and said she wished she weren't either. Nelson asked her why she didn't try to quit, and she asked without malice what made him think she hadn't. She had the monkey, she said, sucking the liquefied heroin into the dropper. After they'd left their kid behind, and she and her shotgun husband had washed up in Chicago, he'd gotten her hooked and sent her out hooking. Those were the words she used, again the wry smile, and she said she guessed that's what he'd meant all along when he said they could make a mint in a big city. You don't grow up in Ohio thinking you'll one day end up being pimped around a city like Chicago by your husband, she said, and shrugged, and jabbed the needle into a vein in her forearm. You ought to quit, he told her. Karl laughed softly through his nose, still drumming to the music. Jack and Patty were both glazed over, heads lolling back. She said if she were someplace else, maybe she could, but she didn't have anything. Her words grew quieter as she spoke the sentence, as the heroin worked through her bloodstream. If you want to quit, if you need a place, Margo, Nelson said, I can put you up.

She'd stayed in this evening to finish a letter she'd started writing to Nelson a few days ago. It had piled up to several pages now, but she hadn't drawn it to a close. Vague thoughts about the novel, telling him how good she wanted it to be, her anxiety that it wouldn't be; anecdotes about the public sneering she still caught regularly on the streets and in the cafés; gossip about Bost, about Michelle and the others; always some lines about Sartre, and Sartre's work. Mostly she wrote about how badly she missed him, how much she wanted to be in the Wabansia nest, reading books and writing and fucking – it gave her a girlish pleasure to write the word fucking. Oh, couldn't she fly across the ocean to meet him on the porch by the alley and the beer advertisement? If he said the word she would book a flight tomorrow and risk the Paris–Shannon, crash in the Irish Sea, Shannon–Azores, crash in the Atlantic, Azores–New York, crash in the Hudson or East River, New York–Chicago, crash in the Great Lakes – all these crashes she would risk, she wrote, for one look at his crocodile smile, a kiss on her frog wife lips.

She worked herself up to the tipping point of crying and put down the pen. It was the red pen he'd picked up from his desk to give her on her very first stay. She ran her index finger along it, as though it were touching him. The door buzzer jumped her from the chair. She looked left and right, panic as though she'd been seen. As though she'd been caught. The door buzzed again.

Bost stood on the sidewalk, holding a large box or crate of some kind. I finally found one, he told her, a good one. One what? She stared. She was still living in the letter. Bost looked like an apparition. Can I bring it in, he asked her. He'd carried it all the way from Montparnasse. His arms were sore. She turned back up the stairs and heard his footsteps behind her, and the door as it caught the latch.

A phonograph, he said as he placed it on the coffee table. Yes, of course. It's a good one, he repeated. I could use a drink. She got a glass and poured him a whisky, and added some drops to her own. He asked her if she was okay, if she'd been crying. She said no, she meant yes, no but she was fine, thank you. As she jumbled out these words she pressed the knuckle of her thumb to her eye. Yes, so she had. Well. The phonograph. She asked Bost to show her how it worked. He'd bought a record, too, Charlie Parker. He set up the player and dropped the record over the spindle, and placed the needle at the edge of the shellac disk. She'd been standing arms akimbo but now she lifted a hand to her chin and felt her face relax into a smile, her forehead uncrumple. She asked Bost if he'd spent everything she'd given him. Plus a little more, he told her, but that's on me. They sat across from one another, the phonograph in between, and listened to Bird's saxophone – it made them feel like insiders to call him Bird – and Roy Haynes's drumming, Miles Davis's trumpet and the dancing notes of the double bass. If only we could send for Algren, she said. Bost joked that he didn't deserve to have his nose punched, but it fell flat.

The local Chicago youth stood in the sunshine on a street corner in Hollywood. He'd be out here for a month or so, working on the negotiations and planning for the film of the novel, John Garfield to play Frankie in *The Man with the Golden Arm*. He'd gotten Acker, another junkie friend, out of jail to come with him and work as an advisor. What a coup. They'd spent the first couple of days at the racetrack, and living at Garfield's mansion, though Garfield wasn't there. Simone had warned him, when he wrote that he was going to Hollywood, that they'd try to take out the dope, that he should hold his ground. That was why he'd brought Acker. Or gotten him into the contract, anyway. To make them do it right. She'd told him not to go without a real contract, either, but he had that. Sort of. He'd refused to sign it after the first week, when they'd finally shoved it in front of him and jammed a pen in his hand; he realised he could do better. After that Garfield's house became unavailable and he and Acker were sharing a motel room.

Simone also told him she wouldn't put him in touch with her friend out here, Nathalie, because Nathalie would just try to sleep with him straight off the bat. Couldn't see the harm in that, but he could see Simone's point of view on it. Anyway, he was standing in the sunshine on a street corner in Hollywood, waiting for Amanda, wife and separated and together again and finally divorced Amanda, no longer using Algren as her surname, to have lunch. Here she came, light brown hair, lightly tanned skin, looking healthy and happy. She waved with a short little flick of the wrist and he felt the fondness for her that had never disappeared, and the faint pang of guilt that he'd twice made their marriage impossible.

But he had movie money, and he could buy her lunch. He met her for drinks a few days later and bought her those too, though the next time they went out she insisted she pay, and only relented as far as going Dutch. She gave him a set of keys to her apartment so he could use it as an office of sorts during the day, making phone calls there instead of paying the premiums at his motel. He took her to parties. He gave her some money to buy a new car – hers was almost twenty years old. It was nice, she said to him, that they could go around town and pay for things. Not like when they were married and broke. He was careful to always kiss her on the cheek when they greeted and departed, and he went home to the motel every night – ostensibly because he needed to keep an eye on Acker, but really to make clear that he wasn't going to break her heart again. He could feel himself wanting to at least suggest they try. He found himself telling her about the various girls in Chicago and claiming they all wanted to marry him, or at least, now that he had a book that sold, they did. He didn't tell her about Simone.

After a morning of trying to write the novel, and of writing to Nelson in California, even though she hadn't heard one word since he'd arrived there, she went out to buy records. Since Bost had turned up with the record player she'd started using any excuse to go out and find records, of any kind, really, but mostly jazz. She scoured flea markets, and some of the bookshops had begun trading in records too. Though she didn't so much scour as vacuum: she would take anything with a name she liked, with a cover she liked, or if she knew who the performer was. She'd bought one Piaf record a few weeks ago but it reminded her too much of the Occupation, of the desperation in Paris during that time, and she'd cried all the way through and for half an hour after, and so buried it under a pile of books and magazines and newspapers in the hope that it might just disappear.

She took a meandering route home, or maybe to the Flore, she hadn't yet decided, winding back, taking turns on whims until she decided to walk straight down Rue du Bac, all the way to Quai Voltaire and along the Seine. The tip of Ile de la Cité and the spire of Notre Dame came into view. She thought fondly, but with a pang of longing, of the gargoyles on the cathedral, the little gargoyles begging across the plaza, Nelson's and her gargoyles. She sat on a nearby bench and fingered through her stack of records, nine in all. One she'd bought only because it had been recorded at a nightclub in Chicago. She didn't recognise the names or the songs. She held it up to eye level, as though she could look into the cover design and find Nelson. Someone said her name. Simone. Not Castor. Simone. For less than half a second she thought, Oh, Nelson! But of course not – no. It was not his voice, it was not his accent. He was in California. Oh, Nelson. Simone. She put the record into her bag. One of the gargoyles was calling her Simone. His face was swollen and his nose splattered with the broken blood vessels of a drunk. *C'est moi – Jacques.*

She stood. Jacques. So it was. Cousin Jacques. My God. How terrible he looked. She kissed him on the cheek, Cousin Jacques, whom she'd loved so much as a girl, as an adolescent whom she'd yearned so hard to marry, until he'd found a beautiful girl to make his wife. She'd heard from her mother, but to see him like this – to see this gargoyle cousin. Let's go for a drink, he said to her, and she went.

She bought him a drink. She gave him some money. She bought him lunch. He told her about going broke, and about his wife leaving, his children, his grandchildren. He still saw two of his boys, but that was all. Cousin Jacques, that handsome boy, the same age as her, looking now like a man of seventy. After lunch she gave him some more money and watched him shuffle around the corner. She knew her money would just buy him another bottle or a day in a café. He was going to get drunk anyway, with or without her money. She went home and put on the record from Chicago and stared at the wall, listening to the saxophone and drums and piano and bass. When the A side had finished she stood to change it over, but first she took her framed photo of Nelson from the coffee table and kissed it.

He was back in Chicago. He was on top. He'd left California early to fly to New York because Eleanor Roosevelt wanted to hand over the first National Book Award since the war. To him. Amanda drove him to the airport in her new car, and kissed him goodbye on the side of his mouth, her hand lingering on his shoulder just long enough. Acker would hang on or find his own way home, or elsewhere. He tugged on his suspenders and picked up the *Tribune*. Stuart had saved it for him. It was a week old, the one with the photograph of Eleanor Roosevelt clasping his hand and kissing his cheek. Stupid grin, looking like a goofball in a tuxedo, but he couldn't deny he was pleased. He was on top. Local youth. Man with Golden Arm.

He smacked the picture twice, quickly, with the back of his hand and set the paper on his writing table. There was a handful of letters from Simone. He'd only read two of them so far, and he'd read them out of order, so they were slightly disjointed. She was asking him to tell her when she could come to Chicago. In the second she was asking; the first was more of a plea, a little alarming. That was what he got for reading non-chronologically. He winced when he read that she'd been kissing his picture. Was she a French intellectual or some kind of schoolgirl? He felt tainted by her idiocy. Some of the letters had cheerful news: Bost this, Giacometti that, Sartre,

Michel and Zette, Sartre again, blah blah blah, Sartre. Could she come for two months in the summer, or three months in the summer? He wondered what Sartre was doing during those months. Oh, if only she could come to their Wabansia nest right away, dearest Nelson! He dropped the letter on top of the newspaper, and brushed it to the side. Yeah, hadn't he made that offer more than once? Only Simone could inflame his irritation so quickly. He would invite her to come in June. He was looking into renting a house in Indiana, on Lake Michigan, for a few months. But she could wait for a reply. Why he should punish her the way he punished himself, he didn't know, but he would do it nonetheless.

There was also a letter from his editor, and one from his agent, both presumably saying congratulations, and another one from Amanda he hadn't opened yet. He picked up the envelope. Yes, it had been good to be friends in California. Maybe she'd like to visit Chicago again. He'd ask in his reply.

Somebody was at the door. He looked out the window but couldn't see. He went down to find Jack and Patty and Karl – he rarely saw one of them without the other two. Margo hung sheepishly behind the three of them, as though they were bodyguards. Jack cleared his throat and looked down the street before he asked if Nelson remembered what he'd said that time. That time? The first time they'd introduced him to Margo, Karl reminded him; he'd said if she wanted to get clean –

Yeah. He'd said she could stay at his place and get clean. He'd meant it. He'd been a little drunk, maybe, and a little smitten too, but he'd seen Margo a few more times since then, and he was still a little smitten for the pale sadsack kid. Margo piped up from behind the wall of junkies and said she'd stay out of the way, she'd sleep on the couch or the floor, she just needed a place where there wasn't a needle and a spoon lying around all the time.

The four of them shuffled up the steps behind Nelson. Karl set Margo's suitcase by the door. I'll clean for you, Margo said, and I can cook too. I'm grateful. Jack cleared his throat again, and scratched his arm, and said they'd leave them to it now, if nobody minded; they'd just shoot off now. Patty pulled the door closed as she left, and Nelson and Margo were alone and staring at one another.

He offered a coffee and she said that would be nice. He turned on the radio. I'll clean and cook, she told him, and he pointed out she'd already said that. He asked her how she thought it would be and she shrugged and said she wasn't really sure. Not great. But I want to do it, she said, and I'm grateful.

A few hours later she was retching and shaking so hard he had to go out and try to find her some heroin. It wasn't something he'd done before, but he knew the guy she bought from, he'd met him before. Where to find him was another story. He tried a few bars, but no luck. There was an all-night drugstore a few blocks from Wabansia, but the guy wasn't in there either. He doubled back towards Division. There'd be some dealer or another mooching around there, for sure. It didn't have to be this one guy.

But he found him before he got to Division, in a diner on Damen, by Wicker Park. It made him feel clumsy, asking the guy, paying and receiving the stuff. The dealer didn't seem fazed by his awkwardness. Once he'd made the buy Nelson hurried across the park, even though it was dark. He cut up Honore and across North Avenue and didn't even think what might happen if a cop stopped him, running around like an escaped convict. When he got home, she was on the floor, pale and sweating and moaning and crying. The radio was still on. He didn't have any syringes or droppers or anything. He mixed it up with tobacco and rolled it into a cigarette. It worked. She lay back on the sofa, soft smile on her lips, her eyes closed. She said thank you several times, and swore in a mumble that she was going to kick it.

Castor sat at her table in the Flore, trying to read. She hadn't been able to write any of the novel for more than a week now. She was too preoccupied by too many things. Sartre had announced he wanted to go away in October, to Egypt, to Tunisia and Morocco and Algeria, and he wanted her, of course, to come with him. She'd persuaded Nelson to let her visit Chicago in June, and he'd rent a beach house in Indiana, where they would work and swim. But now Sartre wanted to move their trip up to the spring. He'd been supposed to go away with Dolores then, but now he'd put an end to it. An end to Dolores: when he told her, she nearly leapt from the table. Sartre and Dolores had made a trip through Guatemala and Mexico, they'd toured around Chichén Itzá and Guatemala City and Mexico City. The same trip she'd made with Nelson two years ago. Dolores had seen Chichén Itzá, Nelson's ants, and Dolores in Guatemala City had eaten spicy food and bought the colourful cloths. Dolores and Sartre had photographs like the ones that had never emerged from Nelson's camera. At least Dolores never saw further than Chichicastenango, would never see their plateau, the tall grass, the shepherdess Olga Maria, the hut, the beautiful clean little lake: these things would remain sacred.

Somewhere things had come unstuck for Sartre and Dolores, or for him. Even he didn't seem quite sure, but in the aftermath he'd cut Dolores off, this time for good. She was leaving Paris; she'd never come back to Paris, or if she did it wouldn't be their problem. Dolores was out. But now she'd had to persuade Nelson all over again, with tears – they dropped on to the pages of the letters she wrote – and anger – his – and frustration – hers – and accusations from both of them, that she move the trip back to July. She didn't tell him about Dolores. She'd had to tell him Sartre's schedule had changed; she couldn't just lie about it. She'd had to tell him, but she was also a little glad that was the case, because he'd written to her of a woman who was living with him, who was looking after him, he wrote, cooking and cleaning in the Wabansia apartment – in her Wabansia nest, she thought, when she thought of it, which was often. He hadn't told her enough for her to grasp exactly who this little whore was. Not a woman he could marry. Not a woman who would give him a child. That much she could tell.

Nelson was back in California. They'd sent him a cheque, and he'd given it to Neal so he didn't blow it all at the track or in the back room at the Tug. Margo was still staying in his apartment. She always insisted on sleeping on the sofa, even though he offered the bed, with or without him in it. The night before he left he changed the sheets and pointed out she might as well sleep in the bed, since she would while he was away. Okay, she said, but you shouldn't sleep on the sofa. It wasn't a come-on, and he knew it, but he lay next to her and thought about it. She kissed him lightly and said goodnight and turned on her back and closed her eyes. He wanted to, all right. If he were half the tough guy he pretended to be most of the time, he probably would've at least tried. But he wasn't. Karl and Patty and Jack knew that, or they wouldn't have brought Margo here. Margo knew that, or she wouldn't have come, three weeks now trying to stay clean, and mostly succeeding, but still getting sick and spending nights here and there screaming in the grip of it. He hadn't had to score for her again, but he knew she was still getting junk, just a little she said to him once or twice, just to see her through. He didn't know; he couldn't say what was best. But she was trying. He made sure Chris or Neal, whom he'd known since their time together on the Federal Writers' Project, would look in on her while he was away, and Caesar, too. Other friends he didn't want to have to get involved.

California held less appeal than before. He knew they were out to screw him, one way or another. Simone had been right about that, and if he hadn't been so proud he would've seen it earlier. Everyone he met held out a hand and a too-broad smile on first meeting, and turned colder by the inch once anything needed to get done. Every asshole in town acted like they were the boss, though none of them really seemed to be, and, every time one of them greeted him with the short laugh and, So you're the man with the golden arm, Nelson considered the option of popping the guy on the nose, regardless of how important a position he held at the studio. He wanted to get this thing made, though. If Garfield played it, he'd have people paying attention to him. Garfield still seemed like an alright guy, even if Nelson couldn't show up at his mansion any more.

He showed up at Amanda's bungalow pretty often, though. They saw each other a couple of times each week. She'd ditched the photographer she'd been seeing. Nelson took her to dinner; she drove him in her new Oldsmobile. He tried to take her to a picture, but she wouldn't go. She laughed and said there was something about working in Hollywood that really put her off the movies. They went for drinks instead. She teased him that the Hollywood bars were a bit more upscale than he was used to, and he teased

174

back that a poor Chicago slob like him could only admire a rich and glamorous woman like her. When she laughed she reached out and touched his shoulder. The next morning he wrote in his letter to Simone that maybe it had been a mistake, after all, divorcing Amanda. He didn't quite believe it, but he wrote it to see what it felt like to put it in words, what it looked like on the page. How Simone might take that he didn't know, but she made him put up with Sartre this and Sartre that, and she was always saying tell me everything. Here was everything. True or otherwise. He wanted to believe it, or thought maybe at least he should. Amanda and he had been happy together, once, and now they weren't poor; they had the money to raise a kid, if they decided to. He spent two more weeks in California. He needed six weeks in Chicago to write the screenplay, he told them. Amanda drove him to the train station. He'd asked her to come back to the Midwest later in the year for a visit, and they could go out to Indiana, and he'd rent a beach house.

Castor took Sartre to Tunis, and to Algiers, but there wasn't a man driving to see his cousins, there weren't crowds of fasters, delirious with anticipation of the moon, no Eid al-Fitr. They took a bus along the coastal road, and Sartre watched the sea, his hands pressed against the glass like a child. After a few days in Algiers, another bus took them into Morocco, and they visited Marrakesh and Casablanca, where they stayed with her sister and brother-in-law. At each hotel she asked for her letters, and at each hotel she was told there weren't any; she made them double-check. She'd sent Nelson all the addresses. No, none, madame. Perhaps they were lagging behind. A pile would await her in Paris, forwarded from each hotel. What good did that do her? Even here with Sartre, she needed a letter from Chicago. The frustration made her cry, and Sartre would spend a half-hour rubbing her back and reminding her she would see him soon. His comfort gave only a temporary relief.

But in Casablanca there was a letter. Her sister had placed it on the bed in the guest room. She tore off the end of the envelope and pulled out a newspaper clipping and a single sheet of yellow paper. Nelson, grinning crookedly, was receiving a kiss on the cheek from Eleanor Roosevelt. He looked sheepish and proud at the same time, black bow-tie around his neck, tuxedo jacket, the little black dots of his shirt studs. The letter she read quickly, greedy for his words. About the National Book Award he wrote in his usual tone of pretending not to care, and he also mentioned this little whore again. She skated over it to keep it from annoying her. He would be going to California again, and was already looking forward to the day he would leave it. He didn't say anything about the house in Indiana, whether he'd rented one yet and that he was looking forward to living with her in it. He should say these things in a letter, he should say them. Her forehead and mouth tightened into a frown. She brushed her finger across the picture, lightly to keep from smearing it, and began laughing: for a second she'd thought how she wished she was Eleanor Roosevelt, that she was jealous of Eleanor Roosevelt.

Chapter Ten

Simone watched Lake Michigan appear below, forest giving way to flat squares of farmland, and then the thin beige edge of beach and the bright blue water, and now she wished she were sitting on the other side of the plane so she could look down and see Miller, Indiana, wherever exactly that was; she could look down and guess which little house might be theirs. Instead she squinted at the sunlight glinting off the water and saw, to the distant north, a couple of tankers moving across one Great Lake to the next. Not long now and she would be landing once more at Orchard Field – no, it had a new name – O'Hare International Airport – it sounded much more grand, whoever O'Hare might be. Not long after that and she would be riding in a yellow taxi cab to Wabansia Avenue, on the lookout for the Schlitz billboard – though that might have changed by now, too – and the wooden porch on the brick house, the crooked smile on the local youth, the Mexican blanket on the double bed. She would be home again in Chicago, or, more accurately, she would be home again with Nelson. The glimmering lake gave way to the western shoreline, docks, factories, stockyards, railroad tracks, boxcars, and down on to the runway.

Yes, there it was, THE BEER THAT MADE MILWAUKEE FAMOUS! – not faded or peeling, but new, repainted, as though to welcome her arrival. She told the driver to stop and as the car slowed she opened the door and stepped out, nearly stumbling into the kerb. The driver said something as he pulled her suitcases from the trunk, but she didn't catch it. She counted out the green bills and paid him a larger than necessary tip because she didn't want to wait for the change. Through the whole process, slowing cab open door suitcases payment, she continually glanced up at the window, wishing to see him standing in it looking down waving or sitting at his desk working. To catch that first windowpaned sight of him, to see Nelson Algren and to know she'd arrived and could be happy.

He took his time coming down the stairs to answer her ring. He hadn't looked down to the street; the first sight of her should be up close, touching distance. So he could decide. It wasn't hot but the stairway was stuffy. He scratched the back of his neck and opened the door.

'Nelson!' Simone dropped her suitcase and flung herself at him, into his arms, he couldn't not catch her, and she pressed her lips against his, hard and long and without noticing that he didn't return the kiss with equal enthusiasm.

He took a suitcase in each hand and followed her up to his apartment. She was talking about the flight, and how relieved she was to be here, and something about Miller, something about the lake but he didn't quite catch it. He wasn't entirely paying attention. He was rehearsing his own speech.

She stood in the middle of the apartment, hands on hips, and smiling. A strand of hair fell across her face. He set the suitcases next to the door.

'Here I am again, at last,' she announced. 'Back in our Wabansia nest!'

'Yes.' He mustered a smile.

'And in a few days we'll go to Miller?'

'In a few days, yes.' He scratched the back of his neck again. 'Do you want something to eat? Or a drink?'

'Perhaps in a little while, Nelson.' For now she was too excited, and maybe a little too tired, to eat. She let her arms drop from her hips and stepped towards him. She leaned forward but her kiss glanced off the side of his mouth to his cheek. An unshaped disappointment pressed gently into her.

'There's things I need to do over the next few days.' Nelson walked to the sink and poured a glass of water. He held it towards her but she shook her head, and he drank half of it at once. 'Writing I need to do. I'm working on this long poem.'

'Of course.' She felt her mouth twitch. 'I have work I can do as well.'

'There's some people I need to see, too.'

'Okay. I don't mind coming with you.'

He waved the glass. 'No. Some people I need to see on my own. Business,' he said.

She felt the shock of no. He was dividing things up. She'd always gone everywhere with him in Chicago before. And all the other places. Even in Paris, hadn't they spent all their hours together? He was pushing her away.

'In Miller,' he said, 'we'll have all our time together. In our little house. There's a lagoon.'

She couldn't shake the prickly disappointment. They went for a walk through the neighbourhood and further, past the Seven Stairs Bookshop in Rush Street – though it was closed for the evening, and Stuart gone – and eventually they went to a diner. She ate a pork chop and he ate chicken, chewing the bones as he always did, and, though she was trying to push it away, the anxiety still bubbled in her, and watching

179

him suck the marrow made her faintly sad. After dinner they found a bar and drank a few whiskies. Nelson gave her a quarter for the jukebox and she chose some songs she'd never heard. On the final number he stood and took her hand and they danced, the only people in the bar dancing, and it made her feel embarrassed but comforted, here in a Chicago bar with her Chicago husband, finally holding her in his arms. It would be okay, yes. After the song they drank one last whisky and walked a little unsteadily home, and up the stairs, and beneath the Mexican blanket as his hand traced along her hip, and up to her breast, she sighed and let her anxiety go.

She awoke alone in the bed, but after a minute she realised she could hear the clacking of his typewriter keys. She leaned against the doorframe and watched him, his grey wool shirt, glasses, tangled hair. He was frowning at the page clasped in the roller, and typing with only his two index fingers. The keys clacked in short bursts followed by longer pauses. It seemed impossible that he was typing a whole word at once. In one of the breaks between typing she spoke.

'Good morning, my crocodile,' she said.

Nelson held up a hand, index finger raised, without looking up. He'd made the decision that he would work, even if he wasn't really doing very much of it. She would have to bend to his schedule, this time. He scratched the side of his face and then began typing again, a long burst of clacking keys, longer than any since she'd been watching. It finally finished and he looked up, and smiled.

'I'll make some breakfast,' he said. 'I haven't eaten yet, only coffee.'

He didn't put on music or the radio, and they ate pancakes – delicious apple pancakes – in a relative silence that made her feel like a little girl again, in that horrible Paris apartment, her father scowling over his plate of food, mother saying nothing and she and Hélène finding excuses to leave the table as soon as they finished. But she had no homework, real or otherwise. She felt herself deflating, slowly, like a bicycle tyre with the smallest of holes. Perhaps she had set her expectations too high, had worked up too much excitement. In those months apart all the letters he wrote, the letters she wrote had made them seem both closer and further away, and made the longing more acute while salving it as well. Was the real thing a disappointment? She looked across the table to him. No. Not for her – for her. Was she a disappointment?

'Nelson, am I a disappointment?'

He removed his fork from his mouth. 'Disappointment?'

'To you.'

He put the fork on his plate and reached across the table to touch her hand. 'Of course not,' he said, though it wasn't quite the truth. A disappointment lurked somewhere between them. It might not be her, exactly, but nor could he separate it from her. 'I have work to do. It's not my vacation. When we get to Miller it'll change.'

If his words didn't convince himself, they comforted Simone. She took hold of his hand and squeezed it.

He cleaned the plates and frying pan while she dressed, and after that they went their separate ways. It was already almost noon. He had to meet some people, he told her, without elaborating. She decided to walk somewhere. She wasn't sure where, but she wanted to walk.

It was hot outside, and she was overdressed. She'd put on one of the dresses she had made from cloth she'd bought when they'd been together in Guatemala, and had hoped Nelson would recognise it, or say something about it. The cloth rustled with each step. Her cardigan was too warm. She took it off.

The sun was bright, the air humid. An El train clattered and sparked as it rolled northward above her. She passed a drugstore and looked at the headlines on the newspapers clipped in the rack outside, but they just seemed like a collection of words without grammatical meanings: KOREA, COMMUNISTS, TRUMAN, KENNELLY. In the bottom corner of the *Tribune* stood a short article about saving bison from extinction. She continued walking more or less towards the Loop, though she had no real intention of going anywhere in particular. After an hour or so she found a diner with fans in its windows and went inside for a BLT and orange juice.

Nelson had gone over to Caesar's to see Margo. He hadn't come here for any real reason, other than to not be with Simone, to show Simone he had competing priorities too. Margo had moved out a couple of weeks after he'd gotten back from California. They were living on top of each other in the Wabansia apartment, and it was no good for either of them. He couldn't get enough work done, worrying over her, buying her food, keeping her company, listening to the radio together, going out to the park or the lake. She started feeling too much like a child, worried over, watched. It wasn't that she was an ingrate, far from it; but the constant attention – the unavoidable-in-that-small-apartment attention – had started to become a gnawing reminder, a complementary addiction. She'd said these things to Nelson – not quite in those words, but they'd discussed it – and he'd talked to Caesar about renting her a room. Caesar owned a building not too far away, and so she'd have a sympathetic and fair landlord. Nelson and others could check on her, come and go as they pleased, and if the neighbours didn't like it, well, the problem stayed with the neighbours, and didn't end with a super calling the cops.

He kissed her on the forehead when she opened the door. She smiled and invited him in and offered to make coffee. An easy new life, he joked, only making coffee and cooking for one. She laughed and said he'd be surprised: it seemed easier to cook for two. Caesar had been good to her, she said, looking in on her every couple of days, but not being intrusive. She hadn't seen Chris or Neal for a while, though. He pointed out they were in Indiana for the rest of the summer. He would be too, the day after tomorrow. After an hour or so he left, and promised to write her a letter or two from Miller. She squeezed his hand as he kissed her cheek goodbye. From the top of the steps he heard her call thank you as she pushed the door gently shut.

Nelson and Simone spent their evenings in the Tug, alternating beer with whisky and playing a few games of pool even though she was terrible. In the daytime he worked, or pretended to, and visited people, or pretended to; she read books, and went shopping on Michigan Avenue, though there wasn't much she was interested in buying, and spent an afternoon in the Art Institute. She stood in front of French paintings bought by rich Americans: Monet, Manet, Renoir, Caillebotte. She might as well be in Paris. She'd rather be in Paris. No, that wasn't quite true. But she'd rather be lonely in Paris than lonely in Chicago, the one place on earth where she shouldn't be lonely, where the entire point was that they could live together, for a time. Yet here she was, standing in front of an enormous painting of rainy Paris, while outside a hot Chicago sun baked the concrete and shimmered off Lake Michigan. Nelson had work to do, she told herself, but she knew that was only part of the story, at best. An indifference had appeared in him, a hint of one. An indifference towards her: no crooked grin, no clownish jokes for her entertainment or at her expense, not even when they were playing pool. He'd danced with her tenderly and he made love to her each night, but he'd become – perfunctory. Did he not understand that she'd come here, that she'd spent their months of separation waiting to come here, that she'd come here so she could be the centre of the world for him, that they could be the centre of one another's world? In Paris, yes, she had her life there, an important life there, but without Nelson across the ocean it didn't have the same resonance. She'd written him that. She was always writing him that. But in Chicago: the other life could drop away, and they could be not Nelson, not Castor, but Simone and Nelson. She was sick of looking at these paintings, these bourgeois Parisians, degraded ballerinas, bridges and landscapes and water lilies. She did everything to make him love her from that distance, and she knew, she felt he loved her from that distance, and always before, she would arrive and that love unfolded the rest of its petals. But these past few days – it would be a slow-blooming thing, she told herself, but it would bloom. This was something new, but only something new. It would bloom.

It was their last night before they went to Indiana, so they went to the Tug. Studs was already there when they arrived, sitting at the bar and talking to Barusz, a long new cigar between his fingers. Nelson clapped him on the shoulder and introduced Simone.

'Of course, of course,' Studs said, and slid off his stool in the same motion as he took hold of her hand to shake it. 'Mademoiselle Beauvoir! *Enchanté, enchanté*,' and the way he said it sounded like 'on-chon-tay,' and she laughed and shook his hand. 'Tell me, Mademoiselle Beauvoir: why fly all the way to Chicago just for Nelson Algren, when there are plenty of men in Paris who actually know how to play cards,

184

and back the winners at the track? But don't answer – ' Studs held up a hand. 'The men of Paris don't take you on tours of jails and electric chairs.'

Studs walked to a table and Simone followed, and once he'd finished talking to Barusz Nelson joined them, carrying three beers. Studs was trying to convince Simone to go on his radio show. 'You can play your favourite records,' he said, 'We'll chat about Paris, about philosophy if you want, those kinds of things – '

'What would your Chicago listeners want to know about Paris or philosophy?'

Studs nodded and waved his cigar, the blue smoke shifting from a line to a small cloud. 'True enough, true enough – nothing, probably. But what they want to know and what they get to hear – how do they know they don't want to know about Paris or Jean-Paul Sartre until Simone de Beauvoir is on the radio telling them? What do the people in Paris want to know about it?'

She couldn't tell whether he was offended, but she didn't think so. She hadn't meant it that way. She drank from her beer. 'Of course in Paris there are many people who don't want to hear these things, too. But there are also many who do want to hear them, or at least will hear them. When I look at the newspaper headlines here, about Communists and Korea and these things, well, I don't know.'

Again Studs nodded. 'True, true, yes. All the more reason, Mademoiselle Beauvoir, all the more reason.'

'Perhaps you are right. But you must call me Simone.'

'Simone it is.'

Stuart arrived a few minutes later, and reintroduced himself to Simone, though she remembered him from the bookshop. Nelson listened to the sounds of his friends' voices and watched the players at the pool table. One of them was a small-time thief he knew. Nelson watched him sink a couple of easy balls and miss a tricky one off the rail, then stood and went to the john, though he didn't really need to go all that bad. He washed his hands slowly, examining the grey cracks along the length of the soap that hung on a rope around the neck of the faucet. The mirror was, as always, spittled with dried soapy water droplets.

When he returned, Caesar and Margo had arrived and were talking to Stuart. Simone and Studs huddled together like conspirators, trying to out-talk one another. That made him smile. He shook Caesar's hand and kissed Margo's cheek, and told them he was glad they'd come.

'Out of the filthy city for the summer,' Caesar said, raising his beer glass.

Nelson waved a hand. 'Yeah, though I don't know why. I like the filthy city in the summer.'

Stuart leaned in. 'Quit griping, Nelson. A house on the other side of the lake? You can cool off instead of trying to type away in that Polack sweatbox of yours. No offence, Barusz,' he added as the bartender set down more beers and cleared the empty glasses. Barusz patted him on the shoulder and laughed.

'I suppose that's the point,' Nelson said.

'The only guy I know who's sorry to escape this humid hellhole in the summer.' Stuart shook his head.

A cloud from Studs's cigar rolled across the table. 'Nelson's just worried he's getting too middle-class for his own good.' He tapped a half-inch of ash into the tray. 'As our esteemed guest would say, too bourgeois.'

Simone flushed. Studs had been talking to her, and apparently eavesdropping at the same time, but she hadn't followed the other conversation. Something about their lifestyle in Miller? That they'd be a little bourgeois couple? She laughed with the others.

Studs left first, a couple of hours later, to go down to the South Side for a poker game. Stuart left not long after that, and it was just Caesar and Margo. Simone had been introduced, but she didn't really know who they were. Friends of mine, Nelson had said, but from where or how he didn't tell her. They struck her as nice. Margo was quiet, and thin. Caesar talked more. She couldn't decide whether they were a couple. It seemed gauche to ask what they did, but she didn't think they were literary people or intellectuals. Caesar was drinking beer, but Margo only drank soda water. They all talked about Indiana for a while, and Caesar asked Simone what she liked about Chicago, and after another round of drinks they went home.

She took hold of his hand as they walked. It was only a few blocks. She felt warm with beer, and the night was still hot, too. Nelson said nothing as they walked, and when she looked at him his eyes were on the ground. She squeezed his hand and smiled, waiting for him to look, but his eyes remained down. When they arrived home they poured a whisky and he turned on the radio. Slow jazz saxophone leaked out into the apartment.

'Studs asked me to go on his radio show,' she said.

'Will you?'

'I don't know. Have you?'

'Yes.'

'What is it like?'

'He's my friend.' Nelson finished his whisky. 'But I'm tired. Let's go to bed.'

Beneath the Mexican blanket she rubbed her hand across his chest. He turned and kissed her forehead, and she lifted her face to find his lips. Her hand moved to his waist, and he traced the line of her leg up to her hip, her belly, her breasts. She pushed her tongue against his lips, against his teeth, but his mouth stayed closed and she kissed his chin, jaw, his ear, his neck, and back again to his mouth. This time his lips parted and his tongue met hers, and her hand slipped down to his penis and took hold. It was soft and she stroked it, slowly at first, but then faster, her tongue pressing harder inside his mouth, her lips and teeth against his. Nothing. He rolled away to face the room and she moved her hand to his back, and rubbed gently. She thought to say something but couldn't think of words that wouldn't sound like an insult to him, so stayed silent and gently rubbed his back.

They took a late-morning South Shore Line train from Randolph Street, down along Lake Michigan, the museums giving way to the stockyards, and the stockyards to the factories before the prairie took over, and the train curved eastward, through Hegewisch, Hammond, East Chicago, Gary and, after Gary, Miller. The city hall in Gary looked to Simone like the architecture of the Italian Fascists, and she said as much to Nelson. He shrugged. He'd hardly said a word since they'd woken up. She didn't know whether to touch him or talk to him or just leave him alone, and hope he'd eventually decide to stop sulking.

As the train slowed into the station at Miller he stood and lifted their suitcases from the luggage rack. Simone tried to take hers.

'No, I'll carry them,' he grunted.

She backed away in shock, one step, but said nothing, and walked ahead of him to the doors and stepped down on to the platform. The concrete was already baking in the hot midday sun. She shaded her eyes and watched Nelson struggle down the two steps, one large suitcase in each hand, too many things to fit gracefully through the door. He dropped them heavily to the platform and wiped his forehead. She laughed.

'Now will you let me carry one?'

'Frog wives aren't allowed to carry luggage in Indiana,' he said, and winked.

The first glimpse of her Nelson returning; the tension jumped from her chest, and she exhaled a large sigh.

Chris and Neal had driven to the station to meet them, and Nelson waved an exaggerated wave across the street to them. Neal took one of the suitcases and Chris greeted Simone. Nelson felt relief. They wouldn't be alone.

The bungalow stood at the end of an unpaved road. It had a small lagoon surrounded by a handful of trees in the back yard, and beyond the lagoon a path led over the dunes to Lake Michigan. They could hear the waves breaking on the beach, a constant pulse like a distant engine. Neal unloaded their suitcases and gave Nelson the key. Chris said they should stop over later for some drinks and dinner.

The house had a small kitchen that led into the living room and dining area. A simple table with four chairs filled the dining area, and beyond that was a sofa and small coffee table. The window faced the back. Simone opened it and stood for a minute or two looking down to the lagoon.

'Do you think it's clean enough to swim in the lagoon?'

'Probably.' Nelson was dragging the suitcases across the room. 'Might be full of leeches though.'

She followed him down the short hallway to the first bedroom. A small nightstand stood next to a single bed. He put her suitcase down and moved to the next room. Another nightstand, another single bed. He dropped his suitcase on to

189

the bed. The next door down led to the bathroom, and next to that was the toilet. There were no other rooms. Two single beds.

'We could move one of the beds into the other room?' She ran her finger up and down the frame of the toilet door.

'Too small,' he called from his bedroom. 'Won't fit.'

'But we could try?'

'We could try. And then we could move the bed back when we discovered the room was too small. So let's not try.'

She continued to rub the doorframe. 'Nelson – '

'Dammit, Simone!' He appeared in the doorway. 'What do you want me to do?'

She walked past him and into her own bedroom. Closing the door behind her, she sat down on the bed and folded her hands in her lap and started to cry as silently as she could.

Half an hour later he knocked on her door. 'Let's go see the lagoon,' he said quietly, and she took it as an apology.

They walked side by side, and halfway down to the water he took hold of her hand. Almost childish, it made her feel, the ripple of sadness leaving her. It would be okay. They would settle. They would make a life here in the woods by this lake. They only needed to settle.

A small rowboat was beached on the edge of the lagoon, and Nelson pushed it into the water and held it steady so Simone could climb in. He mounted the oars on the gunwales and dipped them into the water. She watched the small whorls at the edges of the blades, and the algae bobbing in the turbulence, and dipped her hand in the warm water to let it trail. Nelson rowed a gentle circle around the lagoon, then a straight line across it, beaching the boat by rowing straight to the shore and hopping out to push it once it ran aground. He stowed the oars and took hold of her hand to guide her out. She jumped on to the sandy ground without getting wet.

They climbed the dune, their shoes filling with sand, and at the top, Lake Michigan opened up, glistening in the sun. Down the shore they could see the stacks of the Gary steel mills. They both took off their shoes and dumped out the sand. Nelson's were wet and clumps stuck to them. He scraped them with his hand, but only succeeded in spreading the grit around. Leaving their shoes at the top, they started down to the lakeshore. Simone took short strides at first, then found her legs reaching longer until she was bounding down the dune, each stride a leap, and laughing as she moved faster and faster but stumbled, pitching forward, her skirt flying up, and landing hard in the soft deep sand, to somersault and slide the rest of the way down to the bottom. Several paces behind Nelson had watched it happen, at first in control and then she was less graceful and the fall seemed only inevitable, the bright colours of the Guatemalan or maybe it was Mexican cloth as it flew around her, and once she'd landed giggling at the base of the dune, he decided to join and hurled himself into the air, landing on his ass and sliding down to meet her. He kissed her cheek and they walked along the edge of Lake Michigan, the waves breaking and running up the sand just to their feet. The water was warmer than she'd expected, not as warm as the lagoon but much warmer than the Mediterranean. She put her arm around his waist, and though his hands stayed inside his trouser pockets he let her keep it there and the frustration and confusion and sadness began to ebb away. It would be a nice summer here in Indiana.

They walked a mile or so down the beach, and back again, climbed over the dune and retrieved their shoes. Nelson insisted on rowing back across the lagoon so the boat would be near the house. At dusk they walked down the small road to have a drink and barbecue with Chris and Neal and after a few hours they walked home through the dark, fireflies pulsing around them, to their separate rooms and single beds.

It would take time, Simone told herself as she lay naked under the single sheet listening to the sounds from beyond the screened window. Crickets rubbed their legs together, the waves hitting the shoreline droned. It would take time. The lagoon, the dune, the beach walk: the tenderness was there, if only fleeting, flickering like the strange fireflies, but, like them, never entirely disappearing, only going away for a time, returning regularly. She'd prepared herself for coming here, and had nothing but him in her sights, on her agenda. But he had work to do, his friends to see, and it wasn't the same as it was for her, in Paris. If she remembered that, and respected that, his love would return more steadily. It would take time. It wasn't that he didn't love her.

A mosquito hummed in his ear and he waved it away. He wanted to feel nothing towards her so he could send her away and be finished instead of pushing just enough to make everything worse. Or if he could only persuade her to never leave. He couldn't jam a lifetime of love into a two-months-of-the-year affair. He couldn't separate out his life the way she could, turning the stretches in between into a letter-writing campaign and expecting the taps to be cranked fully open the minute they found themselves together. As long as she didn't ask more than he could give it would be okay. It wasn't that he didn't love her, but love was a slippery thing, hard to hold on to, and it couldn't only work on her conditions.

She could feel the heat of the sun, and see its light through her closed eyes, and she heard the clacking of Nelson's typewriter. After lying stretched along the bed for a few minutes longer she wrapped herself in a dressing gown and went to find him.

'There's coffee,' he said without looking up from the typewriter, fingers still clacking the keys against the paper.

She wanted to put her arms around his shoulders, to kiss his neck and tell him they should just go to bed, or go and lie in the grass by the lagoon. But she knew not to try that when he was working. She sat at the small kitchen table with a cup of coffee and two slices of bread, tearing pieces from the bread and rolling them into little balls as she watched him type. When she'd finished the coffee she'd eaten maybe half a slice and most of the rest dotted the table. She swept the doughy crumbs into her hand and tossed them out the back door for the birds to eat.

Already it was hot, even in the shade and with a breeze from Lake Michigan rustling the leaves of the trees. Simone went back inside and put on one of the dresses she'd had made from the Guatemalan cloth, wrapped her hair into a bun and went back outside. A chaise-longue sat facing the lagoon. She settled herself into it and opened a book, an Agatha Christie novel she'd bought in Paris. She had brought serious reading, though nothing urgent, and the novel she was working on, but until she could gauge Nelson properly, until they found a balance or rhythm to the life they were going to lead here, she didn't think she could start any serious work. The breeze, the waves, the intermittent bird song, the typewriter from inside, and the trees, the lagoon, the rowboat, the little house: it all added up to a perfect setting for the happiness she sought, if only the man at the typewriter would take up his part in their happiness, too.

He walked across the lawn to the chaise-longue and placed his hands on her shoulders, near the neck.

'I put together some lunch,' he said.

She looked up from her book and smiled. 'How did your work go?'

He shrugged. 'It went.'

An answer, she supposed, was better than none at all.

Nelson and Simone ate their lunch with minimal conversation and Nelson returned to work and Simone to Agatha Christie. In the evening they again walked down to Chris and Neal's for barbecuing and drinks. Nelson became his other self once they were out of their house, not just when they got to their neighbours but even on the way: he began joking in his usual way, calling her his frog wife and clowning about the other people who might show up. When they were all together, he talked with his arm around her, and introduced her to the other people – Dave, and a couple, Earl and Janet – with that note of pride and, yes, she felt it, love. At the end of the night when they arrived home he kissed her on the cheek before heading to his room. She'd held his shoulder, hoping to keep him there, to move his lips to her own, but her grasp was loose and the moment brief, and she let him walk away.

Their days continued in this pattern. Nelson got up and made coffee and began working on his long poem, a prose poem really, all of Chicago packed into it. Simone awoke to the sun and the heat and the clatter-clatter-ding-clatter-clatter of the typewriter and after a short greeting moved to the chaise-longue and looked out at the little boat and the lagoon before reading, or trying to work on the novel, or writing letters to various people, mostly Sartre. She found it difficult to do any good work on the novel. In the afternoon they might walk over the dune together for an hour, or Nelson might row around the lagoon, but it was a precarious calm they pursued here in Miller. Most evenings that first week they spent with Chris and Neal and others, either at one of the neighbours' or this little house by the lagoon, and they would drink and eat and laugh and Nelson would put his arm around Simone and without either of them articulating it they would play happy husband and wife, to their mutual enjoyment and disgust; for when it was time for bed they would slink to their separate rooms.

Simone wrote to Sartre that she longed for him, and their life in Paris. It was true, though it didn't seem the complete truth it looked on paper. Were Nelson being Nelson instead of playing this aloof role he'd designated himself, she wouldn't feel quite the same, would she? In Paris she longed for her Chicago husband regardless of who surrounded her and what she did, and, when she wrote to him, all the English words on the page looked exactly like they meant. The French ones she wrote to Sartre seemed tempered by Nelson's inability to understand – not them, but her. He wouldn't understand that she came all this way for no other reason than him. Or if he did want to understand that – she didn't want to countenance the thought that Nelson wasn't playing some game against both her and himself, the thought that he really didn't love her any more. It didn't seem possible.

Nelson rowed the little boat around the lagoon after lunch. They'd been in Miller almost a week now. He'd found a certain peace in the rhythm of work, and in the space. Chris had done well, finding this house. With the dunes so close, it was like the one his sister had owned. And the lagoon would freeze over in winter. Though he wasn't much of an ice-skater.

'Do you think things will change?' Simone asked.

He took some time to reply. 'Change how?'

She pressed her hands against her cheeks. 'To how they were before. I don't like all this silence.'

Again he took time to reply, the oars dipping and lifting, dipping and lifting, several strokes before he spoke. 'I have work to do, that I need to do,' he said.

'I know, Nelson, but even so – '

'When you have work to do,' he stopped rowing, 'you change your schedule, you fly away early, you delay your departure, you make an excuse, you run to Sartre. I have work, and I am not running you back to Paris. I am not fleeing you.'

He dipped the oars back into the water. Her hands remained pressed against her face.

'Your life is quite easy,' he said. 'But you can't just always get things your way or organise them until they do go your way. This is not Paris, and I am not Sartre or Bost or anyone else who will run around in circles to fulfil your every whim. This is not Paris. This is real life, Simone. Sometimes you have to give, too.'

'Please row me back to the shore,' she said.

It took a few minutes to complete the journey, Nelson rowing slow, deliberate strokes, Simone facing him, not sure whether to look into his eyes, which appeared so cold to her now, or down to the bottom of the boat, or across the lagoon to the trees. No view offered comfort. When the boat was close enough she jumped into the calf-high water and splashed to the shore and up to the house. Nelson took his time dragging the boat on to the shore and walked slowly to the house. He could hear her crying in her room, long loud sobs followed by shorter and quieter ones, and he knew from experience that she would carry on until she ran out of energy or tears or anger or sadness or whatever it was that drove Simone de Beauvoir. Damned if he knew. He stood, arms akimbo, looking at the typewriter on the dining table. Probably that was it for work today. He took a blank piece of paper and scribbled a note to Simone, left it weighed down by a bottle of whisky on the kitchen counter, and left the house.

Nelson? She'd called his name a couple of times before she found the note. So she knew she wouldn't find him at the lagoon or over the dune or drinking a gin and tonic with Chris and Neal or anywhere else in Miller, Indiana. She poured a glass of whisky and reread the note, then poured the whisky down the sink. Weighing it down with the bottle was his big joke, probably. Bastard. She poured another glass anyway and drank it. This will be the evening, I suppose. Whisky alone.

Studs, Pharaoh, Saul, Stuart, Leon, some guy Pharaoh had brought along and Nelson: a decent pool of players, a decent pile of money. The usual dealer, a wiry Polish guy named Martin, collected the money and dealt the first hand. Depending on the night, Stuart or Studs or Pharaoh was the best player at the table. Nelson knew he was better than Saul, or maybe anyway, but not worse. Pharaoh's pal was the wild card here, but from the look of him he wouldn't challenge, and Pharaoh wouldn't bring a poker genius to the table. It wasn't in his interest, and it wasn't his style, either. If the cards fell his way he could have a good night. Hell, even if they didn't he'd have a good night. The windowless upstairs room of the Tug was hot and the small fan only pushed the hot air around in a listless way, but it felt more open, a better breeze than off the lake in Miller. He folded his first hand without throwing in more than the ante, and went a couple of rounds of betting before bowing out of the second, but he won the third and fourth. Pharaoh's friend wasn't up to anything at all; he'd been right. Fortune was smiling on Nelson Algren for a change.

Simone turned on the radio and washed down a couple of pills with whisky. After two glasses she'd begun to hope he'd been bluffing and any minute he'd come back in the door with a bag full of groceries, some steaks or something, and they'd have a barbecue here at home just the two of them, Nelson and Simone. She'd realised by the third that he really was in Chicago. She'd called him a bastard a few more times, she'd drunk another glass of whisky and now the radio played some terrible singer, a big orchestra behind him. She should just go and get on a train and go to Chicago and go to the airport and go to Paris and go forever just go and let Nelson Algren rot in hell for being a bastard just go. Go and forget Chicago and forget Nelson Algren and forget just forget forget just go home to Paris go home to Sartre go home go go go go and forget Nelson forget Simone go home to Sartre and Castor, just go and forget and go.

Ah, the night didn't go too well but it had been fun. Only one further hand had been Nelson's for the taking, but he'd played as smart as he could – too many bad hands, nothing he could do – and kept his losses down. Kept his losses down, but kept playing. Okay, he'd blown all his money again. Pharaoh had cleaned up on them all, all of them except Studs, anyway; Studs had done all right. Pharaoh's buddy had tapped out early and gone home. Saul philosophised away about his losses and kept playing. Stuart hung in but got a couple of bad deals he couldn't recover from. Nobody else blew it all, but what was the point if you didn't try? It had been a good night, a long night at the card table. Martin declared the game over and everybody but Nelson threw him a couple of bucks. Out in the morning street Saul and Pharaoh went opposite ways and Studs and Stuart asked Nelson whether he was going back to Miller. He looked eastward and shoved his hands in his pockets. Not too sure, he told them, and felt the shock and nausea as Stuart punched him in the stomach. Don't be an asshole, Stuart told him, and Studs shoved a couple of dollars into his pocket. There's the money, Studs said, now get on the next South Shore train and don't come back to Chicago until it's time for Simone to leave. You don't have to be an asshole to every woman you meet, Studs said. Especially not this one, said Stuart. Don't be a schmuck.

It was late. She could tell from the heat. Her head hurt and her mouth was phlegmy. No clacking of the typewriter. A couple of seconds later she remembered why: that bastard. For another half-hour she lay in bed, the heat becoming less and less tolerable, even with the sheets thrown off, trying to decide what she'd do. If she took the train back to Chicago she could change her reservations and be flying back to Paris in the next couple of days. Or she could wait to see if he came back. And if he did? Probably it depended on what he said. Though maybe it didn't. She could convince herself that she wanted to leave but the task wouldn't be simple, because she knew she'd be punishing herself just as much as him. She wanted to be strong enough to make that sacrifice – but did she really?

She swung her legs to the floor. There was no point in trying to decide before some breakfast and maybe a shower, or, better yet, a swim. She needed to make a clear decision, with a clear head.

Only when she was buttering the toast did she notice his shoes by the door. A little thrill stuttered through her. He'd come home. But she couldn't remember now – had those shoes been sitting there all night? It was possible. She stood, knife against the bread, staring at the shoes, trying to visualise the house last night. It was no good. The drink and the pills muddied her memory. She could peek in his room. But if she woke him he might get angry and that would spoil the homecoming. She'd have to wait. The brown shoes wouldn't tell. Now she realised she wouldn't go back to Paris early. That shiver of pleasure at the sight of his shoes – it gave her away, to herself. She would stay and somehow Nelson would start to love her again. They'd stumbled before. This was no different.

He found her lying on the chaise-longue, reading a book facing the lagoon. She didn't look up until he placed a hand on her shoulder, and when she did look he couldn't read her expression. It seemed impassive. What a jerk he'd been. Stuart was right. Studs was right.

'I thought we could go swimming later,' he said, 'And picnic on the beach.'

Tears welled in her eyes but didn't fall. 'I'd like that,' she said, and smiled.

Nelson squeezed her shoulder and leaned over to kiss her temple before walking back into the house. A few minutes later the clacking of his typewriter joined the whistling birds.

Late in the afternoon they packed a basket with bread and cheese and ham and salami and what remained of the whisky. Nelson insisted on rowing across the lagoon and when they reached the other side they took off their shoes and climbed up over the dune and down to the beach. The breeze blew across them as they sat in the sand and ate their picnic, watching a tanker move slowly across the horizon. After they'd eaten, Simone took off her clothes and folded them into a pile, placing her underwear on top to keep the sand out, and waded naked into the lake. Nelson watched from the shore as she dove in and swam inelegantly to the sandbar that ran parallel to shore about twenty or so yards out. He laughed at her splashy strokes, but then, he wasn't much of a swimmer himself. She reached the sandbar after a minute or so of slow swimming and let her feet sink into the mucky bottom. Nelson seemed further away, sitting on the beach, than he actually was. She waved, her arm above her head, and laughed when he waved back in the same exaggerated style, mocking her.

Yet another sandbar lay more or less equidistant from the first and after resting for a few minutes she pushed towards it. The water felt cool but not cold and almost there she rolled over on to her back to float. Only a few small clouds interrupted the sky and though the sun was halfway through its drop she still needed to squint against it. She used her hands and light kicking to keep the waves from pushing her back shoreward. Each crest pushed her slightly out of the water, and each trough dipped her ears below it, so she heard brief and regular pulses of the peculiar drone that comes underwater. She watched a plane move eastward across the sky. No, she wouldn't be on one soon. She pushed her hand down into the water and rolled to swim to the sandbar.

The cramp bit into her toes and the gasp of pain sucked in water. Her arms flailed above her, hands grasping for the surface, but her toes – her toes were frozen in an angry splayed talon and she couldn't move her leg. She needed to move her leg. Trying to cough out water. Leg frozen. Arms splashing against the surface. Nelson jumped to his feet when he saw the frantic splashing. That wasn't inept swimming. He pulled off his shirt and stumbled as he ran towards the water pulling off his trousers at the same time. He ran into the water and when it was deep enough, dove, keeping his head above the surface so he could see her. He was no good swimmer but he concentrated on making even, strong strokes, and soon reached the first sandbar and continued past without putting a foot down. Onwards towards Simone. Arm hooked underneath her but in her panic she thought what she thought a fish a monster a riptide what she thought but she heard Simone Simone relax Simone it's okay Simone and still she was panicked but moving now which way she couldn't tell Simone but moving and up surface light air Simone she floated atop him coughing spluttering out air and water toes still taloned leg still pained stiff but floating, and now bumping the ground, and yes, okay, okay. Okay. They stood on the sandbar, Simone leaning her weight against Nelson, head on his shoulder, he with his arms around hers. The water reached only to her hips, mid-thigh for him. They remained silent and motionless, a succession of waves rising and ebbing away towards shore.

'I don't know if I can swim back,' Simone said after several minutes.

'Sure you can. We'll go slowly. But only when you're ready.'

They waited a silent half-hour before she announced she felt ready. The cramp had receded, and so had the ghost – the physical memory – of it, though she felt trepidation. She swam on her back, kicking only lightly, and he swam next to her, his hand brushing against her as he stroked. They rested at the next sandbar for a few minutes, and when they set off again she felt more confident. Soon they could touch the bottom, and walked until they were knee-deep.

'I was scared,' Simone said.

'So was I.'

'I thought I was going to drown right there.' She looked back at the lake. 'So close to shore.'

She wrapped her arms around him, pressing herself against his body, and kissed his neck, then, on tiptoes, his lips. They walked holding hands back to the beach and sat naked in the sand by the picnic basket. Nelson took out the whisky bottle, opened it and handed it to Simone. She drank a large mouthful and handed it back to him.

'To your health,' he said, and drank.

She smiled. He smiled. They both felt that old feeling – the thrill of one another's being – creep closer. For another hour they sat silently on the beach, watching the waves break on to the shore, drinking another sip of whisky, eating a little more of the food. The sun was another hour from touching the horizon when they dressed and climbed back over the dune to the lagoon.

Later he boiled pasta and chopped some tomatoes into it and they sat outside in the moonlight, listening to the crickets and waves and slapping at the mosquitoes that buzzed around them and bit into their arms and legs and necks.

Simone folded her arms across her chest. 'The sound of the waves has changed for me. They made a kind of murmur before; it soothed me into sleep, and out of it, in that little bed.'

'And now?'

'And now – I don't know. It sounds more like a roar than a murmur. I wouldn't say angry or threatening, but it sounds different.'

They sat quietly after that, drinking another couple of glasses of whisky, each thinking about the sound of the waves rolling on to the sand in the dark. Around midnight they decided to go to bed. Nothing had been spoken about Nelson's trip to Chicago, and nothing would be.

Simone paused at the door to her bedroom. 'Goodnight, Nelson.' She leaned one hand against the frame, and with the other took hold of his upper arm. 'Thank you for saving me.'

He bent down and kissed her, on the lips and hard. With her right hand she squeezed his arm more tightly and she held the doorframe with the other. His hand touched her hip and she let herself be pulled towards him, against him. She felt his other arm against her back, the hand massaging her shoulder. Like this they moved into her room, and on to her narrow bed, her hands now pressed against his chest, pulling at the buttons, he removing her dress. Soon they were naked, together in the same bed in this house for the first time, and both felt the fervour and love that had guided them for the past five years, but had vanished these past couple of weeks. The strange and uneasy hiatus was over. When they slept, they slept in each other's arms, the sound of their own breathing close enough to cover the breaking of the Lake Michigan waves.

Morning: sunshine, heat, clacking typewriter. The previous day crept into her mind like the return of a vivid dream. But it had not been a dream. No nightmare of drowning, but real; no peaceful slumber of sitting in the night air with Nelson, but real; no dream of their kissing and making love, but real. She got up from the bed and wrapped a bathrobe around her and followed the noise of the typewriter keys to Nelson at the dining table, working. She tousled his hair and he turned his face up to her and smiled before returning to the typewriter.

The routines at Miller altered course. Evenings they still usually walked down to Neal and Chris, but there was no playing at husband and wife; the marriage had become real once more. The arm around her shoulders, the teasing, her playful punches on the arm: they no longer happened as charade or show, but gestures of real affection between them. Daytimes continued superficially the same: he worked at the typewriter, she sat out on the chaise-longue and read, or wrote letters. But after lunch they went together to her bedroom, the narrow single bed. Now and then they pushed the boat into the lagoon and he rowed her around for an hour, but they stayed away from Lake Michigan. She wasn't sure she really would've drowned – the idea seemed ridiculous in hindsight, but then again maybe it wasn't – but either way she didn't want to climb the dune and look out at the water that had scared her. So they kept to the lagoon, and, when the sun had dropped, the mosquitoes and fireflies and the sound – only the sound – of the breaking waves. When it got late they went together to her narrow single bed.

For three weeks their lives together unfurled like this. She wrote to Sartre that her life here, her love here had returned and though she still missed him perhaps their life in Paris didn't feel as urgent as it had. To Nathalie in California she wrote that when she arrived in Miller in a few weeks' time she'd be meeting the real Nelson Algren, the man Simone lovingly and jealously called her husband. Nelson continued working on his long poem, every morning out of bed and to the typewriter, and the work was going well, he liked the shape it was taking.

The night before Nathalie's arrival they had dinner with Chris and Neal, and when they arrived home Nelson kissed her goodnight and went to his own bedroom for the first time since he'd returned from the poker game. Simone wanted to say something, to ask him to bed, but none of the ways

205

to say it seemed right, and she knew well enough that no combination of words would work. She knew he'd made his decision. What it meant puzzled her, though perhaps it only meant that he was tired. Some nights sleeping together in the single bed was too close, too hot, even if neither of them would let it go to sleep in separate rooms. She vowed not to give it another thought.

Nelson spent the morning at the typewriter as usual. He'd made the separation last night because it had to be made. Nathalie's arrival would break it, and he wanted to at least pretend – to Simone, but mostly to himself – that he held some control over this fragile love. She couldn't always think it was her circumstances that decided the force of their passion.

Simone, instead of moving outside to read after her breakfast, began cleaning to prepare for Nathalie's arrival in the afternoon. She washed, dried and put away the pans and dishes. She swept the floor in the kitchen, and she swept the dining and lounge area, and she swept the hallway and the bedrooms. She arranged the newspapers and books into neat piles on the coffee table. She wiped counter-tops and the table that Nelson was working on, leaving his area a dry island surrounded by shiny damp wood. She scrubbed the bathroom.

'Don't forget to wash the outside of the house,' Nelson said when she came back from the bathroom.

She stopped, holding the cleaning rag aloft in confusion. 'The outside?'

He laughed. 'A joke. I've seen the Paris apartment of Mademoiselle Beauvoir, and many a hotel room occupied by the first lady of Existentialism, and on that evidence I find myself surprised to see she knows what a cleaning rag is for.'

Simone threw the rag at him, but it fell short and hit the table before landing on the floor. Nelson looked down at it.

'That's not what it's for,' he said, and looked up at her and winked.

At noon Simone left to walk down to the station to meet Nathalie on the 12:23 train. Nelson remained working at the typewriter, though he didn't get much more done. These weeks had been trying. True, he was responsible in part for making them so, but it wasn't entirely like that. He couldn't pretend to a passion that wasn't there, or one that couldn't find the surface. Maybe it was stupid that it took the near-drowning – if it was even really that dramatic an event; he wasn't sure, but it had felt so at the time – to resurrect his – their – passion, but so it had. The past few weeks he had forgotten that she would leave again, back to Paris; that undetermined space would open up again, filled only with letters proclaiming how much she loved him and missed him and needed him. He'd forgotten, but now the arrival of Nathalie served both as a reminder and an interruption to the bliss, the precarious love they worked to maintain. Nathalie, whom she'd forbidden him to see when he was in California.

He heard them through the open window, giggling and babbling in French, before he saw them coming down the gravel road side by side, each with a suitcase in one hand, their inside arms linked together. He looked at the page flopping halfway out of the typewriter. This was the end of work for today. He typed a period and turned back to the window to watch the two Frenchwomen approach. If only he could go row around the lagoon for the rest of the afternoon.

Nelson stood smiling at the dining table as they entered. He strode towards them, two overexcited women, and Simone introduced them. He kissed Nathalie on both cheeks, and told her she was welcome, and took the suitcases while Simone bustled her around the house showing her the bedrooms, the bathroom, all the places she'd cleaned a couple hours earlier. Nelson began preparing their lunch, which they planned to eat on the Lake Michigan beach, Simone's newfound aversion to the lake notwithstanding.

Nelson, Simone and Nathalie picnicked on bread and cheese and meat and apples and wine. The three of them sat on a large blue blanket while they ate, facing the lake. The women spoke mostly in French, rapidly, not that it would've mattered if they'd spoken more slowly, laughing and touching one another on the arm, on the shoulder. Occasionally Simone or Nathalie would turn to Nelson and translate. He'd smile or chuckle as appropriate but the translation never seemed all that interesting or funny.

After lunch Nathalie announced she wanted to swim.

'*Viens avec moi, Simone,*' she said.

Simone shook her head.

'The high priestess of Existentialism no longer swims.' Nelson reached out and rubbed Simone's back as he said it.

'Nelson, you come and swim with me.'

His hand dropped to the small of Simone's back. 'No, I'll stay here, too. But go ahead. We'll keep an eye on you. Save you from the sharks.'

'Sharks.' Nathalie laughed. 'I live in California.'

She pulled her dress over her head, unclipped her bra and shimmied out of her underpants. Nelson could see why Simone had forbidden him from meeting Nathalie in California. She smiled over her shoulder at the two of them as she trotted towards the water. He watched her hips, her ass. He would've gladly been seduced. But then, he probably wouldn't have spent so much time with Amanda if he had. Nathalie waded in to knee depth and dove across the water, only the ends of her hair dipping into the lake. Simone sat tensely watching. He could feel her shoulder muscles tightening beneath his hand.

'She'll be fine,' he said. 'It was a freak thing, your cramp.'

Simone rubbed her hands together. 'I suppose. I still feel the fear.'

'I can always go and save another Frenchwoman from the Indiana waters.'

'You'd like that, wouldn't you?'

'She is something to look at,' he conceded.

'And a flirt. More than a flirt. You see why I kept you away from her when you went to California.'

'Ah, but there's only room for one frog wife in my small heart,' he said.

Nathalie swam to the second sandbar and back without incident, and they watched her emerge from the lake, water dripping from her hair and arms and legs. Nelson poured three more glasses of wine and Nathalie lay naked on the blanket to dry.

They barbecued by the lagoon in the evening, Neal and Chris and a handful of other neighbours also joining them. Simone and Nathalie stuck close together for the entire night. Even when one of the other guests spoke to one of them, the other would be close at her side. Nelson spent most of the night talking to Neal and Dave, and watching Simone and Nathalie. There they were talking to Chris, Nathalie's hand on Simone's arm; now they leaned towards each other like conspirators, each touching the other's shoulder. Eventually they sat side by side in folding chairs by the table, the rest of the barbecue happening a head above them as they talked.

Nelson finished a beer and told Dave he could swear they might be lesbians. Dave laughed, but Nelson didn't, and Dave said he couldn't be serious.

Nelson opened another beer and shrugged. He wouldn't rule it out. Dave told him he was an idiot, that they hadn't seen each other in years, and that was how women were. Nelson frowned and said it didn't make sense of all the touching. It does, Dave told him, and laughed again.

When eventually the guests had left and the food had been cleared away, they went to bed. Nelson slept on the sofa. He had given his room to Nathalie. Simone had looked to him to see if he'd come to her bed, standing in her doorway until he'd lain down and put the sheet over himself. He didn't offer a kiss goodnight, or even look in her direction. She lay awake for a short time, wondering whether she'd slipped once more from his heart. He lay awake listening for the sound of Simone sneaking into Nathalie's bedroom.

Early the next afternoon Simone took Nathalie to Chicago for a few days. Nelson saw them off at the station. He kissed Nathalie on both cheeks, and couldn't resist putting a hand on her hip as he did so. Simone he kissed on the lips. He'd given them the keys to his apartment.

'What are you going to do?' he'd asked as they waited for the train to pull in.

'See the sights,' Nathalie said. Other than passing through on her way to Miller, she'd never been to Chicago.

'I'll show her the electric chair,' said Simone as the bells began to clang to signal the arrival of the train.

He waved, one hand in his pocket, and watched the train chug eastward, Simone and Nathalie sitting with their hands and their faces pressed to the window like children. For three and a half days he would be free to work alone, sit out back alone, row around the lagoon alone. He stopped at the railside bar for a beer. The rest of the afternoon and evening he spent at home, alone, doing very little: he read for a while, listened to the ball game on the radio, and fried himself a steak for dinner before going to bed early. Tomorrow he could wake up and work, and work all day without interruption.

Simone walked down to Randolph Street after seeing Nathalie on to the New York train at Union Station. They'd see each other again there in a couple of weeks, and Stepha and Fernando. She took a window seat on the left-hand side of the train so she could watch the lake and the steel mills. The few days with Nathalie had been pleasant, but Chicago had seemed different without Nelson; not exactly strange, but almost unfamiliar, as though part of its energy had stayed in Indiana with him. As they'd left the apartment with their suitcases this morning one of his neighbours had come into the corridor and demanded, first in a string of Polish, then in broken English, to know who the hell they were and what they thought they were doing. She'd threatened to call the super, and that the super would call the police. She'd called them thieves. They'd done their best to ignore her, but it was a relief to make it down the stairs and on to the pavement of Wabansia Avenue. She laughed quietly to herself now, and contented herself that she had a story to make Nelson laugh, too.

She hoped he'd managed to get a lot of work done, that he'd be satisfied with what he'd accomplished, and ready to move back into their pattern of mornings and afternoons, of work and play; that he'd be ready to take her in his arms and love her, to sleep again in her bed.

It would not be that way. The typewriter and books and papers were sitting alone on the dining table when she arrived.

211

She called his name, but he didn't answer. She looked in his bedroom: empty. She carried her suitcase to her own bedroom, the curtains closed, the heat filling the space between the walls. He didn't go to Chicago. He couldn't go to Chicago again, no. She'd walked past Chris and Neal's house so she knew he wasn't there. And Dave's. She would've heard them, or seen them. Maybe she should've checked the bar by the station. She went back to the living room and took another Agatha Christie novel from the coffee table.

When she came around the back of the house to sit in the chaise-longue, she saw him. He was rowing back towards the house. She called his name. No response. The wind had picked up; the waves and the leaves must have drowned her out. She waited until he began to turn the boat, and waved, but he'd looked over his shoulder and didn't see. She waved again. Only when he'd straightened out the boat did he see her. He dropped the oars and waved, and even from the distance she could see his teeth in the smile that formed. She waited as he turned the boat around again, and pulled the couple of strokes he needed to beach it. She wanted to run to him, as though she hadn't seen him for months, not a few days, but she stayed by the chaise-longue. He walked up from the lagoon and kissed her. She put her arms around his waist.

'Chicago was strange without you,' she said.

'I've always assumed it stopped existing when I'm not there,' he replied.

'It was still there. Just different. For me, at least. Your neighbour yelled at us this morning. An old woman.'

'Mrs Staslovski,' he said. 'Did she threaten to call the super?'

Simone nodded.

'Mrs Staslovski,' he repeated. 'It'll give her something to tell the other ladies when they meet for pinochle. She threatens to call the super at least three times a week.'

She would've liked to stay at home that evening, but Nelson said Chris and Neal had invited them around for a drink, so after dinner they went. They knocked on the door, and when nobody answered they went around the back.

'Nice surprise,' Neal said. 'I'll fix you drinks.'

'Yeah,' Nelson said, 'we thought we'd stop by on the off-chance.'

Simone stared at him as he said this. The force of his lie didn't reveal itself as a shock so much as a disappointment, a small scratch. She had wanted to stay at home; he'd lied to get away. She liked Neal and Chris, and she would have a pleasant evening – Neal handed her a gin and tonic – but Nelson had signalled, and signalled clearly, a shift, and she would have to navigate the two weeks before she left carefully, instead of simply loving him fully. She pushed her teeth into her bottom lip as the thought landed.

They slept in their separate rooms. In the morning he made toast with butter and a pot of coffee and they sat across the table from one another and ate breakfast.

'Is this how it will be?' she asked after she swallowed the first slice.

'How?'

'Nelson, I'll be leaving in two weeks and then it will be months, maybe a year before we come together again. I'd like to spend it in love, not silence.'

Nelson finished his coffee and refilled the cup. 'You'd always like to spend it how you'd like to spend it.'

'I don't know what you mean.' She held a slice of toast just above the plate.

'I mean that your time, your mood, your whim, always has to be the thing in charge. Like a spoiled little kid. What you want, you have to get or you throw a fit. Nobody else's wants, nobody else's needs, get taken into account in your life. If you don't have work to do, why should anybody else?'

She set the toast down uneaten. 'I make many sacrifices of my time and pleasure in Paris,' she said quietly.

'In Paris.'

'Yes, Nelson, in Paris. In Paris! That is where I live! That is where I work! Sartre needs me there.'

'Yes,' Nelson said. 'Sartre. The exception to the rule.'

'That is not fair.'

'It's entirely fair.' Nelson shifted his coffee cup between his hands. 'If Sartre tells you he's bored, you'll come running from the other side of the globe to make sure he has a game to play. As soon as he says he doesn't need you, you start writing about when you can come to Chicago.'

Simone's eyes had dropped to the table. 'That is not fair, Nelson,' she said, almost in a whisper. 'That is not fair.' She didn't dare to say I love you.

'It's fair,' he said, and took his coffee and walked out the front door. He circled to the back of the house and kicked the chaise-longue as he passed. When he reached the top of the dune he flung the cup towards the lake; most of the coffee had spilled on the climb. It landed five or six feet short of the waterline. It is fair, he repeated to himself. Love can't be built on conditions. If it is, maybe it isn't love, after all. Nelson didn't recognise his own conditions as conditions. But conditions are always there, in love.

The rest of the morning and into the early afternoon Nelson sat halfway down the dune, looking out across Lake Michigan. Simone stayed in the house, despite the sunshine, and tried to read, tried to write some letters, and mostly cried. When she heard his footsteps coming back around the house she went to the bathroom to wash her face.

'Let's have lunch,' Nelson said when she'd come back out, and they ate together at the same table where they'd had breakfast, one slice of cold toast still sitting on a plate.

For nine days they moved in unsteady paths to and from and around each other. Without telling Simone, Nelson had decided friendship was the attitude to strike. Without telling himself, he'd decided friendship would save him from the pain of love. His love for Simone hadn't gone and wasn't fading. But she would disappear without the love vanishing at all, and that was a burden too heavy to carry around without knowing when it might be shrugged off, without knowing the relief of it being shared by the two of them, not distanced by the continent and the ocean, but together, in the same place. Friendship could be the shield against that.

Simone tried to harden herself against his indifference. She knew questioning him would only raise his anger. She stopped trying to kiss him, even on the cheek. Every morning he smiled at her and prepared breakfast, and every night he put his hand on her shoulder before walking down the short hallway to his own bedroom. Each day he rowed around the lagoon but she didn't accept his invitation to join. She felt herself being dragged into a pattern, or a new form that her mind and her heart resisted. She couldn't stand to be away from Nelson, loving him so strongly when they were apart, and only feeling close when she wrote to him, or received a letter; but neither could she stand to be near him when he only offered – what? Breakfast, indifference, a hand on her shoulder, a half-hearted smile. She wanted to rescue her

Chicago husband, pull the local youth from this nothing lagoon and show him love was still possible – not even possible, but there, real, large and passionate and necessary. But she couldn't think how.

The day before they returned to Chicago they held a final barbecue, a farewell barbecue. Farewell for Simone: Nelson would come back to Miller in a couple of weeks. Dave, Earl and Janet, Neal and Chris came by late in the afternoon, with beer and whisky and gin and meat, bread, potatoes and sweetcorn, and stayed late into the night, early into the morning. Simone and Nelson caught an evening train back to Chicago and stopped for a beer at the Tug before returning to Wabansia Avenue.

On her last day in Chicago they went to the track. Simone's flight to New York, where she would stay for another week before returning to Paris, was leaving later that night, so they checked her baggage with a porter at Midway Airport and took a bus the rest of the way to Cicero. Nelson rubbed his hands together as they approached the race course. Simone hadn't much wanted to spend her final afternoon watching horse races, but she couldn't see another idea that might dissuade him, and it seemed pointless to leave town on an argument, especially not knowing if she would ever see him again.

He'd brought $200. He didn't tell her that. She wouldn't want – he didn't want her to know how much. It wasn't her money anyway. He could gamble most of it and, even if he lost, still have money for dinner and a taxi back to the airport. The sun was out and warm, but not hot, and once they got close enough to Sportsman's the damp smell of horses seeped into their noses. It would be a good afternoon, a lucky afternoon.

His first few bets didn't go too well. In the first race he'd picked one to win and another to show, and the winner finished second, the shower somewhere in the middle of the pack. In the second race he'd another winner and the same horse to place, but that one came in a close third. A close third, though – it was close.

'A few inches,' he said to Simone. 'A few inches and I'm a winner.'

'A few inches,' she repeated, and smiled.

He looked at the copy of the *Daily News* he'd bought on the way, wrinkling his nose as he tried to choose the next bet. 'I think I'll sit this one out,' he said after a minute or so, 'and let my luck change in the race after. Don't you want to place a bet?'

Simone shook her head. She hadn't brought any cash with her. She didn't want to lose any. She had her budget for New York.

'Here.' He gave her twenty dollars. 'There's your kitty. Make some bets.'

She didn't want to, but took the two bills and decided she'd place each one of them on a horse she liked the name of to win.

The next race he decided what the hell and put thirty bucks on a trifecta plus another ten on a horse with longish odds to win. The trifecta was a bust but his horse came in, and put him up. Put him up on that bet, anyway. He still had to make back the first couple of races. But his luck had turned a corner, turned a small corner. He turned to Simone.

'My luck has turned a small corner. What did you have in that one?'

She shrugged. 'I didn't bet on that one. I didn't like any of the names.'

Nelson laughed. 'I hope you find one you like soon,' he said, and went back to the betting window to put some money on a handful of straight bets, figuring maybe it was better to stay away from the exotics.

He started winning a few bets, but only enough to claw back a little money, not enough to get back to where he started. Eventually Simone put half her twenty on a horse called Jealous Widow, but it came in second to last. Her other ten dollars she held on to until late in the afternoon, when she lost it on a horse called Brogan. Nelson's luck, meanwhile, hadn't turned any corners, large or small. His hole got bigger and bigger, down fifty, down seventy, down ninety, now one-ten. He tried to box a couple of bets hoping it would pay off and get him back to even all at once, but it only dug him in deeper.

'That's it,' he said with two races to go. 'I'm bust.'

'Bust?' Simone said. 'You're all out?'

'Broke,' he said, and turned his pockets inside out.

'Nelson, you have nothing?'

He shrugged. 'That's how it looks. I guess you'll have to pay for the taxi to the airport.'

'All my money is in my suitcase,' she said.

Nelson ran his hand through his hair. 'We don't have any money.'

She looked out to the track, where the next set of horses were being lined up. There were hours before the flight. No reason to panic. But no money – Nelson. Nelson. 'Nelson,' she said, only once.

'I can call someone,' he said, pushing his pockets back inside. 'I'll borrow some money.'

He couldn't get hold of Jack or Karl, and anyway, they were unreliable. He hadn't wanted to call Studs or Stuart.

Either of them would come down, but he'd get a sermon, and probably another punch in the stomach. But Chris and Neal were in Indiana, and so was Dave. Margo was out of the question, and, if he called Caesar, she'd find out that way. So he called Stuart, and risked the sermon, risked the punch.

They met him an hour later outside the main entrance to the track.

'You owe me one, Nelson,' he said as he approached, but he was smiling and shook Nelson's hand, and kissed Simone on the cheeks.

'I'll pay you back with interest. Double if we go back for the last few races and I cash in.'

Simone clenched her fists and looked to Stuart.

'I'm not watching horses today,' Stuart said.

'Come on, I'll go back in for one last bet. Just give me five bucks and I'll improve it. Guaranteed.'

Stuart handed the cash to Simone. 'You're in charge of this money,' he said, before turning to the street. He flagged a cab and ushered them into it. 'I don't care how you get home from the airport, Nelson,' he said, 'But you're at least going to get Simone there.'

Simone waved at Stuart as the taxi pulled back into traffic. The cab drove down Cicero Avenue towards the airport. Nelson leaned against the door.

'So this is how we will say goodbye.' Simone continued to watch the buildings along Cicero.

'What do you mean?'

'A day of gambling away all your money and a silent taxi ride.'

'I tried to do something fun. We did do something fun. The money isn't important. It's still fun. Now you'll leave, for New York, to Paris, and I'll go back to my life here, you'll go back to your life there. I thought we should try to have fun on the last day.'

'Yes,' Simone said, 'I suppose.'

Simone paid the driver and gave the change to Nelson for the El back North. He helped her carry her suitcases to the gate, and there they said goodbye. She kissed him and he kissed her back, and the hug was tender, but not passionate. She watched him walk away, but he didn't turn to wave a last time, or to blow her a kiss. This might be how it ended, she realised, and in the same thought told herself this would not be how it ended. Could not be how it ended. Half an hour before the flight boarded she heard her name, and when she acknowledged the call she found herself presented with a boutonnière, a large purple flower, and a small card that said, *With Love from Nelson.*

Chapter Eleven

TEN DAYS AFTER he left Simone at the airport, Amanda rang the bell at Wabansia Avenue. He looked out the window and saw her standing on the porch. The next day they went out to Miller. She would stay for two weeks.

He insisted they stop for a beer at the railway bar before they went to the house on the lagoon. He carried her suitcases and his small bag. Most of his things he'd left in Miller, knowing he'd return. The bartender, when he pushed the beers across the bar, raised his eyebrows in private acknowledgement at Nelson, here with yet another woman. Nelson winked in return. They sat in a booth near the jukebox. Amanda reached across the table and stroked the back of Nelson's hand. It's nice to be away from Hollywood for a little while, she said, and nice to be back in Chicago, or the Midwest, at any rate. Nelson curled his fingers around her hand. Miller isn't quite Chicago, is it? he said, and she laughed, and told him it was hard to think of him as a country boy. I think of it as between my roots, he said. Detroit-born, Chicago-raised, now between everything in my Indiana home. I'm thinking I'll buy the place out here. To have it for good.

On the way to the house he pointed out where Dave lived, and Chris and Neal. She knew them, of course, and said she was looking forward to seeing them again. When they arrived he set the luggage by the door. Before we go in I have to show you the best part, he said. He took her hand and they walked around the back, past the chaise-longue and down to the lagoon. He helped her, giggling, into the boat, and pushed it into deep enough water to start rowing. He rowed a couple of laps while they chatted about the trees, the sound of Lake Michigan, the dune that rose up from the far shore of the lagoon.

He set the suitcases inside, next to the dining table, and showed her the house. First he swung open the door to the small bedroom that Simone had occupied, the narrow bed and night table and wardrobe. Next he showed her the other – his room – equally small, no night table, small chest of drawers, single bed. After that he quickly showed her the bathroom and they went back to the living room and dining area. Nelson, she said, can't we move those beds together, into one of the rooms? We'll have to move the other furniture around too, he said, and before he finished she interrupted, and said she hadn't come from California to sleep down the hallway. Yes, he said, if we move the wardrobe and the night table we can probably squeeze the two of them into the front room. It took a little over half an hour, but together they carried out the wardrobe and night table, and, with three pauses to rest, they brought the bed from Nelson's room into the front bedroom, manoeuvring it sideways through each door. They shoved it next to the other, and it fitted with almost a foot of floorspace on the other side. That's better, Amanda said. That's how it should be.

It was winter now in Paris, mid-February. The new year, and Castor's birthday, had come and gone. Almost five months since she'd been in Miller and Chicago, since she'd flown to New York clutching a purple flower that had wilted and died before the plane touched down at LaGuardia Field. Despite him – no, despite the way he'd acted and because of him – she'd wanted to go back almost immediately when she'd returned to Paris. In New York she'd stayed in the Hotel Lincoln, where she'd stayed on her very first trip to America, not in the Brevoort. She wouldn't stay there without him. She returned and started to work on her novel. She was transforming her life – parts of her life – into fiction. Yes, but not exactly. And now she was writing about Nelson, about herself and Nelson. And only longing to be in Chicago with Nelson. She wrote a letter each day, asking when she could come. It hadn't been left well, yes, she knew, but they could make that up, they could regain what they'd had. She wrote this in letters, she wrote this into the novel, where it looked flat and obvious and stupid, so she rewrote and rewrote. Nelson never left her mind.

Nelson hadn't written back, not since his last letter, in which he claimed – was it a true claim? – that he'd taken up with a woman, that she was helping to support him. That had been two weeks ago, and she'd written every day, pleading for another letter, wanting to know more details, all the details, wanting to hear of his life. She went to the Flore in the morning to work, her manuscript in a canvas bag. She could work for a couple of hours before anybody came by looking for her, and, when they did, hopefully she'd be gone. She didn't want to see anybody. Only Sartre, whom she had to meet at his mother's home later, and Gallimard, whose office she would visit before that. And Nelson. If only! Nelson Nelson Nelson. She began work on a new paragraph, but it was no use. After an hour she'd still only written one short sentence, and retraced the accent marks and punctuation several times over. She took out the latest letter she'd been writing to Nelson and read it, adding a further page about her inability to concentrate on her work, her eagerness for his answer to whether she could visit, to when she could visit, that she wanted this novel to be the best thing she had written, that it was a gift for him. If only she could concentrate. If only he'd write; then she could.

She paid her bill and collected her belongings together, the manuscript in the canvas bag, everything else – papers, pens, keys, books – in another. A walk might clear her mind. She had a little while before she needed to see Gallimard. She could stop at home and see if Nelson had written. That was what she would do.

She didn't stop at home. She hadn't paid much attention when she left the Flore, and found herself walking in the opposite direction. By the time she realised, it seemed foolish to change directions, or find a way of looping back. Anyway, it didn't matter. She'd only have time to stop by, and she didn't want to read the letter in public. Regardless of what it said, it would make her cry. She knew that.

She reached Gallimard fifteen minutes late, and couldn't concentrate during the meeting, all of twenty minutes. She kept wondering if a letter awaited her. She kept imagining the yellow envelope, the stamps with numbers and the letter 'c' with a line through it, USA, a return address of either Wabansia Avenue or Miller, Indiana, the yellow paper with Nelson's handwriting inside. Somehow she assured Gallimard the novel was going well. He advanced her the money she needed for the plane tickets for her and Sartre, and she left. He ran after her thirty seconds later, holding the canvas bag aloft. I can't advance you money for a manuscript you leave lying around, he joked. She took the bag and smiled sheepishly and departed, manuscript in her left hand, the other bag dangling from her right. She took a taxi to Madame Sartre's apartment. She needed to see Sartre, but really only wanted to go home now, to go home and have a drink and hope the letter had arrived, and rest.

Madame Sartre was cordial and pleasant as always, and her cook served a delicious meal of *coq au vin*. Sartre chatterboxed through most of dinner, in between bites and even while chewing. He talked of their upcoming vacation, and she assured him she'd received the money from Gallimard; she waved the cheque in the air to prove it, as though waggling a newspaper at a naughty dog. He talked about the writing he was doing, and asked her when she'd have time to read through it. She told him she could take whatever he had home with her, and work on it tomorrow. He jumped up from the table, his mother exclaiming not for the first time about his rudeness, and returned with a packet of papers, tied with string. After dinner they drank a brandy, and she gathered up her things, adding Sartre's papers to them, and he walked her to the taxi rank, where she piled them and herself into the back seat.

No letter from Nelson when she arrived home. No yellow envelope, no American stamp. She dropped her bag by the doorway. Nelson, please write to me, she said aloud, in English. She could only hear the clock ticking in reply. After pouring a large glass of whisky and using part of it to wash down some pills she placed the arm of the record player over the smooth edge of a Miles Davis record and watched it slide until it caught the outer groove and the music jumped above the sound of the clock. She sat down on the couch and listened to the drums, bass, piano, and trumpet and wished – now she could feel herself about to cry – that she were in

Chicago, in a basement bar in Chicago. Nelson. She stared at the door, as though he might walk through it. Silly, but she stared. She looked at the bag leaning next to the door, her pens and pencils, her books and papers, Sartre's work. She thought about the work she couldn't do this morning –

She jumped up and ran to the door. Only one bag. The manuscript, the novel. No. Only one bag. She thought back to the Flore, yes, she left with it, yes Gallimard, he'd carried it towards her when she left it there, yes, she'd had it in the taxi to Madame Sartre's, yes, she'd had it when she left, Sartre had tried to carry it but she wouldn't let him, yes, she had it in the taxi – she left it in the taxi. She didn't remember the driver, hadn't paid attention. Her manuscript was sitting on the floor of some taxi. Her novel for Nelson was sitting on the floor of a taxi, or not on the floor of a taxi, picked up by someone else, read by someone else, and she would have to rewrite everything, remake everything. She sat on the floor next to the one bag she had brought home and drank her glass of whisky. When it was empty she walked back to the table and refilled it, and took two more pills. The record stopped. She flipped it over. She sat down. She drank whisky. She stared at the bag on the floor by the door. She cried.

He spent most of the autumn and winter in Miller rewriting the long poem. He'd take the train to Chicago a few times a month, depending on poker games or whim. He'd visit Margo for a couple of hours here or there when he was in the city, but couldn't persuade her to travel out to Miller for a week or two. She was still trying to stay clean, and yes, it would be impossible to get junk out in Miller but that was the point, she told him. He didn't get it, but knew well enough to let Margo do things her way. He would stop by Wabansia, even if he wasn't staying the night, to pick up mail. Always it was mostly letters from Simone, envelope after envelope with French airmail stamps, or one fat envelope full of letters masquerading as a single one. She complained that she missed him, she asked when would be good for her to come visit again, she talked about Bost, about Sartre, about her sister's paintings, about André Gide dying. He couldn't think of a useful thing to reply, so he didn't. Instead he wrote to Amanda, letters that sent uncomplicated news, and received uncomplicated replies. He'd go back to Miller and find more letters from Simone waiting for him there. She was hedging her bets.

She found it. Thank God. She found it. She'd called the dispatchers but they couldn't tell her which taxi she'd taken any more than she could tell them. They told her where the lost property office was, and she went there. Nothing. She spent the rest of the day washing amphetamines down with whisky. The next morning she worked on Sartre's essay in the morning and after lunch went back again to the lost and found. Nothing. By the fourth day the lost property attendant – an old woman, probably a collaborator, Castor decided after the third day, but changed her mind the next – had taken special interest in Castor's problem. Nothing new today, she said by way of greeting. But look around if you wish. The same routine followed on the fifth, sixth, seventh times she made the trip over to the office. She went on Sunday, forgetting it was Sunday and the office wouldn't be open. Every night she drank whisky and listened to records. She couldn't work at all, except for an hour or two on Sartre's writing. She would have to start the whole novel over, try to reconstruct every word, every sentence. She should cancel the vacation with Sartre, she should forget – Nelson didn't write anyway, not a word – going to Chicago. She would have to go somewhere quiet – to La Pouèze, maybe – and do nothing but retread all the steps, thousands and thousands of words. On the eighth trip the attendant clapped her hands together. I have two different sheaves of paper arrived overnight, she said. One must be yours – must be yours. But neither was. The woman wrung her hands in apology. I was sure, she said; how could one of them not be? Castor left the office while the woman continued to mutter apologetically.

She hadn't been to the Flore. She'd forgotten a meeting with Gallimard, and she'd skipped the radio. She'd missed a deadline for a short article for *La Libération*. She'd deliberately skipped the *Temps Modernes* meeting because she didn't want to face those men, and put up with their squabbling. She couldn't do anything anyway. She couldn't concentrate on anything anyway.

The woman in the lost property office had nothing for her again on the ninth day, but on the tenth she leapt from her chair. This time I know I have what you are looking for, she told Castor, who doubted it. I know it. This one came in, and it has your name on it. The woman couldn't stop talking. You see? I know, I know. I've been taking special care because I know who you are, I recognised you, remembered your face from the newspaper. This one – she disappeared behind the desk for a moment and reappeared with a sheaf of papers – this one has your name across the front page.

It did. This was it. Castor stood perfectly still. The attendant disappeared below the desk again. Also, your bag? It was in this bag. She carefully placed the papers into the bag and handed it across to the dumb Castor. Only when she felt the weight of it pull against her shoulder did she reanimate. She reached into her pocket and removed some money – not coins, but paper money. Take this, she said to the attendant, in gratitude. This has saved my life. The attendant refused the money. It is my job, Mademoiselle Beauvoir, I merely do my job. No money is necessary. She waved her hand at the cash.

Castor stepped on to the street in a trance, clutching the bag across her chest. It was raining. She was exhausted. She would go home, and sleep for an hour or two, and maybe then go to the Flore. She could relax. She could start working again tomorrow.

When she arrived home, still holding the bag across her chest, as though someone might rip it from her grasp, she found a yellow envelope, littered with stamps bearing the 'c' with the line through it. Samuel Gompers looked at her from one, and Cadillac pushed his canoe ashore in front of Detroit skyscrapers on another. The postmark bore the name Gary, Indiana. She had it torn open and was already reading before she'd reached the couch.

The letter ran to several pages, and she had a hard time concentrating on so many words, so much information, after all the stress of the last days and the excitement now beating inside of her. Nelson, beloved Nelson. Paragraph after paragraph, but only one sentence that actually mattered, at least right now: *I thought you might like to come again to Wabansia and Miller in September, and row on the little lagoon.*

Chapter Twelve

SIMONE ARRIVED, as customary, to Wabansia Avenue, keeping an eye out for the Schlitz billboard, Chicago presenting its familiar tall buildings and elevated rail lines. The driver stopped outside 1523 Wabansia Avenue and helped take her luggage from the trunk. She climbed the short set of steps and rang the bell.

'Hello,' he said after opening the door, and she watched his mouth turn to a smile, one corner a little higher than the other. He leaned down to kiss her and she moved towards him, but no, he picked up her suitcases and she had to stop to keep from headbutting his shoulder. She followed him and her luggage up the stairs and into the apartment. His typewriter sat on the writing desk, within reach of the sofa. The record player sat on the desk as well. She followed him through to the bedroom and smiled to see the Mexican blanket spread across the bed. He set her baggage on the floor and turned to face her.

'I'm glad you're here,' he said, and from the flattening out of his tone in the last two words, she expected the conjunction that followed. 'But,' he added, 'we can only make this work for the next month on the understanding that what we have here is a friendship. A good friendship, but only a friendship.'

For months he'd tried to convince himself that friendship was the answer to the pain their love scored into him whenever she left. He could endure the pain of only a friend departing. He could try.

She looked at her suitcases. 'A friendship, Nelson.'

'A friendship, Simone.' Where once he might have said this in a joking tone, she could see and hear that he was only speaking seriously. He was making an offer of friendship, when she had flown across the ocean for love.

Nelson slept on the sofa, and Simone beneath the Mexican blanket, alone in the double bed. In the morning they took the train to Miller, where the single beds crowded against the walls in separate rooms. The chaise-longue sat in its familiar place in the backyard, facing the lagoon. They walked past it and down to the lagoon, and Nelson steadied the dinghy while she climbed in. They rowed twice around the lagoon, Simone letting both hands drag through the warm water, her head back and looking up at the red and yellow and brown autumn leaves.

Nelson ran the boat aground on the far shore. He helped Simone out and they took off their shoes and climbed the deep sand of the dune until they reached the peak and could see down the shore and across to the blue horizon, shielding their eyes from the late afternoon sun. An Indian summer had broken, and the sand was hot, so they couldn't pause long at the top, and as they walked along the beach, had to keep near the waterline, where they could cool their feet. They walked eastward, towards Gary, towards Chicago. They reached Marquette Park, and walked around the concrete two-towered pavilion, constructed of blocks put together like a puzzle, and Nelson made a joke about the Aquatorium.

'It's the most grandly named bath house in the world,' he said as they watched a couple of children emerge with their mother, clothed to go home after one last day of swimming. 'Or at least in northern Indiana.'

For half an hour they watched the lake, and the lone remaining swimmer pushing back and forth through the water parallel to the shoreline, and then they turned their backs on Gary and Chicago and walked home towards Miller, the sinking sun heating their shoulders.

In the morning they awoke and breakfasted and worked, Nelson at the typewriter on the dining table, Simone in her familiar station on the chaise-longue. She was writing an essay in which she evaluated the Marquis de Sade. He hated and loved women in equal measure, she had decided, and kept writing in prison about those things he could never do, about his loves and hates. When she felt particularly maudlin or self-pitying she would try to imagine, reading these words over, that she had written them about Nelson, but it didn't hold; the fake analogy didn't have claws. She'd found one of the Agatha Christie books in the house, and reread it in small doses when she'd grown tired of writing.

Nelson mostly pretended to work. His long poem had been published in *Holiday*, but the editors had butchered it. No matter: the real version would be out as a book in a couple of months. A hell of a Christmas present. He fooled around with a few poems and short stories, trying to rewrite things, but he wished he had something new, a new idea, to work on. He spent a lot of time looking out the window at Simone, writing longhand, using a stack of magazines on her lap as a writing table. Friendship. He'd decided on that answer before she arrived, and wouldn't go back on it now. So far it worked.

Friendship worked for them both. They talked about their work, and they enjoyed their walks along Lake Michigan and their rows around the lagoon. As the previous summer, they hosted a few barbecues for Dave and Chris and Neal, and were themselves hosted by their friends for drinks and meals. They made only a few trips into Chicago, and, when they did, Nelson slept on the sofa. But they went to the Tip Top Tap, and talked about the first time they'd gone there, on Simone's second trip to America, the first she'd made just to see Nelson. They talked about it nostalgically but without heartbreak, laughing over her surprise that Stuart had known her work, about Nelson's attempts to impress her by eating his chicken bones. They played the same game they'd played before, watching the other couples and making up biographies for them: the sausage baron and his wife, the heir to the brush factory trying desperately to get laid. They made another trip to visit the Art Institute, and another for Nelson to deliver a talk to a club of law-abiding middle-class citizens who turned out to be less interested in the truths behind *The Man with the Golden Arm* than their invitation had suggested; nor did they notice the world's most famous Frenchwoman in their company. An unspoken agreement kept them away from the track, and away from the Tug.

Simone's day of departure arrived both quickly and at last. They breakfasted together quietly, both unsure how to frame the conversation of their remaining few hours together. No plan, no promise of the next occasion to bring them together raised itself, and neither of them could think of a thing to say about it. After he washed the dishes, Nelson came into the room where Simone was packing her remaining things into her suitcases. In three hours the taxi would arrive and she would leave for the airport.

'You should read this before you go,' he said, holding a book towards her with both hands. 'The introduction.'

She stood and took the book. It was an edition of Dostoyevsky's shorter novels, and an essay by Thomas Mann formed the introduction. She looked up at Nelson.

'I read it a few days ago,' he said. 'Mann talks about Dostoyevsky and criminality. It's worth reading.'

He turned and walked back into the other room and once again Simone was alone with her suitcases and now this book. She set it on the bed and continued packing. Nelson sat at his desk and looked through a stack of papers – letters, mostly. He stared for a while at the photographs pinned to the wall, among them a few of Simone, of him and Simone, one of him and Eleanor Roosevelt, clipped from the newspaper. He had letters from Amanda, and letters from his publisher, and letters from Simone, a letter from Richard, a letter inviting him to deliver the talk he'd given last week. He picked up the issue of *Holiday* with his poem in it. Sandburg had contributed an essay, and Gwendolyn Brooks. But so had Robert McCormick and there was some crap by Irv Kupcinet. They'd titled his own contribution 'One Man's Chicago', and he had to laugh over that – Ken wanted to distance his stupid magazine from the idea that Chicago was something other than McCormick's and his loyal puppies' view of things. Gwendolyn had done the job right, though: 'They call it Bronzeville'. But they'd really done her wrong with the photographs, making the place look like a circus show. At least this man's Chicago got Art's photographs like it should. He looked again at the cover painting: racing white and red lights of traffic zooming from and to Chicago, the blurry skyscrapers forming a skyline across the top third of the page, the blue lake and ink-black shoreline to the right-hand side. For comparison he looked out the window at the brick apartment buildings opposite, two storeys high, and the lone thin elm tree planted in the sidewalk. One man's Chicago. Simone's taxi would be arriving soon. Looking at a magazine wouldn't change that. The chair creaked as he pushed out of it to go into the bedroom and say his goodbyes.

She sat on the bed, newspapers, magazines and the Dostoyevsky book gathered around her like eager pupils. She was reading a page of the *Daily News*.

'I read the essay,' she said, and smiled.

'It's almost time for you to go.' He held the doorframe, and rested his cheek against his hand.

She set the paper to one side. 'Yes.'

One of the magazines slid on to the floor as she shifted, landing on the spine and flopping open. They both watched it.

'I'm glad we can have a friendship,' she said, looking back to Nelson. 'I'm glad we know our friendship works.'

'I can't offer you friendship,' he mumbled, his head still pressed against his hand.

She didn't understand. He'd spoken too quietly, and into his hand, and whatever he'd said didn't sound like words, just noises. 'Nelson,' she said, about to ask him to repeat himself.

He dropped his hand from the doorframe, took three steps towards the bed, and squatted like a baseball catcher. He picked up the magazine and set it, closed, on the bed. 'I can't do it,' he said. His face muscles moved into an expression she couldn't recognise – unlike any he'd made before. 'I can't offer you anything less than love, Simone.'

'Nelson,' she said. 'Nelson.'

They remained like that, Nelson crouched at the side of the bed, his hand rubbing the orange and yellow and red and green and blue Mexican wool, Simone among the papers and magazines, her back cushioned by pillows, without either knowing what to say, until the sound of the taxi engine, and the horn blasting twice, entered through the open windows and forced Simone down the stairs, carrying both suitcases while Nelson sat on the floor of his bedroom.

After paying the cab driver she walked as quickly across the departures hall as her two suitcases would allow. She dumped them outside the restroom door and charged to the nearest toilet stall, her face now wet, and already stiff and sore from the clenched muscles. She lifted the seat and leaned over the bowl and retched twice. With the third, she vomited. Another retch and her stomach was empty, and only small streams of bile emerged on the next two, three, four – she didn't know how many times she heaved towards the water. Always so much water in American toilets. She rinsed her mouth at the sink, washed her hands and collected her suitcases. Walking towards the main concourse, she knew better than to expect a flower-bearing messenger from Nelson Algren.

Part Three

October 1951–September 1959

Part Three

Chapter Thirteen

NELSON STAYED IN Chicago for a week, and, when he returned to Miller, Jack, Patty, Karl and Margo made the journey with him. Margo had managed to stay clean for several months now, but she still struggled. The others, when they needed a fix, took themselves away from the house, out into the trees around the lagoon, or over the dunes; or they tied off when Margo and Nelson had left for the lagoon or the beach. He spent hours rowing her around the lagoon, or walking the beach – they walked to Marquette Park, where the beach lay empty now that the weather had returned to autumn, and no swimmers pushed through the waves. Nelson took photographs of Margo, pretty, young, thin Margo, in the dinghy, atop the dune, mouth open in a toothy smile with Lake Michigan waves breaking behind her. She was shy about it, but enjoyed Nelson's attention, liked having her photograph taken. They sat, towards the end of afternoon, on the sun-warmed sand and looked out to the lake, chopped into whitecaps by the wind. Margo wrapped her arms around herself and sighed. It's nice to be out here, Nelson, she said; even with the others around, and their junk, and the temptation, it seems possible to stay clean. Nelson rubbed her shoulder. I'm glad, he told her; it's nice for me, too. They stood and walked back along the beach until they reached Nelson's dune – as he thought of it – and after taking a last look at Lake Michigan for the day they climbed back over and down to the lagoon, where Nelson insisted on making the unnecessary boat journey instead of walking along the little shore.

When Jack, Patty and Karl left after a couple of days, Margo stayed, sleeping in the back bedroom while Nelson slept in the front. When he wanted to work, she rowed herself around the lagoon, or dozed on the sofa. She read half of *Murder on the Orient Express* while he sat at the typewriter. They rowed in the lagoon, or sat in the cold wind on the beach. He didn't see Dave or Chris and Neal for the week that she stayed. When it was time for her to return to Chicago, he walked her to the station and waited with her for the westbound train. It's like something in a movie, she joked: people waiting for a train to say farewell. Except I'll be in Chicago again next week, Nelson reminded her. I'll look forward to that, she told him. Let's go for dinner with Caesar when you're back in town. The train arrived, and she climbed up the steps and sat in the window seat nearest the door, waving at him until the train pulled away, next station: Gary. Nelson stopped in the bar for a couple of beers before he returned home. No women today? the bartender joked, as he'd grown fond of doing now that Nelson was a regular. No women today, Nelson provided the standard reply.

The routines started up again upon Castor's return to Paris. Every morning she took her work to the Flore. She'd finished the Sade essay and now returned to the novel. The daily writing proved difficult; she knew what she wanted to do, where the story was heading, but she couldn't write any of it without thinking of Nelson, constantly of Nelson, of the friendship she thought they'd developed from their love, and of Nelson crouched next to the bed in Wabansia Avenue, shattering that friendship with his love. If he wanted love, she could give him love, and if he wanted friendship, she could give him friendship, but to love him so intensely from Paris, only to make an annual trip to Chicago not knowing whether love or friendship or hatred awaited her – no.

In the afternoons, people would begin to drop by, and she could distract herself, more or less, from the question of Nelson, and from the struggle of turning her emotions into fiction. Bost came by most days, and Sartre would move from his table on the other side of the room to take lunch with Castor. Inevitably strangers would stop to talk as well: students eager for wisdom, journalists who only wanted to harass the Great Beauvoir-Sartre Couple, and others who simply knew they were famous. She accomplished very little work in the afternoons, and eventually Sartre would mutter that they needed to send for Algren. Bost still found this joke hilarious, and would repeat it with glee, but, though she would smile, it made Castor glum to think she couldn't, even if he were in Paris, count on being able to send for Nelson to punch noses. She wanted to write to him to tell him so, but, after a long letter written in New York, in Newfoundland, and above the ocean, trying to explain herself, trying also to explain Nelson to himself, she could only muster the energy for silly gossip, or what looked like it, anyway: updates on all the people he knew in Paris, Bost this and Olga that, Jean blah blah, Michelle such and such. Nights she listened to records and drank the whisky she'd smuggled through customs.

The new year arrived, and shortly thereafter, her birthday. She found a lump in her breast. Her hand brushed against it as she pulled on her dress, and she registered the strange feeling – a little hard spot. She hated touching her own body, but pressed her finger against it anyway. Yes, a lump. A small hard pebble. There had been pain, a slight pain, for a couple of months, but it seemed like nothing. She touched the same place on the other breast for comparison. Nothing. One last press, as though it might have disappeared. She looked at her face in the mirror. Old. And now a lump in the breast. She sat down on the bed. She didn't want to touch it again, but she did. She looked at the framed photograph of Nelson on the nightstand: standing in front of the lagoon, and the little boat resting on the shore in the corner. She began to cry, her thumb unconsciously stroking the silver ring on her finger. She needed her Chicago husband now. Not Nelson the friend, not Nelson the lover: Nelson the unconditional husband. She didn't go to the Flore.

Nelson wrote back immediately when he read the letter. Go to the doctor, he wrote, go to the doctor right away and find out what it is. Already a week had gone by before she'd sent the letter, and it had taken the damn thing two weeks to get to Chicago. She hated going to the doctor, he knew it, he wrote, but dammit, go. He took the letter to the post office and wished he could put it on the airmail plane himself, or courier it himself straight to the Rue de la Bûcherie. Paris seemed very far away.

Chicago felt closer when she received the letter at the end of February. Every morning for weeks she had pressed her finger into the lump before getting out of bed. She knew she should go to the doctor, she'd known that since the first morning, pulling the dress over her head. But still she wished it would just go away, that if she pressed it each morning, one day, instead of feeling a lump, instead of it feeling bigger, and the surge of nausea it gave her, she would feel only flesh, and her life could continue. She'd told no one, except Nelson. His advice was sound, and his concern warmed her. Still she needed two more weeks to work up the courage to make the appointment. Another letter had arrived in the meantime, asking whether she'd gone yet.

Now it was March, and every day he waited obsessively for the mail to arrive. He wanted to spend more time in Chicago, but he knew she'd write to Miller, so he stayed put. He hardly even left the house until the mail arrived, sometimes late morning, sometimes early afternoon. He'd try to work, going over his first novel and revising, and rewriting whole passages. It was starting to become a new story. But he found it difficult to concentrate. Nights he'd go to the bar by the train station, or visit Dave or Neal and Chris. A few times he took the train into Chicago for poker at the Tug, coming back out in the early morning so he'd be home when the mail arrived. Finally a letter arrived covered in French stamps, three weeks after she'd written it, sitting at her desk or a table in the Flore at the same time, no doubt, that he'd been pushing more chips into the middle of the table for Pharaoh to bluff him out of. Damn Simone, she never wrote in three or four words what she could say in seven hundred: he had to read two and a half pages of unimportant details before she came to the point that the lump was benign, and now removed. The letter went on for several more pages, but he set it down. He took a bottle of whisky from the kitchen counter and poured two fingers, plus a little extra, to celebrate.

Sartre had brought a handful of young journalists on to the board of *Les Temps Modernes*, all left-wingers, to try to keep the magazine moving in his own direction. Castor sat in Sartre's apartment, measuring up the new faces. Merleau-Ponty looked unhappy, arms crossed over his chest, trying

not to glare at these fresh little boys. She could see him –
imagine him, anyway – thinking: Sartre's henchmen. They
had the good grace to keep mostly quiet during the meeting.
Good grace or timidity. Mostly the new boys watched Sartre,
nodding when he spoke, aping his frowns or smiles as he
listened to others. When Castor spoke she felt their eyes
alternating between her and Sartre. This one here, black hair
and blue eyes, he leaned forward as she spoke, eyebrows
pulling together in concentration. She knew him to be a
friend of Bost, who had recommended him for the board. A
bright and ambitious young journalist.

When she stopped in the offices a week later the secretary
told her that Claude had said she was beautiful. Don't be
stupid, Castor said, I'm too old for jokes. But at the next
meeting she noticed he watched her more than others, and he
took his cues from her as much as from Sartre. The flattery
warmed her, even if it struck her as silly. He spoke well in the
meetings, always supporting Sartre's view, but intelligently,
not slavishly, the way some of them did. Bost had chosen well.
She didn't think about it much outside of the meetings. She
had her own work to do: six or seven hours a day she was
working on the novel, she met Sartre in the afternoons to read
through his work, and still there was more reading, articles,
books. Nights, in bed, she would reread Nelson's letters,
this one or that, for bittersweet pleasure. She chose them
randomly and read them instead of drinking, which she'd cut
out in order to rise earlier and work harder. The letters gave
her the right amount of melancholy to help her to sleep.

Bost and Jean were flying to Brazil to research for a book,
and Olga hosted a farewell party. Castor asked her to invite
Claude, whom, after all, Bost had brought into the *TM* circle,
and who would be doing more work in Bost's absence. She

spoke to him briefly, asking him how he found working with the various personalities that dominated the magazine, and what he thought of Sartre, really, not just what he thought people – she – wanted to hear about Sartre. She asked him how he'd met Bost. Olga had brought out a good bottle of whisky – one that Nelson had sent last year, smuggled in the bottom of a large package – and Claude swirled his drink in his glass, answering politely and thoughtfully. They spoke for ten minutes or so before Bost engaged her in another topic. She noticed Claude watching her, now and again, when she happened to glance in his direction, and it seemed sweet, to have this young man so attentive.

Her telephone rang the next morning and she was surprised to hear Claude introducing himself and asking if she'd like to go to see a movie. She thought she understood his meaning. I'm going away next week, she told him, and don't really have time. She felt the disappointment in his silence, and said, look, we could meet for a drink the day after tomorrow, after lunch. He agreed, his voice sounding again, more brightly, she thought. They arranged a café – she didn't want simply to meet him in the Flore – and she placed the handset back on the receiver.

She tried to ignore the stack of letters and the framed photograph on the bed stand but even without looking she could see them. She sat down at the desk and stared at the page she'd been writing, one-third filled with her handwriting, and at the stack of completed pages next to it. For at least half an hour she sat, and watched the page blur, and looked out of the window until the Rue de la Bûcherie blurred. She could hear the Arab music and chatter from the café. Claude, this young man, wanted to love her. Nelson Algren had crouched on his knees by the side of the bed in

Wabansia Avenue, Chicago, Illinois and declared he could never offer anything less, and even across the ocean he could offer her nothing less than love, contingent upon not even the ocean. If she were to allow Claude to love her, and if she were to allow herself – another dreadful goodbye to Nelson Algren, that was what she was making right now, sitting at this desk, her back to his photograph, her back to his letters. Holding on to those days of 1947, of 1948, regarding them as a current and living love, would now be impossible. The past would be something to let go of, and Nelson Algren would be someone – love for Nelson Algren would be something to let go of, for ever. They would have only each other's friendship, and the memory of the past.

The second afternoon she met Claude he came back to 11 Rue de la Bûcherie and spent the night. She let him sleep when she awoke and moved to the desk to begin work for the day. When she heard him stir she told him he could use the bed for his own work, if he wished. She didn't want to confuse him, nor was she trying to pretend indifference. Simply, there was work to do. He would need to understand that. In three days she would leave for Italy, and she needed to complete so much work before then. She didn't tell him these things, but he seemed to understand. There is coffee, she said, waving her hand more or less in the direction of the coffee pot. For a couple of hours two scratching pens, as though duelling, formed the only significant sound in the apartment. When Claude left just after midday, she looked up, and smiled, and returned to the page. It seemed close to perfect. She would see him again once more before she left, and when she returned in the autumn they could pursue their affair more properly. Maybe she wasn't quite so old and useless for love as she'd thought.

He met Amanda's train and they stopped in the bar, though she drank a ginger ale while he had his beer. Afterwards he carried both her suitcases home, where the two beds had been pushed together in the back room. Dave hosted a barbecue at his place to welcome Amanda, and Chris and Neal came as well. For the first three days of her visit they spent their time enjoying the peace of doing nothing: leisurely breakfasts after late rising, the obligatory row on the lagoon, a beach picnic or sitting in the sun reading books and watching the waves scuttle up the sand. As they moved into the second half of the first week he returned to work on his essay, and Amanda cooked dinner each evening, steak and mushrooms or pork chops and onions, unless they went to Chris and Neal's, or if the neighbours came over to their house. They made a trip into Chicago to see a ball game, and afterwards a too-expensive meal in the Palmer House before catching the last train back to Indiana.

The letter arrived on Monday. Amanda set it, along with the others, next to his typewriter. He shuffled through, saw the letter from Simone, and decided it could wait along with everything else. They were going for an afternoon swim, and then to Dave's for another barbecue. He only got around to reading it a day or so later. She'd found herself a toy boy and was already acting like it was the love of the century, never mind Nelson Algren, never mind Jean-Paul Sartre. The ambivalences and contradictions of her other letters evaporated here: goodbye to you, Nelson, since you only want friendship. Which wasn't true, either, but at least simple. For her. Maybe for him, too. There was nothing he could do, and no sense in waiting around for a frog wife who would no longer arrive. Good luck, young journalist. I hope you're a better man than I am.

The rest of the morning he sat at the typewriter, half-filled sheet curling over towards the keys. He didn't write anything. Raindrops fell through the leaves and spattered the window intermittently. They'd planned to walk down the beach to Marquette Park. Amanda swept the kitchen and the hallway, and wiped all the countertops. She filled the sink and washed some clothes, both her own and Nelson's, and hung them around the house to dry. Shortly after noon she placed her hand on his neck and rubbed the tiny soft hairs. The typewriter has been quiet this morning, she said to him. Nothing to write, he told her. I doubt it, Nelson. She ruffled his hair. Let's go to the park anyway. We've got umbrellas. I don't want to sit around watching our laundry dry.

Two weeks after he and Neal had driven her to the airport, stopping at the track for a few hours before returning home to Indiana, he wrote to Amanda and asked whether she'd marry him again. Maybe this provided the answer. They both knew better who they were now, and this time they could do things the right way, in their little house in Indiana, a perfect place for a child. When he received her letter saying she would, he took the train to Chicago and packed what few things remained in Wabansia Avenue. Miller would be their home.

When Castor returned, the first thing she did was sift through the accumulated post looking for American stamps and a yellow-papered letter, the first in months. American stamps she found, but not a yellow letter. Nelson still had not written. But Claude was in Paris, and seemed as eager as she to pursue their love. She met him the afternoon following her return, and told him everything about her trip, even though she'd written everything already: every city and village she and Sartre had visited in Italy, from the mountains in the north all the way to the south coast. The way his expressions changed with her inflections coaxed her into telling more and more detail, though she tried to restrain herself from embellishing. After dinner they walked through the darkening streets to Rue de la Bûcherie and once inside the door to her apartment she felt as though she were a woman half her age, though when she'd been half her age she wouldn't have known what to think.

Amanda arrived in early December by plane. She'd sold her car in California and the rest of her belongings would arrive by train in another week. Neal drove Nelson to the airport to meet her. She's visiting again so soon, Neal said as the car crossed into Illinois, but Nelson only stared out the window. The two of them stood by the gate, Nelson holding a bouquet he'd bought outside. There came Amanda, shivering from the walk across the tarmac from plane to terminal, wearing her California short-sleeved dress, her coat folded neatly in the suitcase she carried with two hands. Nelson kissed her on the cheek and handed her the flowers. She tucked them under her arm while she unfastened the suitcase to pull out her coat. You didn't forget Chicago winters, Neal said, and added, How long are you staying, Amanda?

Nelson looked at his shoes; her mouth moved open and slowly closed. Neal didn't get an answer. They drove back to Miller listening to the hum of the tyres on the highway. Once in the house Nelson put her suitcase in the back room and sat down at the typewriter and threaded a page. Nelson, you're not going to work right now? It's an important idea, he said, I've been working solid. True enough, even if not quite. He'd started turning Margo's story into a novel, loosely based. Amanda sat down on the sofa, her hands folded in her lap. Only for an hour or so, he said, but I can't let this get away. Amanda asked whether he'd told Simone they were getting married, since he hadn't told anybody else. I did, he said, and continued punching at the keys. And? And? he repeated without pausing. What did she say? He shrugged, and stopped typing for a second. I haven't heard back. Let me work now.

Early in the new year they were married by a judge in Chicago. Nelson insisted they go to the Tug for a drink first, and had a whisky and a beer while Amanda drank ginger ale. Apart from Barusz there wasn't anybody in there he knew. Margo and Caesar stood witness and afterwards they dined in an expensive French restaurant. Nelson ordered a bottle of decent champagne and they drank three bottles of wine across the course of the dinner as well. Amanda had never met either of the witnesses. Margo responded to her questions with as few words as possible while still remaining polite. Nelson sat mostly silent, worrying the base of his wine glass with his thumb and forefinger and watching Margo's lips as they formed the words she spoke to his new-old wife. The first course made him a little less drunk but by the time they were halfway through the main he'd grown bored of Amanda's curiosity, bored of the steak he was chewing, bored of the wine that the waiter kept pouring into his glass as fast as he could dump it down his neck. Now she was telling Margo how pretty she was, that if she were out in California everybody would be trying to put her in movies. Margo looked at her plate, flattered but bashful, and probably a little too worldly-wise to buy that crap, he thought as he stretched his foot across to stroke her calf. Her eyes flicked up at him briefly and as she put another forkful of steak into her mouth she moved her leg away. Oh, Nelson, look – Amanda was swaying and reaching over: he'd spilled gravy on his tie and she dabbed her napkin into the stain. For fuck's sake, I'm not a child, Amanda. Her hand shot back to her lap and the table became quiet apart from the sound of chewing and cutlery. Nelson watched Margo's hands, wrapped around knife and fork. Caesar rescued the silence with some questions to Amanda he already knew the answers to. Yes, she told him, the lagoon really was lovely, and Lake Michigan just over the dune. Neal and Chris were sweethearts, and their boy was darling.

The waiter returned to clear the plates and Nelson took hold of his elbow. I just got married, he told him, and the waiter uttered a congratulations. My wife worked in the movies, he said, and moved all the way out here to be with me. Can you believe it? The waiter said something noncommittal and moved away with the plates.

Once the dessert wine had been poured out – Nelson drank a cognac – Caesar stood and raised a toast to the newlyweds. He congratulated them on their new start, and told Amanda that the renewal of their relationship and now of their vows had brought Nelson calm and happiness. He wished them many years of love together in their Indiana home. Though the two women watched Caesar as he spoke, and Amanda reached over to her husband to squeeze his hand, Nelson stared at Margo through the whole speech. When it ended he stood and raised his glass towards Caesar, then towards Amanda and thirdly towards Margo. To a long and happy married life, he said. The husband will now kiss the bride and bridesmaids. He leaned over and kissed Amanda; she moved her mouth towards his but he aimed for the cheek and awkwardly caught the corner of her lips. He lightly clipped the corner of the table as he moved to Margo. She shook her head and Caesar said, Nelson, but as Amanda watched he kissed the helpless woman on the mouth, long, and moved back to his seat, his eyes still on her, Margo once again looking down at the space where her plate had been. Already chasing other women, Amanda said with a brave laugh.

Eventually an American-stamped envelope arrived, return address Miller, Indiana, postmarked Gary. She closed her eyes for a moment, her finger wheedling the seal, to imagine the yellow paper that she had only seen in the old reread letters. Sitting at her desk, she finished opening the envelope and read Nelson's news. He'd decided to remarry Amanda. One more small moment in the death of their love. She thought it as a fact, not as pathos, though the sadness of the thought might have pushed her to tears had Claude not been lying on the bed reading the newspapers. Those were not tears she wished yet to explain to her young lover. Oh, but if they were the kinds of friends who met daily for coffee or lunch or dinner, who shared a drink and ideas, not only beautiful letters; if they could share their fondness for one another together. For Nelson to be sitting around a table in the Flore with Bost, with Sartre and Michelle and Claude and Jean. Amanda too of course. A real friendship.

They had pine-scented garbage bags. He must be the only writer in America with garbage bags that smelled like chemical pine trees, but Amanda insisted on them. He chalked one up for California. It seemed like the kind of thing people did out there. He tried to remember if Garfield's house had pine-scented garbage bags. He couldn't drop a banana peel into the trash without getting at least a little irritated.

His writing desk and typewriter now stood by the window in the front room, with a view out to the lagoon. Amanda didn't want to listen to the clacking keys when she sat in the living room, and, even when she wasn't around, she didn't like having the typewriter and stacks of papers and books on the dining table. He preferred the little room anyway. It was cosy, and he could close the door and nothing would disturb him for as long as he wanted. He had two projects: a longer, book-length version of the essay on literature, and the new novel. Slow work, but good. Instead of a five- or seven-day pot of bachelor stew for dinner, each night Amanda made a full meal: steak and potatoes, pork chops and apple sauce, fancier things and casseroles. No, it wasn't all bad. But when the writing was going slowly or not at all he'd look out towards the lagoon and see that chaise-longue, falling apart and piled with snow because he never bothered to bring it in, and he could see Simone stretched along it reading one of those stupid Agatha Christies. Christ, he could still love her if she were here. Not be fond of her and enjoy her companionship like with Amanda, or gawp at her frail beauty and tragic soul like Margo, but love her, flesh and stubborn beautiful mind. But not across the ocean. He couldn't love like that. And now across the ocean was all they had, since he and Amanda couldn't travel to Paris, despite an invitation from Simone to honeymoon there. His passport had been denied: the FBI called him a Communist and person of suspicious behaviour. It'd be funny if he were twenty years or even ten years younger, if he weren't living in a house in Indiana with a wife he shouldn't have remarried and the idea of producing a child, writing letters to the only real wife he'd ever known, and whose arrival, for the first year in six, he wouldn't await, or whose gargoyle neighbourhood he wouldn't see. Instead, there was a broken chaise-longue, piled with melting snow.

In September the rejection came. He saw it coming. After all, he was officially a suspicious person peddling left-wing ideas about literature to a publisher run by reactionaries. They'd sent a kid out to help polish it up – that was their word, polish – and so they spent a week sitting in the living room polishing the thing dull. The editor spent so much time casting glances at the joint in the ashtray that eventually Nelson just decided to light it up in front of him; that was what suspicious persons did. He left with a weary handshake and carefully constructed smile, and a few days after that Nelson got the phone call saying they were dumping his book into the pine-scented garbage. At least they let him keep the advance money. He needed it. More to the point, he didn't have it any more. It had vanished at a poker game in a rich lady's basement a few months ago, along with five hundred bucks he'd borrowed from Dave. Amanda had driven him into Chicago for the game, and he'd come back two days later flat broke. He'd sort of tried to hide it from her, but his perverse pride in fucking up so badly meant that he'd baited her into trying to guess the damage. He added it to the list of arguments she'd forced him into. He'd earned the money, and he could lose it however he wanted.

He locked himself in the little front bedroom every day and worked, or tried to work. Some days he sat at the desk and looked out at the lagoon and played records. Without turning it up too loudly he could drown out the sounds of Amanda doing whatever she did: banging pots and crockery in the kitchen, walking the house like an elephant. Roy Acuff sang 'House of the Rising Sun', the line about the only thing a rounder needs, and, when the song finished, Nelson moved the arm back to the outer edge and watched it glide towards the grooves again. And again. He did this over and over and over some days, closed in the room pretending to work. When he wanted to feel further away from Indiana and closer to

Paris, he would read some of *The Second Sex*, seven hundred pages of translated French. At night, after Amanda had gone to bed, he sometimes called Dave and they'd sit on the sofa watching the late-night fights on television. Month after month dragged on this way. The novel was going nowhere. When he looked out at the lagoon, he knew his life was going nowhere. When he took the train or forced Amanda to drive him into Chicago, and blew what little money he had in the upstairs room at the Tug or the basement of the rich lady – a benefactress of a magazine, who he'd met at a fundraising party and who for some reason let him run poker games in her house – he knew his life was going nowhere.

In the summer he stopped staring at the lagoon and put himself on a flight to Houston without telling Amanda. He wrote her a letter when he got there and told her he'd be away for three weeks. He hitched down to Laredo and across the border and spent two nights in Mexico doing nothing, just sitting at a table in a bar with his portable typewriter for silent company. He took the bus back to Houston and another into Louisiana. The heat and humidity of New Orleans pressed in on him and made him feel like puking all the time. He'd been stupid to think he could recapture the feeling he'd had twenty years ago. Back then he had been too hungry to puke and too young to care; he could roam the streets and markets and watch turtles getting decapitated for soup all day. Now he could only lie on a bed in a crummy motel sipping warm water and watch the occasional roach skitter across the wall or floor. Even when he managed to get outside in the marginally less oppressive evenings, he couldn't find anything of the place he'd known. New Orleans had changed too much, and so, he supposed, had Nelson Algren. The last two days he wrote letters to Amanda, to Margo, to

Max in New York, to Simone in Paris, a city that seemed to drift further and further away.

Through spring and another summer in which she thought of Miller, Indiana without visiting, and the same again through autumn, winter, a new spring, a third summer without the lagoon. In October the novel was published, to acclaim and scandal, but nothing like the uproar four years earlier. The right people liked it and the right people hated it, and in December she received the Prix Goncourt. She'd expected it and yet still it came as a surprise, vindication, and most of all as a pleasure: the best work of her life, the book she'd written with love, for Nelson, had won the prize. But it also felt, now that she had Claude and Nelson was married to Amanda again, that a little more of their love had vanished for ever. If only he were here to share in it; if only he could read it now and know the beautiful thing their love had created.

She could have used his help with the publicity attention, too. More than once over the previous days – when photographers and reporters began to camp out in the café across the Rue de la Bûcherie from number eleven – and following the announcement, when she escaped to the apartment of a friend of a friend, where nobody could find her, Sartre or Bost would mutter, Send for Algren. Even Claude had adopted the motto. Photos of her appeared in the papers, articles and articles, and constant demands on her concierge to let them into her apartment, on Gallimard to force an interview. She gave them all the slip, and felt a little like a spy. After a week or so the hype settled down, but she received letters from well-wishers and old friends, a mountain of mail from every corner of France, though none, as yet, from Chicago. He had no reason to know, but even then it had been months since she'd received one; the last had been a glum announcement that he was a suspicious person and unfit for travel. Once the mayhem of the prize settled, she sat down and wrote to him.

In February he went back out to Hollywood. The bitter irony wasn't lost on either him or Amanda. If only she'd never left the place. If only they hadn't trapped themselves in a little house in the middle of nowhere, if only Nelson could avoid being the depressing asshole he'd become to himself. In California he was getting what he deserved, surrounded by assholes of all stripes, and their chief, Otto Preminger. This guy seemed to think buying some film rights made him an artist, and buying them at the biggest rip-off rate he could made him a better artist. But Nelson needed money. He'd blown most of what he had at poker tables or the track, and it didn't look as though a book advance would be forthcoming soon. Book reviews paid a little, but the inevitable divorce was going to cost him a bunch of pennies, albeit only with himself to blame. These movie assholes would have to pay out. They'd promised a grand a week in the telegram that got him on the train. Now they said seven-fifty and they wouldn't acknowledge the telegram when he waved it under their noses.

A kid from an agency took him around to some studios to see if he could get some other work, too, as long as he was out there, but they didn't drum up anything. It made the kid glum. He'd read *The Man with the Golden Arm* and he wanted to do good by an award-winning author. He was an aspiring writer himself, he told Nelson as they drank manhattans in an uncomfortably swish bar. He wanted to save up some money, he said, enough so he didn't have to work for a while, and could get a boat over to France. He'd live there like Fitzgerald and Hemingway had, and camp out in the cafés until he

257

found Simone de Beauvoir and seduced her. That was his big ambition. Nelson picked up his cocktail and drank to hide his smile. Might get in over your head there, kid, he said. Nah, I'd show her, I'd show her, the kid told him. Yeah, that's what they all think. This kid was okay, the only decent person he'd met out here, as far as he could tell.

The couple of months writing the script and maybe longer working on the film turned into a week, less than a week: he wrote a treatment, Preminger told him he couldn't make it, Nelson told him then Preminger wouldn't make it, and Nelson left town without any money, just further in debt. Hollywood assholes. Preminger made the movie anyway, without permission, without the rights, and now he needed to finish this novel and get some money to hire a lawyer to sue the big chief asshole.

Lawyers. Amanda had hired one and, when the divorce got filed in June, it was only a matter of time before she owned the house by the lagoon and he became homeless. He didn't go back there; he couldn't go back there. Now he found himself in Missoula teaching creative writing classes to enthusiastic and talentless summer school students: eager undergraduates, bored housewives and retired accountants, all of whom were burning to tell their boring autobiographies in a form that made them handsome, smart, and experts in the sack. A recent divorcee stalked him all over the place, never shutting up in the classroom, coming to the entirety of his obligatory office hour, even following him to the bar, where the only escape was a smug and condescending academic who thought Saul Bellow, that overrated show-off, was the future of literature, and didn't care when Nelson told him Saul was the one guy you could count on to hand over his money in every single game of Texas Hold 'Em he ever played. For five weeks he sat on top of a desk for an hour every other day telling these people they showed promise, that they needed to move some commas around, that they ought to read Richard Wright and see that Bigger Thomas was twice the man that wimp Augie March thought he was. Everybody in the room knew he was a fraud, but what could he do? He needed the money.

She moved. They moved; Claude had convinced her to buy an apartment, that the dripping, crumbling, tiny place in 11 Rue de la Bûcherie couldn't hold the two of them, and wouldn't do anyway, now that she had the money for a better place. He'd been living there for almost a year now, working on the bed each morning while she sat at the desk working and looking out on to the little street, the gargoyles, and the Arab men in the café below. Now they hired a man to load all of her things into the back of a truck and drive down the Rue St-Jacques so she could settle into a new number eleven: she and Claude would share a big studio apartment in 11 Rue Victor Schoelcher, with an enormous floor-to-ceiling window that overlooked a skinny tree and the wall, overflowing with ivy, of the Montparnasse cemetery. Without living neighbours opposite the street was quiet, and a breeze blew in from the cemetery to ease the August heat. They both had enough space to work, she at her old table and Claude at the small school desk she bought to help fill the apartment. She hung one of the Guatemalan blankets on the wall, and on the edge of the desk arranged a collection of framed photographs of her family of friends: Olga, Bost, Sartre, Michelle, even one of Boris, and three, in the centre, of Nelson: in Chicago, in Paris, by the lagoon in Indiana. Claude ran his finger across the top of one of the frames. She hadn't included a picture of him; after all, he lived here.

For two months Claude would live there on his own, under the watch of the trio of Nelson Algren photographs, because almost as soon as they'd moved in, she left, with Sartre, for two months of travel in China, and first, a week in Moscow. All this, as the guests of Communist governments. The thought, as they sat in the plane hurtling towards the Soviet Union, made her laugh. Like Nelson, the FBI will call me a suspicious person. She turned her ring one full rotation around her finger. Yes, but it only seemed funny for a moment. The end of another year without travelling across the ocean to the Wabansia nest or the Miller lagoon, another year of only writing and receiving letters, and when Nelson wrote that she had become a kind of ghost to him – well, it made her want to assure him she was real in the only irrefutable way possible. Again she rotated her ring around her finger.

Chapter Fourteen

ANOTHER JUNE, and he flew out to New York. The new novel had just been published, and a theatre production of *The Man with the Golden Arm* was about to hit the stage. He wouldn't get any work done, but for a month he had an apartment in Greenwich Village and the prospect of these New York schmoozers putting their money where their mouths were for a change.

A scrum of reporters and photographers met his flight. The only thing they wanted to know about was Simone de Beauvoir. She's a French writer, he said, and tried to push through. One of them thrust a book towards him: *The Mandarins*. Inside was the dedication to Nelson Algren, and, further in, the character of Lewis Brogan. I'm not a character in a novel, he told them and pushed past to collect his suitcase. The questions pummelled him: how did he and Mademoiselle Beauvoir meet what did he think of Sartre how closely did Lewis Brogan's conversations resemble his own what was his view of *The Second Sex* why hadn't he discussed Mademoiselle Beauvoir before how did her ideas influence his writing how did Sartre's how often did he go to Paris how often did she come to visit him did she show him the novel before it was published?

He escaped into a taxi and watched the gravestones of St Michael's Cemetery as the car drove through Queens towards Manhattan. No, she had not shown him the novel before it was published, but he wouldn't have been able to read it anyway. She'd written about it enough in her letters, though. He looked at the hardcover in his hands. The man on the cover did look quite a bit like him, and that seemed unnecessary. People he knew had read the French version and nobody had said much about it; some asked him to sign it, and he always did: his handwriting, her name, and a joke about him being her ideal man. He traced his fingers across her name on the title page and looked at his own name on the dedication page before flipping through to find out what kind of mirror Lewis Brogan was.

After two days in New York he called Margo from a payphone in a drugstore around the corner from his apartment and told her he felt ill. See a doctor, Nelson, she said. I'm not sure what I'm supposed to do about it. It's not physical, he told her. I'm just ill in my head. It's the regret, the damn regret. I read her book. She's made up all sorts of words that I never said, but the situations – the regret, Margo. I should've done everything in my life different. Nelson, she said, Nelson, don't be that way. Don't be dramatic. Maybe it's her you should call. Tell her, if you regret. He wanted to say more, or listen to her more, but the connection broke.

He had to go to literary parties where everybody treated him like he was Lewis Brogan, some caricature Simone de Beauvoir drew, and not Nelson Algren, a man, a writer with a National Book Award from Eleanor Roosevelt, a sold-out play on Broadway, a lawsuit against the chief of the Hollywood assholes Otto Preminger and a new novel about to hit the shelves. Nobody wanted to talk about his work, and nobody wanted to talk about him; they wanted to talk about Simone de Beauvoir and a fiction called Lewis Brogan. He wished he could escape to a poker game.

He went back to the drugstore to call Simone. He'd told reporters she shouldn't be digging in her own garden if she was a decent novelist, and he wanted to tell her the same thing. He also wanted to tell her to come to Chicago; he wanted to tell her his regret. He wanted her to help him bring his life and his work into order. It took about twenty minutes to even get the operator to understand the call, and another half-hour for her to set up the connections to England, to France, to Paris. He imagined the bundles of cables running below the ocean, sharks and whales and squid swimming above, crabs and lobsters crawling on and underneath. He waited. The operator came back on and told him that the other party had not answered the telephone, but she'd arranged to try again in exactly two hours. He needed to call from the same phone.

He walked around the block several times but it only killed ten minutes so he headed downtown and watched people coming out of the Staten Island ferry terminal. Her voice would echo down the line and he didn't know how hearing it would make him feel. He should've convinced her to live in Chicago. He could've done it. There was nothing in Paris she couldn't have in Chicago. He would've stayed out of these stupid entanglements with Amanda, a disaster he'd seen coming when it was still a speck on the horizon, but allowed to approach as though he were a helpless and drowning swimmer. But no, he couldn't blame Simone. The regret. Now every literate American could look into the one good private thing he'd had, and claim some kind of ownership of it. If he'd held on to it, they wouldn't, and he would still have it. He walked slowly back in the direction of the drugstore, trying to reconstruct Simone's voice in his mind, as some kind of preparation.

Please tell her the call is from Chicago, he told the operator. He'd had to wait an extra five minutes while somebody else jabbered into the phone before he could get his second chance. But sir, you're phoning from New York. I know, he said, but you need to tell her it's from Chicago so she'll know who it is. She might not take it otherwise. The operator sighed and agreed; he could imagine her rolling her eyes in the sound of that sigh. He waited and listened as the connections were attempted and made again, along those cables beneath the ocean. He listened to the operator announcing she had a call from Chicago, and he listened to the unsilent gap before a European operator repeated the words. He heard the faraway Paris ringing. It interrupted and a man's voice said, *Bonjour*. He heard the French operator rattle some information in which he could only pick out the words Mademoiselle Beauvoir and Chicago.

A call from Chicago, Claude said to her, and stretched the handset towards her. Nelson. She looked in the mirror and touched her hair. Five years. Oh, Nelson. Her stomach contracted and she rubbed her hands together in a vain attempt to keep them from shaking so hard. She tried to imagine his voice, and what it would sound like after five years and down a telephone line. Dearest Nelson. She took the phone from Claude and held it to her ear. She took a deep breath. 'Nelson?' she said, 'Hello, Nelson?' Her throat tightened as she listened to a series of echoing clunks down the cables and waited for Nelson's voice. The operator's voice returned: the other party has disconnected, she said. Disconnected, Simone repeated, and felt the corners of her mouth pull hard, and the tears rise. Oh, Nelson, she whispered, and placed the handset back down on the receiver. She looked at the silver ring on her finger and then she began to really cry.

Her voice down the line: no, he realised, he didn't want to hear it. He did want to hear it. He couldn't stand it, though, to hear her voice and not see her face, not touch her body. He wouldn't add further to the regret that pressed down on him.

When he arrived back in Chicago he had no place to go. His tenancy had run out and he didn't have enough money to rent a place. He rode the El to Austin and paid up front for a room of his own in a dormitory for working men. The only sink and toilet were at the opposite end of the hallway. He stayed there for two weeks, trying and failing to write. The landlord was suspicious of him because he didn't go to work. When his two weeks had run out he left and got on the train to Miller Beach. There was no place else to go, and he hoped Amanda would let him live there, at least for a week or two. When she answered the door he could see in her face that he was the last person she wanted to see, but he could also see she'd let him stay. Amanda was too good to let somebody go without a roof, no matter how much he'd berated her, blamed her, no matter how much, they both knew, he still would. She let him have the front room, his desk and a single bed. He was a guest in his own house now. He tried his best to stay out of her way, most of the time, but he let her cook him dinner when she insisted. When she wasn't around he watched baseball or boxing or Mexican bullfights on the television, and sometimes he played cards with Dave and Neal, but always at one of their houses. Every morning he sat down at the typewriter and looked out at the lagoon, but he rarely touched the keys. The most he did was put on the Roy Acuff record and watch the grooves as it played. He stared so hard at the grooves his eyes would water. He stared at the lagoon so hard his eyes would water. He stared at the typewriter keys and his eyes watered. Hell, everything made him cry.

He got so bad at sleeping he didn't bother trying to go to bed any more; once Amanda had turned in he'd just put on the television and watch whatever was on it, or not really watch but look at the television, anyway. He didn't bother getting dressed, either, because he didn't have any place to go to; his grey bathrobe and slippers were enough.

At the end of August Margo came out to visit, and he managed to sleep a little, now on the sofa so she could have the front room. They walked along the beach and over the dunes, and he took some photos. It felt a little bit like old times, and he felt almost happy, but after a few days she left to go back to Chicago and he stopped getting dressed again. When he wasn't listening to Roy Acuff telling mothers to tell their babies not to do what he had done, Nelson walked laps of the house, from his little room to the kitchen, tracing his fingers along the counter, to the table, the living room, around the sofa and the chair, down the hallway to the bathroom, where he'd lift and reset the toilet seat, past Amanda's door and back to the little room. He'd sit down for a moment and get up and pace the lap again, the open backs of his slippers slapping gently against his heels.

Amanda knocked on the door. 'The House of the Rising Sun' spun on the turntable, but he hadn't dropped the needle. Neal's here, she said; he wants to talk to you. Neal opened the door. Nelson looked at his friend, standing above him, and he looked back to the silent and spinning record. I haven't slept in days, Nelson said. I can't do anything. Why don't you go to the hospital, Neal said, and get some pills, get some rest? It'll do good for your work, Neal said. I just need money, Nelson said, I haven't got any money. If I get some money I can work, I can go to Paris, I can buy this house back. Loan me some money so I can put it on a sure thing and come up a winner again. Neal put his hand on Nelson's shoulder. Why don't you get dressed, buddy, and we'll go to the hospital. You can get money later. You need to rest. Nelson looked from the hand to his friend's smiling face. I just need a bit of money, Neal, and a little luck. You need to rest, Nelson, you need to sleep. Neal tugged gently under his arm. Come on, get dressed, how about it?

Nelson stood and walked a small circle around the room. Amanda stood behind Neal in the doorway. He picked up a pair of grey wool pants that were draped over the chair and sat back down on the bed. He pulled one leg on and stood abruptly and walked another lap of the room, sat down again and pulled on the other leg. He stood and hitched the pants over his waist and did up the flies. He sat down. I just need a little luck, he said. Some money and some luck. He stood and walked around the room. He found an undershirt and put it on, sat down, stood up, walked another lap and picked a checked shirt from a hanger. He put his left arm through the sleeve and stood up again. He stopped his lap at the window and looked out to the lagoon. Some luck, he said, I just need some luck. He felt the sting in his eyes. Some luck, Neal. He pulled the other sleeve over his right arm and completed the circuit of the room. Seated on the bed, he began to button the shirt, but when he got to the top he'd misbuttoned and one side of the collar was higher than the other. I can't even button a goddamn shirt! he yelled. Neal and Amanda jumped. He undid all the buttons, quickly, and started to rebutton his shirt, slowly, one button every half-minute or so. It took several more minutes to pull on his socks and shoes. Each move required a lap of his small room, sometimes a pause at the window. The entire dressing had taken more than forty minutes.

Half an hour later Dave arrived in his car. Nelson had spent the intervening time pacing laps of the entire house: a lap around his room, then kitchen, living room, hallway to the bathroom and back down to his own room. Neal took him by the elbow, as though he were an old man, and helped guide him into the front seat of Dave's car. Before he closed the door he squeezed Nelson's shoulder. You're going to be okay, buddy, he told him. Amanda got in the back seat and Dave drove down the road, towards Highway Twelve and the two hours to the psychiatric hospital on the North Side of Chicago. Nelson played with the radio knob, choosing one station, then another. Finally he settled on WBEZ and his old friend Studs's show. He could trick himself he was going to visit Studs. He didn't want to go to the hospital. He didn't want to be a loony in the loony bin. They'd only gotten as far as the Gary airport when he told Dave to stop and turn around. I can't do it, he said, I don't want to be in the hospital. I don't want to do it. I can't do it. Dave made a U-turn and started back, but he said to Nelson that it might be worth going at least to see the place. He didn't have to go in if he didn't want to, but they could at least drive up there and have a look. Nelson relented and Dave pulled another U-turn and they headed back towards Chicago.

The reception area looked like a hotel lobby, but with tiled floors. A large wooden desk stood at the end of the room, directly opposite the entrance, and twin doors stood either side of the desk. A nurse who wasn't dressed like a nurse sat behind the desk and smiled as Nelson walked in, closely trailed by Dave and Amanda. He stopped at the desk and placed his hands on the edge of it. The nurse continued to smile. I'd like to check myself in, Nelson said. Very good, sir. Please fill in your address and sign your name at the bottom. He wrote down his – Amanda's – address, slowly, in block capital letters, and set the pen down. Please sign at the bottom, sir, the nurse said. Nelson turned to Dave and Amanda. They smiled back at him, both with the same pitying smile, fragile on their faces. He couldn't blame them. He turned back to the sign-in book and made the vertical line of the N and set the pen back down. The nurse, patient, continued to smile. He picked the pen up and made a connecting V to complete the N, set the pen down again and turned around. I can't, I can't, I can't, he said, and walked between Amanda and Dave and towards the door. They remained still. At the door he stopped and looked back. Okay, okay, he said, and walked back to the desk and made the loop of the *e* and set the pen back down. He bit into his bottom lip painfully as he made the taller loop for the *l*. When he completed it he put his face in his hands, elbows resting on the desk. Amanda massaged the place where his neck and shoulder met. Half a minute passed and he picked up the pen once more to make the *s*, followed several seconds later by the *o*. When he'd completed the rounded curves of the *n* he put the pen down and walked back to the door. I can't do it, he said. Dave, just give me some money and I'll make good, he said across the lobby. He walked around the edges of the room and back to the desk. *Nelson*, he'd written. He picked up the pen and made one slant of an *A* and set the pen back down. He made the second slant and the line across. He made the tall loop of the *l* again. To make *g* took three or four minutes. Adding the *r-e-n* took another ten. His whole name had taken more than twenty.

Two orderlies appeared, large men in white, and each took hold of an arm. No! he yelled, and looked back at

Dave, trying somehow to plead for help. Amanda had sat down in a chair by the wall. They dragged him through the door, too strong for him, even though he kicked and tried to squirm free. Their fingers dug hard into his arm – there'd be bruises. No, goddammit, no! Dave! Drive me back! The door slammed shut and they manhandled him down a yellow-lit corridor. He was still yelling for Dave, for goddammit, for no, for anything. They were saying things, but he didn't know what, over the sound of his own voice, over the sound of his own despair. They put him in a room and locked the door behind him. It felt worse than when he'd been in jail twenty years earlier. He'd always known he'd get out of jail.

The hospital did nothing for him. He tried and failed to sleep. They wouldn't give him any medication because his doctor was away someplace and they couldn't do anything without his doctor's say-so. Not even a goddamn sleeping pill, when all he needed to do was sleep, just to sleep. The other inmates he avoided; he couldn't stand the mirror of his own looniness in their faces and dejected shuffles. He was too exhausted to read, and didn't have any books anyway.

After a few days he'd had enough. At the end of the hallway, only two doors down from his own room, a window led to the fire escape. The window was locked, he knew that much, but he could break it, or at least he could try. Late one afternoon when nobody else roamed the corridor, no orderlies, no nurses, none of the other losers trapped in here with him, he sauntered to the window to see what he could do. He placed both hands at the base and gave it a hard push. He yanked up on the handles as hard as he could. He stood on the sill and kicked at the latch with his heel. On the third kick, it jumped loose. He pulled up the window and climbed out on to the fire escape. His floor was only two storeys up and it was easy enough to clamber down to the bottom, then drop into the alley.

He couldn't go back to Indiana. They'd look for him there, or Amanda and Dave and Neal would try to persuade him to go back. He couldn't go to Margo, not like this. Paris – Paris was so far away. He walked to Jane's place. He'd known her for years. She'd written a novel about this kind of thing. She'd let him stay for a night. She could talk to him. She could listen to him.

She did let him stay, and she did listen, and she did talk to him, but he couldn't stay with her indefinitely, and after a few days he took the train back to Indiana and knocked on Amanda's door. She let him in, and told him she was relieved to see him. She'd been to the hospital to visit and they told her he'd run away. She'd thought he might have died. He could see the tears building in her eyes, so, before she cried them, he went into his room. A new letter from Paris lay on his desk, but he didn't read it. Later Amanda cooked him dinner. They didn't talk about the hospital. Dave stopped by the next day, and they talked about boxing. He tried his best, over the next few weeks, to do some work, to act normal, to keep out of Amanda's way. It didn't work. He yelled at her at least twice a day for walking too loudly, for asking if he wanted something to eat. She found another place to live and told him he could stay in her house. In her house that used to be his. Now he lived alone in it.

A respite from keeping his own company arrived in November when he got asked to be a guest on Irv Kupcinet's television show. He didn't like television much, and he didn't like Irv much, either, but the attention was nice, the fact that somebody wanted to talk to him publicly, the recognition that

Nelson Algren was still a writer – it made him feel less like an escaped mental patient. He took the train up to Chicago the day before and stayed at Margo's place, sleeping on her sofa, though she offered to let him share the bed. In the early afternoon, before the show, they walked along the cold grey lakefront. He wanted to tell her that she made him less depressed but they walked without talking very much, only occasionally pointing out something, a bird wheeling above the waves, an empty paper bag pushed by the wind along the hardened sand.

Caesar and Margo both accompanied him to the studio. They hailed a cab outside Caesar's building. Nelson sat between them in the back seat. As the taxi turned off Division on to LaSalle, he squeezed Margo's knee. Thanks for letting me stay, he said, and for the walk on the lakefront. She touched his hand briefly and smiled. It's no problem, Nelson. He took hold of her hand. We should get married, he said. She laughed, but he was serious. Marry me, he said. Margo's laughing smile quivered into a frown. Nelson, she said. You can't. I'm serious, he said. She pulled her hand out of his and looked out the window. Please stop the car here, she told the driver. They were at the corner of LaSalle and Chicago. She opened the door and got out. Nelson, she said, and he looked at her. She was crying. Nelson, she repeated, and closed the door. He watched her walk away in the direction of the El. Caesar told the driver to continue and the car pulled back into the traffic and around the corner.

It was the last time Nelson would ever see Margo, though she phoned him once more, in December. She was getting married, she told him, to a good man with a good job. Would Nelson come up to Chicago and meet him? They could have lunch or go for a drink. No, he said. Nelson, it would mean a lot to me, she told him, for you to meet him. He knows all you've done for me. He knows what you mean to me. No, Nelson said again, and added, he'll get by on you telling him whatever I meant to you. Nelson hung up the phone.

A few days later a letter arrived from Simone. He put the envelope on his desk, next to the one that had arrived a couple of months ago, also unopened. He didn't want to read about Sartre this and Bost that and the young man blah blah, a very serious discussion at Les Temps Modernes over whether crossing tees or dotting eyes was a bourgeois affectation. Instead of reading her letters, he wrote her one. Margo was gone for good. He'd driven Amanda away enough times. Simone remained, across the ocean, but nonetheless: Simone.

In the morning on New Year's Eve he walked to the grocery store to buy some drinks and food to take to the party he was going to later. A thin layer of snow, enough to cover the grass but not much more, covered the ground. The temperature had been hanging around the low twenties for days. If he cut across the lagoon instead of looping around on the road he could shorten the walk by ten minutes or so. Neal had told his kids not to play on it, but that was because they were kids. The ice must be thick enough by now. He walked straight across the middle. When he stepped on to the shore again he shrugged and said aloud, No big deal. He bought a bottle of whisky and some cheese and bread and cold cuts and a jar of olives and headed back by the same route, stepping on to the ice carefully, but with the confidence that he'd crossed it once already.

The moment when his foot pushed through the ice a brief and euphoric incomprehension fluttered across his mind, but horror submerged it as the cold water clutched his waist and chest. He screamed; he shrieked, high-pitched and wordlessly, just vowels flashing across the lagoon. He reached across the ice but it broke off in his hands. The burning cold became numbness and still he shrieked. A couple of men in hard-hats appeared and threw him a rope, but when they pulled it slipped through his numb hands. Finally he managed to wrap it around his waist and tie a good enough knot, and slowly they pulled him across the ice as it cracked beneath him. He shuddered uncontrollably with the cold and his mouth felt too numb to talk properly but he conveyed to the men where he lived and they took him inside and ran hot water into the bath and helped him climb into it. Is there a neighbour we can call, or a friend? they asked him. Nelson sat shivering and naked in the bath. Neal and Dave were both nearby. Amanda, even, wasn't far away. They'd ask him, though. They might accuse him. No, he said. I don't know the neighbours. I could call somebody in Chicago. He thanked them, and wished them a happy new year. Make sure you keep this water hot, they told him before they left. The numbness in his fingers and toes had disappeared, and was creeping away from his limbs. His skin had turned red from the heat of the water. He'd just broken through the ice, that was all. It was an accident. He drained some of the water and added more from the hot tap. He hadn't actually tried. They couldn't hold that on him. He hadn't meant to do it. When he'd been in the bath long enough for his body to return to pink and normal heat he dried and dressed himself, and threw the soaking clothes in a pile in the snow outside the door. It wasn't on purpose.

Soon she would turn fifty. My God, she'd felt old enough at forty, and never really considered for a serious moment that fifty would arrive. Here she was nonetheless. Sartre had already passed the mark. Claude wouldn't arrive here for years. Nelson would meet her at it shortly, though they might not ever actually meet again, it seemed. She looked at herself in the mirror and smoothed her hands down her sides to her hips. She turned the silver ring a single rotation on her finger. It was a fifty years she could take pride in, or at least satisfaction. From her childhood through her studies and until now, it was a life she had moulded for herself, a life that she and Sartre had moulded for themselves – and for others. Sartre. Most evenings she spent together with him, discussing and polishing drafts of their work while they drank vodka or whisky, until finally the energy for work had been spent and she would place the needle on to a record and they'd listen to music, classical or jazz, depending on their mood, sipping the final drinks of the night. Claude didn't spend his nights in Rue Schoelcher very often any more. Sartre spent a lot more time speaking at political meetings, something she found herself having less and less patience for, though she didn't take up the subject with him, and still supported him at many of them. She began to think about what she could create for her next big project; the essay on women had consumed her for several years, as had the novel, and to live another large project through seemed the perfect idea – but without, it seemed, an idea. Nothing pressed her, nothing urged itself upon her the way the 'women question' had, the way the need to shape the experiences following the war and the emotions of her life with Nelson into a coherent story had. France and its reactionary politics consumed Sartre, but not her – let her help him and leave the main work alone. Her own life remained her only focus, but that was hardly a project for writing. Though it could be: to reflect, and to shape and reconsider the events and ideas of her life from the vantage point of fifty years would breathe new meaning into her life, would help her to understand her own development, and perhaps, yes, as with her other work, in looking at herself she could lead others to examine their own lives. She touched the ring again. She could make it a worthwhile project.

Part Four

March 1960–September 1960

Chapter Fifteen

FINALLY HE WAS ON a boat across the ocean to Europe. Somehow the lawyer had gotten some documents pulled, or some statements interpreted favourably, or anyway: whatever the FBI had on Nelson Algren, the lawyer managed to get it to look okay enough for them to let him go be a suspicious character in foreign lands, and the passport had come through. Simone's young buck had left her, or they'd had an ideological difference, or something like that. Nelson had written and asked if he could visit for a couple of months, whenever it suited her. A last gamble: Paris, Simone; maybe he could still come up a winner in France, even if only for a short time. At least it would be better than sitting around in Chicago as the biggest loser in American letters. In a couple of weeks they'd dock in Southampton and he'd take the train up to London for a few days, then a train and boat across to Ireland. Back to London for a few days and finally – yes, finally – to Paris. For eight years the city had shimmered just outside his vision, flickering only in his imagination. Not that he had any idea what he wanted from Paris, other than Simone. A place that wasn't the United States, where lawyers demanded fees, film producers sold everybody out, governments denied freedom to travel or think. But most of all: Simone. The anguish of their separation would vanish when they found themselves together; it always did. They would reconnect the disparate pieces of their love, the pieces of paper sent across this same ocean on which he now floated, and rebuild that whole thing that existed only when they lived, no matter how briefly, together. It could save him.

He arrived in Paris on the tenth of March, on a train from Calais into Gare du Nord, a different station from his arrival of 1949. That long ago. This time he knew she wouldn't be there to meet him. For ten days he'd be on his own until she got back to the city. Paris remained Paris, but he sensed a gap, a space the size of a little Frenchwoman that nothing and nobody else could fill; the city would not be the same until she returned. But here came Bost, waving like an idiot with his hand as high in the air as it would go, yelling, Algren, Algren, over and over, Hey, Algren! The two men clasped hands and pounded each other's backs. I'll show you to her place, Bost told him, and you can put down your bags and then we'll go drinking, yes? Yes.

France, Paris, home: where Nelson awaited her arrival. God, she'd become old in the last eight years, and she'd arrive puffy and tired from the transatlantic flight; what would he possibly think? Eight years was such a long time, especially when one passes through her forties. He'd imagine the already old but at least younger woman he'd fallen in love with in 1947, some ideal picture, and when they met, finally, he could only be disappointed, would only be disappointed. He wouldn't want his frog wife. She was crossing the same ocean as he'd crossed, nonetheless – the same ocean he'd crossed to see her.

She knocked on her own door and took a deep breath as she waited. She heard his shuffling footsteps and set down her suitcase so she'd be ready; ready for what?

He smashed his shin against the coffee table. Dammit. Unless something stood in front of his face he couldn't see it. He wished he'd brought his glasses to Europe, but there they sat on his writing desk in Chicago. The contact lenses were hard and hurt too much, so he'd given up wearing them. Now he'd have a bruised shin for his stupidity. He limped to the door. There'd only been one knock so it must be Bost, who knew he'd be in; but it was too early for Bost.

The door swung open and his face appeared, handsome as her memory and squinting into the dark corridor. She stood with her arms at her sides, her hands shaking right to her fingertips. Was she waiting to be invited into her own home? Her throat felt too dry to ask, tongue too big in her mouth. Nelson. He gripped the door frame and squinted in silence.

'Nelson?' she said in a hoarse whisper.

'Wee?' he said, still squinting.

'Nelson!' she exclaimed.

His eyes opened round in recognition and she pressed herself against him, her arms gripping his as they wrapped around her.

'You're blind,' she said, laughing, and kissed him.

'My contact lenses hurt my eyes.'

'Oh, poor and blind Chicago husband.'

He picked up her cases from the corridor and followed her inside.

'You've been comfortable?' she asked.

'Yes. I miss the Arabs and gargoyles of the slaughterhouse, though.'

'We'll walk up there while you're here.' She looked at herself in the mirror. Puffy. Grey around the eyes. She touched her hair. 'I must look awful to you.'

'Never,' he said, and, watching her pat her unmessed hair into the same shape, he noticed the silver ring on her finger.

For the first handful of days, though they shared the bed, they moved carefully around each other; the memory of their last parting wasn't fresh, but its marks were indelible. They regarded one another delicately, as though it were 1947 once more, and two infatuated strangers needed to guard themselves against their own feelings and the unknown onward path; though now that path stretched thirteen years into the past as well. Each morning Nelson rose first and made breakfast, squeezing oranges, boiling coffee and running down to the bakery; the necessity of his first week alone in her apartment had improved his French as far as *'une baguette et deux croissants, s'il vous plaît'*, though not much beyond that. After breakfast they set to work, Simone at her large writing desk, Nelson with his portable typewriter set up on the school desk. In the afternoons they took walks – around the cemetery, along the Seine, or across it to Les Halles – and usually ended up in a café for a drink or three. The patterns helped, and they settled into their old, pleasant way of being with one another.

The Cuba trip had invigorated both Sartre and her and now they'd devised a plan for a series of articles for *France-Soir*. It was too much work for one person, and even for two, so each afternoon Sartre and Claude arrived at Rue Schoelcher to discuss, to write, to edit. For her it seemed the perfect arrangement: mornings after breakfast she and Nelson could work, he at the little school desk clacking his typewriter, she at her large writing table looking over the cemetery wall. In the afternoons Nelson continued at the typewriter while the trio huddled over their sheaves of notes and photographs, mapping out the best lines of argument, dividing the work, developing the theories.

Whatever kind of domestic routine they'd managed to develop got shattered once Sartre and Claude started coming over all the time, as far as Nelson was concerned. He got it, he got it: she needed to work, and her work was important, and, not just to me, Nelson, not just to Sartre, but to many people, to France. The damnedest thing was that, when she said that, he couldn't dismiss it as an idle boast: nobody laughed at her in the streets the way they had in 1949. Her enemies scorned her, but they didn't mock, they couldn't mock her, because she was too important, she was right: her work mattered. But goddammit, he'd floated all the way across the ocean on a boat to see her, to live with her, and some of this important work could wait, or she could give him some more of her time. Often the three of them huddled around the table until well into the night, and then it was, Let's stay in, Nelson, and listen to some records; we've been working all day and I'm very tired.

He knew she included him in that we, but he wasn't working much at all. Oh, he pounded the typewriter for hours, but mostly he wrote letters, full-of-crap letters to Studs, to Amanda, to Dave and Neal and Malcolm, to Janet and various others. He didn't have anything to say, and he knew it. When they read his letters they must've known it, too. When he grew sick of his own stupid words, he read. He made sure to go and get himself an orange or an apple, or fill a water glass from the sink every so often, just to remind the trio he was there, to remind Simone she was neglecting him. He'd walk in and listen to them blah blah blah, Castor, blah blah blah, *oui, Sartre, mais* blah blah blah, and interrupt to ask something inane. He resented himself for it at least as much as it annoyed the three of them.

After a week she moved her afternoon work to Sartre's. Nelson was too much of a distraction – too much of a child, to put it more honestly. He demanded attention when he got bored, jealous of Sartre and Claude. She'd told him half a dozen times already that it was work, and it was necessary, but he persisted with his regular interruptions, so she suggested that they move their afternoon sessions out of the Rue Schoelcher. Each day at noon she kissed Nelson goodbye, and returned at six, or seven, or eight, or nine, or sometimes arranged a time to meet him somewhere for dinner.

He sat at his typewriter for entire afternoons, writing nothing. He walked laps of the apartment, and laps of the cemetery opposite. Sometimes he walked up to the Luxembourg gardens but it remained too early for spring to have pushed full leaves or buds on to the trees, and the fountains were still boarded up against the winter. He would've liked to watch the children pushing canvas-sailed boats around the pools, or to have prodded one around himself. Instead he would sit on a bench until he got too cold, or wander back to Rue Schoelcher and hope Bost might swing by for lack of something better to do.

Simone would return, and sometimes it was better; they'd drink whisky together and listen to jazz and she'd listen to him talk about everything going wrong in America; she really listened, and the pleasure of that also reminded him of what he lacked so badly at home. She would listen to this sad man that her Chicago husband had become, and realised that only love made his complaints tolerable. The crocodile of thirteen years ago, who charged around the worst parts of Chicago and who ate chicken bones to impress her – this man had not vanished, but he'd shrunk so small inside the Nelson Algren-shaped body that he'd become difficult to find and release. He thought so little of himself that he couldn't reach high enough to let others help him; to let even his frog wife, his Simone,

284

help him. Though sometimes he grew big enough, forgot his misery, and forgot to tell her about it, and they had fun: they walked up to Rue de la Bûcherie and he posed outside number 11 while she photographed him, and they persuaded one of the Arabs in the café to stop playing backgammon long enough to snap one of them both. She took him out in her beloved car, and they drove all over Paris, Nelson leaning out the window with a small movie camera, filming passers-by, tourists, prostitutes who gestured and swore at him. Some evenings, after a Saturday or Sunday spent together, or even just after a normal day, they rediscovered the passion they'd often shared so many years ago, and removed each other's clothes and made love in her bed.

He arrived back at Rue Schoelcher after an afternoon in the cinema watching a film about a thug who wanted to be Bogart and an American girl who didn't know what she wanted. He didn't understand a word of it, but the images were good, and told the story. He liked it, even if it seemed to want obsessively to be American in some strange kind of way. Nelson nodded to the concierge as he came through the door, and sauntered down to Simone's door. The footsteps of people coming down the stairs reverberated above him and he heard voices, women, speaking English. He pulled the key back out from the hole and waited for them to descend.

They were both attractive, one a little taller, and also a little older, about his age, probably, and the shorter one maybe in her late thirties. Hello, he said, and they smiled as they passed. You're Americans too? he asked, and they stopped. Yes, the older one said, a smile spreading across her face, and she added, Do you live in the building, too? I'm staying for a few months, he told them, here, and he patted Simone's door. The women inched closer. You're staying with

Simone de – with Mademoiselle Beauvoir? The two faces now beamed with both awe and curiosity, their eyes widening. Yes, I am, he said, and extended his hand to introduce himself. Nelson Algren. The older woman took his hand and glanced briefly at her companion. Nelson Algren the writer? she said. He replied that he was indeed, and felt the tiny swell of pride, and hated himself for it as much as he enjoyed it. The younger woman put her hand on his arm. You'll have to meet Jim, she said, and the other woman added, My husband, Jim – he's a writer, too. Oh, you must come up for a drink this evening. Number three – *numéro trois* – she giggled. We're on our way out just now, but do drop by, say around seven? He said he would. And do bring Mademoiselle Beauvoir if you wish. It took no imagination to predict the gossip that began the moment the door to the street closed behind them.

The Americans were okay. Jim turned out to be a writer Nelson had read but didn't think much of. They were friendly enough people, not bitchy or backstabbing from what he could tell – they didn't gossip about people. The few hours he spent in their apartment that evening passed pleasantly enough. They talked about literature for a while, and about home – they always called the US home, even when they were disparaging it – and they talked about Paris, and of course they wanted him to talk about Simone, who hadn't come, because he hadn't invited her, and Sartre. He found ways of telling them what they thought they wanted to hear without actually telling them anything – without giving away any of his and Simone's privacy, let alone that of Sartre.

He returned to Simone's apartment around ten or ten-thirty but she still wasn't home so he poured a whisky and put on a Miles Davis record. He flipped through some of the French magazines that were lying around, mostly to see if there were photos of beautiful women, and he studied the Spring Training box scores in the *Herald Tribune*. When she finally arrived home he'd replaced Miles Davis with Dave Brubeck, even though he didn't like it, and the second whisky stood half-drunk on the table.

'You're home,' he said when she came through the door.

'Yes,' she said, 'finally. We worked very hard.'

'I met the neighbours.'

'Who are they?'

'Americans, so at least I could understand what they were saying.'

'Are they interesting people?' She poured herself a whisky and sat in the chair opposite Nelson.

He shrugged. 'Not really. But it's better than talking to myself all the time.'

'Nelson.' His unmistakable accusation stung her. She picked up the whisky glass and set it back down without drinking. 'We have important work to do, and deadlines. I can't leave it all to Sartre. It's not fair.'

'Yeah, it's not fair. Eight years.' He pressed the heels of his hands against his eyes. 'I'd think I'd merit more than a spare hour here, or a late-night drink there.'

'Nelson, I cannot put all of our work on hold for you. If I could, perhaps I would, but it simply doesn't work like that.'

'Perhaps.' The record finished the side so he stood and flipped it over. He'd accidentally put the B-side on first, so now the hectic 'Blue Rondo à la Turk' belted forth from the speakers. 'Perhaps,' he repeated over the music. 'Or perhaps you'd find some other excuse.'

She set herself against letting him make her cry. 'You are being unreasonable, Nelson.'

'I am not!' he exclaimed, and once again he picked up his whisky and set it back down. 'I am being lonely. I am being bored. I am being miserable in the only place on the whole of the goddamn planet where I can think I might find the hope of being happy, with the one person in whom I can find the love I need to continue. I am – ' He picked up the whisky and drank one large and swift mouthful. He didn't know what else to say.

Neither spoke for some time. He didn't expect her to reply; he didn't even know what he'd say to himself. The slow build of Joe Morello's drum solo – kicks spaced far apart, snare, cymbal – filled the room.

'I am trying,' she said eventually. 'It is not easy, Nelson, for me, either, even if it appears so. And I do care about you, and I do love you – ' She cut herself off before she said 'but'; she didn't know what might follow that word. 'Tomorrow,' she said, 'I'll try to get away earlier and we'll go to eat steak, and drink a nice wine. We'll have the whole evening and night for ourselves.'

She knocked on the door at nine the next night. He hadn't eaten lunch and felt light-headed with hunger. Why she knocked instead of coming in he didn't know. Maybe she'd decided to make a game of it. Maybe she didn't want to dig around in her bag to find her keys. He got up to open the door.

Two sheepish kids stood there. They were probably in their late twenties. Monsieur Algren? the boy asked. We've come on behalf of – Castor sent us, the girl told him. She apologises. We'll take you out for dinner. *Je suis* – I am Florence, and this is Serge. We work for the magazine. He shook their hands. All right, he said, but let's skip dinner and just go for drinks.

They took him to a bar where the average age fell short of his by ten or fifteen years, but so what? He was out on the town, he'd have fun with the kids, whatever Simone might be doing. He ordered a beer and a whisky, knocked them back and ordered another round. Florence and Serge each sipped their beers. They'd turned down the whisky. Serge asked whether he didn't want to go eat somewhere, either after this round or later. Nah, Nelson said, no need. Florence said that Castor had told them Monsieur Algren had wanted to go for a steak. She'd given them the money to pay for it. What Simone de Beauvoir thinks Monsieur Algren wants, Nelson told them, and what Monsieur Algren actually wants, are not necessarily the same thing. He waved at the waiter for another round. His empty stomach meant he felt pretty drunk already but he didn't give a crap. You keep her money, he told Florence and Serge, the drinks are on me tonight. Now finish up before the next round comes. This is how we do it in Chicago.

The two young people shared a look, and Serge shrugged and finished his beer; Florence quickly followed suit. You don't call her Castor, Florence said. Everybody else does. I thought you were close friends, no? Castor is everyone else's name for her, Nelson said. I haven't called her Beaver once in thirteen years, and I'm not going to start now.

Florence and Serge provided good company. They drank several rounds before moving to a different bar, Nelson already staggering, though staying upright as he followed them down a boulevard, into a small back street and down into a basement club with live jazz. They asked him questions about Chicago, and they asked him questions about literature – they'd read the things Bost and Sartre had translated for *Les Temps Modernes*. They asked him about American politics and what he thought about the elections coming later in the year. They drank one round for every two Nelson put away. When the night ended they put him in a taxi and accompanied him to the door, keeping an eye on him as he dug around in his pockets, one hand propping himself against the wall, trying to find the keys. They didn't come inside, but only left once he'd gotten the door open, found the way through, banging against the frame as he went, and shut it all too loudly behind him.

The next night he went out drinking with Bost, and the night after that he met up with the Americans from upstairs and some of their friends, all of them Americans as well. He realised this second time that the only thing these Americans did was visit with other Americans. They lived in a noplace, neither Paris nor America: they complained about the United States, they gossiped about people they knew there and events they'd heard of, and they ran it down like good Frenchmen or expatriates should, but they knew nothing of Paris, except where the other Americans lived. None of them spoke much French, none of them had any actual friends who were French; the closest they had to that were waiters they knew by name and who sneered at them when they placed drinks and food in front of them in the Deux Magots or Brasserie Lipp or the Closerie des Lilas, places they went to in order to talk almost incessantly about the fact that Hemingway ate and drank there. They did nothing in the first person; they were third-person people drifting through third-person lives while insisting they'd discovered a smarter way of living than anybody else. They were shits, and spending time with them made him feel like a shit too, or, even worse: made him an actual shit, a third-person shit.

Their patterns of life continued: in the morning Nelson awoke in a hungover and dark mood but made breakfast, going first to the bakery to buy a baguette or croissants, and squeezing oranges for juice. After breakfast and small talk Simone settled to her work at her desk while Nelson pretended to work at the school desk, banging out letters in which he made things up or complained about the Americans, the French, his life, to various people back home. Afternoons she left for Sartre's to work and Nelson counted the hours until she might return, or until he could find Serge and Florence or Bost and Olga and their friends Monique and Juan and go drinking. Some evenings Simone arrived home early enough that they ate dinner together and listened to records, or went out with the group that now constituted her family, as she called it. Rarely did he see Sartre, whom Simone kept away from the socialising for the sake of his health. Nelson would've liked to box with him, or sit around telling jokes that one or the other only half-understood, and he took it personally, felt snubbed by the little man.

She didn't know what to do about Nelson. She felt sorry for him. He didn't seem to be accomplishing much, and the happiness she could bring him seemed minimal. When she'd visited Indiana and he'd worked at his typewriter all day, even when she didn't want to work she could amuse herself by the lagoon or over the dune on the lake. Nelson couldn't seem to find contentment in Paris. Even the Americans he'd found annoyed him more than anything – though this didn't surprise her. He understood, or said he understood, that she needed to work. And she did need to work: she fielded requests for interviews, wrote articles and prefaces for various women's groups, pamphlets and causes, and spoke at meetings. She found herself in the position of not being able to – and not wanting to – turn down these requests, mainly from young women who had read *The Second Sex* and were organising themselves; she needed to continue, for herself, and for them, for the wider causes, much in the same way she needed to continue Sartre's work for him, for her, for them, and for the broader circumstances.

But when she arrived home each evening or night she would find Nelson sitting next to the record player, listening to jazz or blues records, working through a bottle of whisky or wine. It pained her to see him so miserable, and it pained her to feel so sorry for him – never had their relationship based itself on pity. Where in previous times of difficulty – with Hollywood, with Amanda, with publishers – her responses and advice had arisen from a real sympathy, she now felt a distance – no matter that it was small, it was also real – between his melancholy and her attitude. Feeling sorry for him hurt them both.

Late on a Saturday afternoon Nelson and Simone walked together up Boulevard Raspail and over to the Jardin du Luxembourg, where after walking past the queens and saints Nelson insisted on sailing a boat in the fountain. The boards had been removed and children scampered everywhere, following and pushing the canvas-sailed boats. One boat turned a listless circle at the base of the fountain, caught in a waterfall eddy.

'That's for children,' Simone said.

He put his hands in his pockets to find some coins. 'Then I'm a child.'

'Yes, you are.' Simone laughed.

He examined the coins in his palm. 'I have enough for you to be a child, too,' he said.

Simone put her hand on his shoulder and shook her head. 'You go ahead, little boy.'

She sat on a bench and watched him push the boat with a stick, towering over the kids who scurried around him.

Every few minutes he'd turn around to wave at her, peering over the glasses that she'd insisted he buy a month ago, a few days into his stay. She waved back each time, and blew him kisses. After half an hour he turned in his boat and they left the park via Boulevard St-Michel, making a detour past Rue de la Bûcherie before crossing the Ile de la Cité and walking up to Les Halles, where they dined in a restaurant known for its steaks.

'I have a proposal for you,' Simone said partway through the meal, wiping her mouth with the corner of the napkin as she spoke. 'An opportunity.'

Strange language: proposal, opportunity. He set his knife and fork on the edge of the plate.

'Monique has invited you to a conference in Spain. A group of writers and publishers are trying to establish a prize. You could go, and they will pay.'

He took off his glasses and cleaned them on his napkin before replacing them. 'Are you trying to get rid of me?'

She was unsure whether he was joking or not. 'Nelson, no – I will join you there. I have work to do here first, but I will come after a few days and we can travel for a time. It will be a nice way to end your stay.'

He picked up his cutlery and sliced a piece of steak and chewed it. 'Okay,' he said eventually. 'Okay. When do I go?'

The conference in Mallorca: writers and publishers and who knew who else earnestly discussed European politics that he didn't much understand, often in languages he didn't understand, though he could follow some of the Spanish. He and the other Americans in attendance played the roles the Europeans expected, nodding along in condemnation of American policy in Korea or Indochina whenever it arrived in translation. It wasn't hard, but it wasn't interesting, either. Mostly he counted the time until the next drink or meal.

After a few days he travelled alone to Barcelona. To be alone and anonymous felt like a gift. He spent most of his first afternoon drinking light, cold beer in a café on La Rambla, watching the pickpockets as they trailed tourists, looking for easy targets. He walked without aim through the Gothic Quarter, escaping the sun in the cool and narrow alleys, smiling and nodding at the old women who leaned out of their apartment windows to catch the breeze. On his second day he awoke early and walked without much aim, mostly along the seafront, trying to decide where exactly the Balearic met the Mediterranean, and eventually finding himself at the port. For an hour he watched cranes lift containers from the ships, and walked around the perimeter fences until he found a place where he could sneak in. With no particular intentions he wandered among the machinery and containers, nodding in what he hoped looked an authoritative way at every person he passed. He watched close up the containers from China and Africa and India being lifted off the ships and moved around the enormous port. How much of this stuff was contraband, he wondered while he watched men with clipboards logging each container; how many of them vanished from the books, and how many never made it into the books in the first place?

In a bar on the edge of the docks he again sat drinking cold light beer and talked to some of the sailors and prostitutes who made it their Barcelona home. English had more currency as a language in the port than at the literature conference, and the Spanish that many of the sailors spoke was on a par with his own. He talked to them about where they travelled from, and for how long, and what kind of cargo they shipped. Neither the sailors nor the stevedores could be drawn on the issue of contraband, though one of the sailors sold him a small block of hashish. He talked to the prostitutes about their young lives – they were all young here – and their aspirations, which were never to be a prostitute for ever, even if the pay at the docks made it worthwhile.

He met Simone and Juan in Madrid, and, despite the easy and aimless floating that he'd made into a comfortable lifestyle for a few days in Barcelona, he found himself glad to have companions again. The city was hot but also beautiful, and each felt strange and wary in the fascist capital: Juan had only left, exiling himself voluntarily, five years earlier; Nelson had felt insulated from Franco to some extent in Barcelona, where everyone seemed to hate him anyway; Simone felt uncomfortably like a tourist of the very politics and philosophies she and Sartre spent their life and work pushing against. For a few days Juan served as guide, taking them to cafés and restaurants where they could speak freely, and showing them the tourist sites as well. From Madrid Simone and Nelson travelled together to places they'd been back in 1949: first to Seville, then Tiana, Malaga, Torremolinos, Almeira and Granada. Over the weeks they spent in Spain, neither of them working, or not trying to work, or not trying not to work, but only trying to enjoy themselves and one another, they both relaxed into their old ways of being together: joking, teasing, loving. Out in the sun and with activities and companionship to occupy his restless mind, Nelson slipped enough away from depression to forget it lurked there, and Simone, free from the daily pressures of work and babysitting unhappy Nelson in Paris, could look on him once again as her local youth and crocodile husband, and feel herself once again his frog wife.

When they arrived back in Madrid to fly to Paris, they spent a day apart, Simone visiting markets while Nelson, unbeknownst to her, went to the American consulate to persuade them to extend his passport, which had only been granted for three months of travel, for another three.

'I have a surprise,' he said when they'd arrived back at Rue Schoelcher and dropped their luggage to the floor.

She covered her eyes with one hand and held out the other.

'Not that kind.' He looked at her outstretched hand, the silver ring wrapping one finger. 'I extended my passport. I can stay until September.'

She uncovered her eyes and hoped they wouldn't betray her. 'Good,' she said after a long silence, and repeated it, 'Good,' as though emphasis could convince her.

Her summer of work turned into a summer of balancing work against Nelson, though she tipped the scales heavily on the side of work. No longer did her involvement in politics consist mostly in supporting Sartre and helping to redraft his essays. She now found herself writing about, speaking about and standing up for women's right to contraception, arguing against men left and right, Communist and Catholic, all of whom had their own spurious ideological reasons that they thought gave them the authority to control uteruses. Algeria, too, began to claim her attention; a longstanding colleague had tried to convince her and Sartre to involve themselves in the Algerian struggle, though they – and she in particular – had avoided doing so, in part, she had to admit only to herself, because of Camus. But now the situation became more urgent daily, and the rights of women pulled themselves into the question too, as French soldiers began torturing, raping and mutilating Algerian girls accused of what they called collaboration, as though the Algerian struggle for independence could be equated, even rhetorically, with Vichy. So she began to expend efforts in this direction as well.

All of which left her with less – with little – time for Nelson, and that more and more seemed just as well. He hardly pretended to sit at his typewriter any longer, but started his day drinking red wine earlier and earlier. He visited the boring Americans upstairs, and himself became more boring with each visit, or so she constructed it in her mind. When she did spare time for him – and she never reminded him that he, not she, had extended his stay – he complained that she didn't carve out enough for him. She tried, several times, to explain that their work was important, and there was much to be done before her August trip with Sartre to Brazil. 'Sartre avoids me too,' he complained, and she didn't tell him that she was keeping them apart, because together they would only indulge each other in drinking and silliness, and Sartre's health wasn't strong enough for boxing with Algren, no matter what either man might have thought.

Once again, she pawned him off on Bost and Olga, or Monique and Juan, or the kids, Serge and Florence. He also went dancing with Michelle from time to time, when she wasn't busying herself with Sartre. He kept telling himself he was having a good time, and when he got drunk enough, and when he was out with other people, he did, more or less. Though he began to wonder whether he should've just gone back to Chicago at the end of June. He felt trapped between two places that didn't need him. Whichever part of their love had been rekindled during their travels around Spain, Simone had let it drop as soon as she'd arrived back in Paris; the way she'd said 'good' to his announcement proved that clearly enough. In Chicago he had just as little purpose. He didn't want to go back, but neither could he stay. He sat in bars with Bost and Olga getting drunk and cracking jokes, sometimes wearing a battery-powered bow-tie that spun around when he pressed a button, and made them laugh. Serge took him to the race track, but he still could never understand the French betting system, so had to stick with trying to pick winners most of the time, and felt like a mug. He'd stumble in late, and if Simone was still awake they'd have another drink together while he complained about himself. If she'd already gone to bed he'd wake her up trying to get into it, and pass out. Once the hangover subsided the next day he'd start again.

This brooding, stubborn, obnoxious drunken man: yes, she still loved him, she could understand enough of herself and of him to know she couldn't stop loving him. But he made it no easy task. Paris dragged him down. It wouldn't, so much, she was sure, if he'd ever bothered to learn French. He might have done that, and been happier. She knew that wasn't really the answer, though. Poor Nelson, poor Chicago husband, poor crocodile and local youth. Again her pity demeaned them both, demeaned their love.

Once more she got him out of Paris. She worked hard and found enough time for a short vacation, a last trip before she and Sartre left for Brazil and Nelson would be on his own in Paris. They flew to Turkey, Greece, and on the way back, Marseille, that old city of strange magic for them both.

Istanbul teemed with noise and people. Simone hated it. In restaurants the waiters would only talk to Nelson, no matter what she tried. The mornings were foggy, and rang with the calls to prayer from the mosques, but after a few days lying in bed and listening it began to seem a false idyll compared to the hot and sexist city outside the bedroom door.

In Athens they climbed up to the Acropolis and looked back down on the city before walking around the monuments. They'd left it too late – almost midday – before they'd started, and now the afternoon sun bore relentlessly on the rock and on their heads. They found a sliver of shadow on the eastern side of the Parthenon and rested.

'It's impressive,' Nelson said, wiping his forehead with a handkerchief. 'But not as much as Chichén Itzá.'

'But maybe as hot, or even hotter,' Simone said. That trip now seemed a very long time ago.

'Remember the ants?'

'I remember the ants. The stubborn ants.'

'The Mexican ants are more ambitious than their Greek cousins, it would seem.'

After another week in Greece, watching the fishing boats come and go in Heraklion, drinking ouzo and eating enough grilled lamb and fish to keep them going for a year, they returned to France via Marseille. The magic had run out of the city, though. In 1949 it hadn't felt much different from when Nelson had been there at war's end, and they'd walked past some of the dives where he'd sold his cigarette rations and stolen uniforms, or bars and cafés that looked close enough the part. Those places were gone now, and their 1960 equivalents operated on codes that he didn't know and wouldn't be able to find. For Simone, too, the place belonged inexorably to the past. Almost thirty years had gone since her unhappy time in Marseille, where the only relief had been long hikes in the nearby mountains, and eleven years now since she and Nelson had discovered their own spirit in the city. He had turned it from a city she'd hated into a place she wanted to spend more time – with him. Now they looked across the harbour to Château d'If and neither wanted to go there; each thought silently and sadly of the choppy waters that had churned Nelson's guts on the return trip so many years ago. Marseille had changed, and they had changed, and walking around the city together made that change painfully apparent. Marseille had once again become a city she didn't like, and Nelson Algren could no longer rescue it.

They returned to Paris, and August arrived, and Castor began preparing to leave with Sartre for two months in Brazil. Packing and preparatory meetings and logistical errands filled her days: trips to the Brazilian consulate to collect their visas, to the American Express office for the traveller's cheques, to the Air France office three separate times until their tickets were finally ready. Not only that: she had signed a manifesto declaring her opposition to the government's policy in Algeria, and now received invitations to speak on the subject to various student groups. She attended meetings with Sartre, who also had signed the manifesto and who also spoke, when he was well enough, and she also went alone, and discussed women's issues as they pertained to Algeria. *Les Temps Modernes* demanded her time as well, with articles she needed to complete before they left, editorial decisions that she needed to make, and of course satisfying herself that the magazine would function smoothly enough in their two-month absence. Each day became a sprinting marathon journey from her writing desk to an office, to another, to another and back to her writing desk, and left her little time for anything apart from a brief meal in a café.

Simone didn't have any time for him so Nelson began knocking on the doors of the upstairs Americans again, even though he didn't like them much. They seemed to enjoy him, though, so what the hell. Sitting around or going to a restaurant with them meant he didn't have to sit at the little desk in Rue Schoelcher pretending to write – though he'd started trying to put something down about his few days in Barcelona, a kind of essay – or getting bored with whatever he could find to read. Better to be bored in company than to be bored on your own. Sometimes, when she wasn't busy looking after Sartre, who was ill and trying to recuperate in time to get on the plane, he could get Michelle to go out dancing with him. Serge didn't have much time to spare because of all the work Simone was dumping on him at the magazine, but Bost was usually good for a crawl around from bar to bar to jazz club. He'd stumble through the door at three or four or sometimes five and sleep until long after Simone had left for the day. He didn't care. She'd made it clear she had too many things to do – too many important things to do – Nelson, I have too many important things to do – to carve out any time for him, so why should he bother? Why he should bother, he knew, was because he still loved her. God knew he still loved her, despite everything, despite himself. But he stayed morose and drunk instead, and then it was time for her to leave.

The morning of her flight they ate breakfast together, in the old manner: Nelson got out of bed early and walked down to the bakery and to the greengrocer, returning with baguette and croissants and several oranges. He sliced the bread and put out cheese and butter and boiled eggs. He brewed coffee and squeezed the juice from the oranges, removing the seeds with a teaspoon. When everything was ready he roused Simone with a kiss on the forehead and waved his arm at the table.

'It feels strange to be leaving you behind in Paris,' Simone said as she spread butter on to a piece of baguette. 'What will you do on your own?'

He'd been on his own for months. But he didn't want to make a scene, not today. 'Maybe I'll go find the prostitutes I filmed, and see if they remember me.'

'Nelson!' She dropped her knife, but she was laughing. 'What will you really do?'

Nelson picked a flake from a croissant and let it dissolve on his tongue. 'The track with Serge, the bars with Bost. Go out for a last tedious meal with the Americans, and let them pay so I leave a good impression. Pay my respects at the grave of Baudelaire. It's only two weeks, Simone.'

'Yes, I know. And you're a grown man. It just seems funny to me, flying across the ocean and knowing you're not on the other side but here, in France, in Paris, in Rue Schoelcher. Like a fingerprint I've left behind.'

'The scene of the crime,' he said, and drank some juice. 'I'm a fingerprint?'

She touched his hand, the silver ring clacking his juice glass as she reached across. 'Not a fingerprint, Nelson, no, but a – I don't know, but it will feel very much as though I've left something behind. Someone behind. A trace of myself.'

'Me.'

'Yes, you.' She took her hand away from his and rubbed the silver ring with her thumb. His obstinacy and obnoxiousness and childishness, the frustration and obstruction he'd caused during his stay: even so, there was the boat in the Jardin du Luxembourg, the pleasant time in Spain, the nights they'd drunk whisky and listened to records together. Even so, there still was love. 'Will it be a long time before we see one another again?'

The memory of 1947, opening the door to his Wabansia apartment and seeing Simone, and Simone's French consulate limousine, announced itself in his head with a suddenness of association that shocked him, and he coughed. 'It will,' he said, 'probably. You can spend the summer in Miller if you like,' he said. 'You should spend every summer in Miller.'

She tore a small piece from the baguette and rolled it into a ball between her fingers. 'It seems so far away, the summer, and Miller.' Chaise-longue, lagoon, rowing boat; dune, beach, lake. 'Soon you will be, too.'

'Soon you will be, too,' Nelson echoed.

When her taxi arrived he helped carry her suitcases out to the street and lifted them into the trunk. Before she stepped into the open door of the car she reached her left hand to Nelson's right shoulder. Her other arm reached towards his waist and she hugged him, and they kissed. She slid into her seat still watching him, and he pushed the door shut and smiled crookedly. He grinned, she thought, as though she were narrating the moment. She instructed the driver and the taxi drove off towards Sartre's, and from there to the airport, and the plane to Brazil, and she watched out of the back window for the fifty metres until Nelson disappeared from view. When the car had turned the corner he walked back into the building, removing his glasses so he could rub at his eyes. In two weeks he would travel alone back to Chicago.

Epilogue

1964

Epilogue

FOUR YEARS AGO, on his last night in Paris, they'd thrown him a party: Bost, Olga, Serge, Florence, Michelle, Monique, Juan and a handful of others he'd met but didn't know as well. They'd gone out for a meal, and then bar-hopped, ending up in a cellar jazz bar drinking wine and cocktails at a steady pace. He'd worn the battery-powered bow-tie one final time, and periodically set it spinning. Around two his Paris friends began to filter away, hugs and kisses across both cheeks and well-wishes and come back soon, until only he and Michelle, his faithful interpreter, former wife of the trumpet player, mistress of Sartre, remained. They took to the dancefloor for half an hour before they, too, found a taxi to take them each home. He watched the other cars and the buildings pass, and he turned to look at Michelle, her right thigh bare beneath the slit in the cloth of her skirt. He reached his hand over and touched her skin. Massaged, lightly, the muscle. She touched his hand and then lifted it back to his own thigh. Not me, Nelson, she said, and squeezed his shoulder and smiled. The next afternoon he took all the francs he had and left them on Simone's bedside table. Rent money. He met Bost at the station and gave him the key to Simone's apartment and boarded the train to Le Havre, and the boat back across the Atlantic.

Last month he'd received the issue of *Harper's* with an excerpt from Simone's memoir, and this month another *Harper's* had arrived, with another excerpt. He'd known it was coming; he'd already been bullied into allowing some small parts of his letters to be quoted in them. Even so, he hadn't been prepared for this bullshit. Their love was, according to Existentialist Queen Simone de Beauvoir the Great, a mere contingency arrangement. Her Chicago husband, her local youth and crocodile – in her presentation of their private lives together for public gossip he became Nelson Algren, a silly American man bewildered at everything she showed him, and appreciative of her expertise and knowledgeable explanations, eager for her pats on the head, a pleasant enough sideshow, and useful proof of her shabby and shitty theory that she and Sartre were better than everybody else. What he read was a burlesque – a careful and artificial stripshow in which nothing would ever be revealed except the arrogance and vanity of the dancer and the grubby hands of everybody clamouring to pay or make a dime off her. Whores didn't pretend they weren't complicit in what was going on, and had the decency to keep it behind closed doors. Simone de Beauvoir would strip everybody else naked so she could look at their cocks and cunts and display them under her light, and only under her light, and all the while she'd be donning those clothes she'd taken, layer after layer, so she would only ever be seen fully dressed, as she wanted. That wasn't how life worked. That wasn't how love worked. She could dress him up as Lewis Brogan and strip him bare as Nelson Algren, but damned if he needed to have anything to do with it any longer.

He never wrote to her again, and as the years passed she became to him what she became to everyone else: someone they knew about, someone they read about, someone they heard about. He would see her in a magazine, and he would see a book review, and he would read a little news of her in a letter from Stepha, from Michelle, or from Bost. He would play it off, when asked during interviews, and make jokes at her expense. It was over. It no longer mattered. Though no, it wasn't quite like that. He could stop loving her, but the press of her life against his would never vanish. He would marry again, and it would fail, and there would be other women, but they could only ever be other women. As he spoke or wrote, dismissing Simone, and dismissing what they'd had, or when he was alone and watching a ball game or having a drink, he would think of that blue wool dress, or he would think of the mountaintop lake in Guatemala, and he would wonder whether she still wore the ring, the silver ring he'd given her, long ago on a street in Manhattan, and he would admit he was dismissing the one love that had been the most real. He wondered about the silver ring, and hoped she still wore it.

MORE FROM MYRIAD

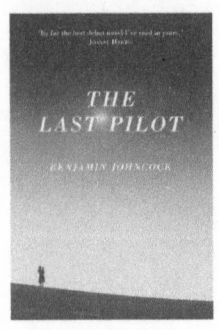

Sign up to our mailing list at
www.myriadeditions.com
Follow us on Facebook and Twitter

DOUGLAS COWIE was born in Elmhurst, Illinois, and since 1999 has lived in both England and Germany. He teaches in the Department of English at Royal Holloway, University of London. He is also the author of the novel *Owen Noone and the Marauder* (2005) and two linked novellas, *Sing for Life: Tin Pan Alley* (2013) and *Sing for Life: Away, You Rolling River* (2014).